DEFLECTING THE DUKE

Dukes Done Wrong
Book 2

Alexa Aston

DRAGONBLADE PUBLISHING, INC.

Dragonblade Publishing, Inc. is an imprint of Kathryn Le Veque Novels, Inc.
P.O. Box 7968
La Verne CA 91750
ceo@dragonbladepublishing.com

Produced in the United States of America

First Edition July 2021
Trade Paperback Edition

ARE YOU SIGNED UP FOR DRAGONBLADE'S BLOG?

You'll get the latest news and information on exclusive giveaways, exclusive excerpts, coming releases, sales, free books, cover reveals and more.

Check out our complete list of authors, too!

No spam, no junk. That's a promise!

Sign Up Here

www.dragonbladepublishing.com

Dearest Reader;

Thank you for your support of a small press. At Dragonblade Publishing, we strive to bring you the highest quality Historical Romance from the some of the best authors in the business. Without your support, there is no 'us', so we sincerely hope you adore these stories and find some new favorite authors along the way.

Happy Reading!

CEO, Dragonblade Publishing

The Heir
The Bastard

Medieval Runaway Wives
Song of the Heart
A Promise of Tomorrow
Destined for Love

Knights of Honor Series
Word of Honor
Marked by Honor
Code of Honor
Journey to Honor
Heart of Honor
Bold in Honor
Love and Honor
Gift of Honor
Path to Honor
Return to Honor

CHAPTER ONE

Amberwood, Kent—July 1796

WYATT STANTON STOOD before his father, the Duke of Amesbury. He had stopped listening to his father's rant because it was always the same. Wyatt was impulsive. Reckless. Selfish. The lecture never changed. Only the circumstances.

This time, he had been called before the duke because he'd gotten into pies which Cook had baked. They had been cooling when he spied them. Cherry was his absolute favorite and the temptation to taste it had proven too great. Soon, red juice had run down his chin, staining his cravat and shirt and the fingers he used to gobble up the pie. He'd moved on from the cherry to the apple one and then the peach. By the end, all three pies had been devoured and his stomach ached as he stood in the study, trying to look contrite.

"The pies were for our guests tonight," the duke continued. "Not meant for the likes of you." Amesbury frowned. "You are far too rash, Wyatt. Did you not think of how hard poor Cook worked to bake them? Or how if your wrongdoing hadn't been discovered, we would have had no dessert to offer our guests?"

He wanted to say that most of his father's friends were too fat and didn't need any slices of pie but refrained from doing so.

"I don't know what I am going to do with you," the duke said, throwing his hands helplessly into the air. "Thank God you are away at school most of the year."

Wyatt preferred school to life at Amberwood. He had nothing against the estate itself. In fact, he thought it was situated on a pretty piece of land and that most of its tenants were decent and kind. It was his family he couldn't abide. His father tended to be a perfectionist and was never satisfied with anything his younger son did. His mother simply didn't care about anyone but herself. And at nine years older, Clive was a stranger to him. His brother had never played with Wyatt or allowed him to be around when Clive's friends visited. They were strangers to one another.

For these reasons, Wyatt had learned to create his own fun—which usually turned into mischief. He didn't think he was badly behaved for a ten-year-old boy. Just lonely and in need of entertainment.

He did like Cook, though, and said with sincerity, "I am sorry, Father, for eating all of Cook's pies. I know she works very hard for our family."

The duke sniffed. "Well, this isn't the first time you have proclaimed to be sorry for being so thoughtless. Go to your room. You are restricted to it and the schoolroom for your meals for the next week."

"A whole week? But can't I ride at least?" he protested, knowing it would be like a death sentence to be confined to his room during the beautiful summer days of Kent.

"You may not," his father said sternly. "Go. But first apologize to Cook."

"Yes, Father."

Wyatt left the room and made his way to the kitchens. He spied Cook and went to her, wrapping his arms about her. She was the only one in the household who had ever showed him any kind of affection. A hug from her could chase away the dark storm clouds of any sad day.

"I am very sorry, Cook," he told her. "I truly mean it. It's just that cherry is my favorite and your crust is so light and flaky. I couldn't help myself."

She squeezed him to her ample bosom. "That's all right, Lord Wyatt. I'd rather you like my pies than not. What's the punishment this time?"

"A week in my rooms," he said glumly. "And it's summer. I will go mad being kept inside."

"No restrictions on your meals?" she asked.

"No. Just that I take all of them in the schoolroom."

She hugged him again. "Then I'll see that you have pie every day, my lord."

Wyatt thanked her profusely and took the back stairs to his room, passing his favorite maid along the way.

"Hello, Joan," he said.

"Good afternoon, Lord Wyatt," she said cheerfully. "In trouble again?"

"Yes."

"Don't worry. Your punishment will be over quickly. And school will start before you know it. I know you miss your friends."

She was right. He did miss his friends and wished the new school term would hurry up and arrive.

"Stay out of trouble, my lord," she said and continued down the stairs.

Wyatt arrived in his room and threw himself onto the bed. He pillowed his hands beneath his head and stared at the ceiling.

He must have fallen asleep because when he opened his eyes, his stomach growled. He went across the hall to the schoolroom and found a tray on the table. Despite having eaten three whole pies, he was already ravenous again. He knew it was a growth spurt because he kept needing new trousers all the time.

After he finished the meal, he wandered back to his room and played with his toy soldiers for a while. Bored, he read a chapter in the book resting by his bedside but it didn't hold his attention. He closed it and sat by the open window, watching as the summer sun sank below the horizon. He continued watching as the night came to life, with the hooting of an owl sounding nearby and various creatures scurrying about in the bushes. Eventually, the two carriages carrying the dinner party guests departed.

For an hour, he stared out the window and decided he should turn in for the night. Then movement caught his eyes. He spied Clive, his fingers around some female's upper arm, dragging her along. She stumbled and fell to her knees. Clive yanked her back up. As he did, Wyatt saw it was Joan.

Where was his brother taking the maid?

A sick feeling washed over him. He'd heard murmurings from the servants about his brother's bad behavior. Several maids had up and quit in the last few years. One had been let go. Thanks to eavesdropping, he learned the unmarried girl had been with child.

His brother's child.

Naturally, Clive had not been held accountable for his misdeeds. He continued to strut about as if he had done nothing wrong in ruining a young girl's life. Wyatt knew his father would never have paid to see the girl and her child taken care of. To do so would admit wrongdoing on Clive's part—and the duke would never want his heir associated with a bastard child.

Now, he worried that the same thing would happen to Joan. The servant had always been friendly and hardworking. It wouldn't be fair for Clive to force himself on her. Especially if it cost her livelihood and meant she would birth a bastard. Wyatt was young but he knew how all levels of society would reject Joan if she had a baby out of wedlock. She would be shunned. No man would marry her. He couldn't stand the thought of her suffering so.

He had always possessed a strong sense of right and wrong. Despite his father's edict that he was confined to his room, Wyatt couldn't let this happen. He had to intervene and protect Joan.

Opening his door, he glanced out and saw the hallway deserted. He knew with his parents' guests now gone, they would have retired to their separate chambers. Slipping down the staircase, he reached the bottom floor and crept out the door, closing it softly behind him. Fearful of what might already have happened, he ran toward the stables. It was the direction Clive had headed and Wyatt figured it would give his brother the privacy he wanted.

He reached the open doorway, peering inside. Though darkness surrounded him, he could see light coming from the far end. Anger surged through him.

Without lighting a lantern, he moved along the pathway, his hand brushing against each stall he passed as horses nickered at him.

As he came closer, he heard Joan begging.

"Please, my lord. Please. Don't. I don't want this. It hurts."

Wyatt heard a slap. "Shut up, you little bitch. You know you wanted this. Sashaying past me all those times, your plump little rump calling out for my attention."

Joan whimpered as Wyatt reached the doorway and stared at the scene before him.

Clive sprawled atop the maid, his trousers pushed past his knees. He kept ramming into Joan. Tears streamed down her cheeks as she squeezed her eyes shut.

"Stop!" he cried.

His brother growled, whipping his head to face Wyatt.

"Get out of here," he said, his voice low and deadly.

He looked to Joan. The front of her gown was torn open, her breasts spilling out, parts of them marred with what looked like bite marks. Her skirts were hiked to her waist. She shook her head at him.

"Leave, my lord," she urged, her eyes dead and empty, so unlike the girl he saw every day. "You're too young to see this. You don't belong here."

"You heard her," Clive said.

He stood his ground. "She doesn't want you to keep hurting her."

His brother's smile sent a chill running down Wyatt's spine. "She loves this, Wyatt. All women do. They say they don't because all women are liars. That's a good lesson for you to learn, little brother."

"You are hurting her, Clive. Get off. I won't leave until you do," he said bravely, though his legs shook.

Clive roared with laughter. "You are just a scrawny little boy. One who always finds himself in trouble. Leave now—or I'll show you exactly what trouble is." He paused. "I am going to be Duke of Amesbury one day. You don't want to cross me."

"I'm not leaving," Wyatt said stubbornly.

His brother's eyes darkened with anger, his cheeks growing red and splotchy. "Then I will make you."

Clive scrambled off Joan. As he did, he knocked against the lantern sitting on the ground. It fell into the hay, which immediately caught fire.

Clive jerked up his trousers as Joan rolled away from the fire. The edge of her skirts had brushed against it, though, and her clothing began to burn. She screamed and began hitting the flames with her hands.

Wyatt rushed toward her but Clive slammed his fist into Wyatt's face. The blow knocked him to the ground. Clive kicked him repeatedly and he felt his ribs snap. He cried out in agony.

Suddenly, Clive rushed away and Wyatt saw that the stall was becoming engulfed in flames. Joan leaned down and latched on to his elbow, bringing him to his feet.

"Come, my lord. We must get out of here and sound the alarm."

"Clive must've done that," he said, holding his hand against his broken ribs to cradle them as they stumbled from the enclosed space.

Already, dark smoke billowed through the air, causing them both to cough as the blaze quickly engulfed the stall they had inhabited moments ago.

"Run!" Joan cried. "We must get out." She coughed deeply and gasped for breath.

Horses neighed shrilly as they made their way down the row

of stalls. Wyatt wanted to stop and open each one but the maid kept pulling him along. They reached outside and her fingers dug into his flesh as he tried to turn and race back inside.

"I can't let them burn," he shouted.

"You'll die if you go back," she warned. "I must leave you. Promise me you'll stay outside."

He saw her bruised cheek and the swelling about one eye.

"What will you say?"

"That I fell down the stairs. You mustn't say differently. Lord Clive will already have it in for you, interrupting him like you did."

"I didn't keep him from hurting you," Wyatt said, tears rolling down his cheeks.

"You tried. No one else would have," she said simply and released him, turning away and rushing away from the stables but not heading toward the house.

He wondered why until he saw servants running his way. Shouts and confusion abounded as they tried to form a line and pass buckets of water along it in order to put out the fire. He moved away from the burning structure, the sound of the dying animals tormenting him, echoing in his ears as he collapsed to the ground.

He hadn't saved Joan, who'd lost her innocence to Clive. He couldn't save their horses. He fought against the helplessness that coursed through him, his sobs lost in the chaos as the stables burned to the ground.

"Here he is!" a voice called out.

Wyatt looked up and saw his brother hovering over him.

"You're in for it now," Clive said, his loathing obvious.

Staggering to his feet, still holding his side, he said, "Why? I didn't do anything. You're the one who knocked over the lantern."

Suddenly, he felt his father's presence and turned. The duke looked at him with such hatred that Wyatt shrank back.

"You would blame your *brother* for this?" his father roared.

"Clive started the fire," he insisted.

Amesbury slapped him. It hurt Wyatt's pride as much as his cheek. "You don't believe me? He did this, Father. Clive. He was—"

"You are a monster," Clive said, cutting Wyatt off. "Starting this blaze. All our horses are gone. Thousands of pounds worth of horseflesh burned to a crisp. And you would blame me? You are despicable, Wyatt. I am sorry I am related to you."

"But—"

"Stop," the duke said, glaring at him. "Just stop, Wyatt. Your mischief has gone far beyond fun and games. Tonight, you have destroyed valuable property. Cost the lives of two dozen horses."

"But I didn't—"

"Silence!" His father shook his head. "The only reason you won't hang is because you are the son of a duke. A worthless, bloody fool that I never wish to see again."

"Father, please," Wyatt begged.

"No. No more from you. Ever. I have my heir. I have no need of you."

"Don't abandon me," he pleaded. "I've done nothing wrong. I'm telling the truth."

Amesbury closed his eyes and then opened them slowly. Wyatt shivered as his father gazed upon him.

"You are dead to me as of this night. I won't ignore my duty to you. God knows I wish I could. But I can cast you from this family for your thoughtless, reckless, damaging behavior. You are poison to everyone you meet and no longer my son."

The duke glanced to Clive. "Take this boy to his room and see he's locked inside. Place a footman to guard the entrance. He is a danger to us all."

Clive roughly grabbed his arm. "Come along," he ordered and began dragging Wyatt toward the house.

He heard a loud noise and looked over his shoulder. The stables collapsed inward. The panicked noises from within ceased at once. Only the burning fire continued.

As Clive marched him back to the house, Wyatt felt the eyes of everyone they passed on him, knowing they would all believe he had caused this massive death and destruction.

Clive tugged him inside the house, which was eerily silent, all the servants having fled outside to help fight the fire.

"Are you satisfied with yourself?" he asked his older brother. "Blaming a boy for what a man did. Except you aren't man enough to claim responsibility."

Clive snorted. "You've always been a troublemaker. This was too easy to set at your doorstep, little brother."

"Joan can tell them the truth," he said stubbornly. "She saw everything."

"She won't talk. If she does, I will slit her throat."

Cold spread through him, hearing Clive talk so candidly of murdering their maid. He realized if the servant stuck up for him, it would be a death sentence for her. His heart wanted her to do so but his head knew he must trade his reputation for her life.

"Don't hurt her. I will accept the blame if you promise never to touch her again."

They had reached his bedchamber and Clive said, "That's easy to do. She wasn't any good anyway. Inside now."

Clive opened the door and shoved Wyatt in. The door slammed behind him and he heard the lock being turned.

His father had disowned him. Everyone thought his behavior criminal.

Wyatt sank to the floor and curled up in a ball, wishing he had died along with all the horses.

CHAPTER TWO

September

TWO MONTHS HAD passed. Wyatt had seen no one but servants during his confinement. With school starting soon, he wondered if he would be allowed to go or if he would remain locked in his room indefinitely.

A light tap sounded on the door and it swung open quickly. Joan hurried inside and closed it behind her.

He rushed to her and threw his arms about her. The maid hugged him tightly and then released him.

"I've come to say goodbye to you, Lord Wyatt."

"Are you . . ." His voice trailed off. He couldn't say the words.

"No," she assured him. "I am not with child."

"Where are you going?"

"I'm going to be a dairy maid for one of the neighboring farmers."

Disappointment filled him. He knew it was a giant step down for a duke's parlor maid but he understood why she had to leave Amberwood.

"I also came to apologize to you."

Her words puzzled him. "For what?"

Her face flushed with guilt. "I didn't stand up for you. I could have come forward. Told His Grace who really started the fire and deserved the blame."

"No, you did the right thing, Joan. My father would never have believed you. He would have sacked you without references. Besides, Clive told me if you did speak up, he would cut your throat."

Her eyes widened. "You believed him." It wasn't a question.

"I did. It's a good thing you are leaving Amberwood. With him here, you aren't safe. He might take it in his head to have his way with you again."

Tears brimmed in her eyes. "I thought so, too. He's avoided me so far. I know he's off to university again soon but I just couldn't take the chance, my lord."

"I understand. Thank you for coming to tell me goodbye."

He wished he could do more for her and remembered he had a few coins stashed away and went to the drawer where he kept them. Removing them, he placed them in her hands.

"It's not much. I have never been one to save my coin."

"I cannot accept this, my lord."

"Please do. It's all I can do for you. I am so sorry my brother hurt you, Joan."

She wiped the tears from her face. "I will never forget your kindness and generosity, my lord. You are the true gentleman. Not Lord Clive." She gazed at him wistfully. "I only wish you could be the duke one day and not your brother."

He shook his head. "I would never want to be a duke," he said vehemently.

She bid him farewell and slipped from the room. He was grateful she was gone when their butler appeared.

"You have been summoned to His Grace's study, my lord."

Trepidation filled Wyatt as he followed the servant downstairs. He had thought he would never see his father again. Hope filled him. Maybe his father had forgiven him. Maybe Clive had done the right thing and confessed to his careless actions.

When he entered the study, though, he saw the stern look on his father's face and knew no forgiveness would be forthcoming. He went and stood before the man he'd never truly known.

Amesbury had kept to himself and spent very little time with Wyatt. He had heard his father tell others that he had no patience with children and he only spent time with Clive because he was the heir apparent.

"You are here so I may inform you that I am fulfilling my duty to you, you worthless piece of scum. Polite Society would frown upon me if I abandoned you. You will be educated at my expense—but you will never be allowed to set foot upon Amberwood lands. Ever."

Wyatt didn't really care. Amberwood was just a house. He had always known that one day he would leave it because he knew Clive would never allow him to stay once their father passed.

"You will be attending Turner Academy. My solicitor found the school. It is a place where wicked boys are sent."

He didn't protest, clamping his jaw so no words would spill out.

"You will remain at this place during holidays. Clive and I agree that you are no longer to be recognized as a member of the Stanton family, though you will be allowed to retain usage of that surname. You are not to tell anyone you are related to either of us. You are never to speak of Amberwood as your former home. You will leave Turner Academy and continue your education at university before entering the army."

"Will you purchase my commission?" Wyatt asked, having known for several years as a second son that he was destined for the military.

"My solicitor will handle that affair."

Relief swept through him, knowing he could enter the army as an officer and gentleman, despite the circumstances.

The duke studied him. "You never looked a thing like me. Or your mother and her side of the family, for that matter."

The mention of his mother did not stir his heart. She had always been cold toward him and hadn't made any attempt to see him these past two months.

"I doubt you are mine."

His father's words struck an almost physical blow and Wyatt recoiled.

"Remember, once you leave this house tomorrow, you are never to acknowledge our relationship. I will provide for you financially, but you are cut off socially from all members of this family."

He held his tongue, knowing if he said the wrong thing, his future might be endangered. Instead, he bowed his head and then nodded curtly.

"Thank you, Your Grace."

"You are dismissed."

Wyatt left the room and returned upstairs to his bedchamber. At least he had learned where he was being sent and knew the expectations required of him. He wouldn't think about the other boys who might be sent to such a place. What they might have done. All he knew was he would finally be free of this place, one he never wished to see again.

⟫⟫⟪⟪

As THE CARRIAGE turned into the drive, Wyatt spied the imposing building in the distance and knew they had arrived at Turner Academy. His eyes cut to his traveling companion, the family butler, who hadn't spoken a word since they'd entered the vehicle early this morning.

The driver brought the carriage to a halt and a footman opened the door. Wyatt exited without a backward glance and the footman shut the door.

"Greetings!" a man called out as he came toward them. "I am Mr. Smythe. Welcome to Turner Academy."

"Hello. I am Lord Wyatt Stanton," he told the servant.

"You will be Mr. Wyatt here," Smythe informed him. "The academy chooses not to recognize titles."

The man's words surprised him but he welcomed them all the same. He would be a boy without a family. Having no title would help him distance himself from where he had come and he wouldn't have to explain who he was—or wasn't.

The footman retrieved his trunk and Smythe insisted upon taking it, handling it with ease. He led Wyatt through the front door and up a wide staircase.

"You are new to our school and will be placed in a room with four other boys who also are in their first year at Turner Academy."

He wondered what those four might have done to be exiled here but kept silent.

They went the length of the corridor, stopping at the last door on the left.

"This is yours," Smythe said, opening the door and ushering Wyatt inside.

A boy with blond hair sat on a bed, his hands braced against his legs and his eyes cast downward. He remained still, not acknowledging their presence.

"Your bed is here," the servant said, indicating one.

He saw his name on a placard above the bed. At least this would be one less thing to fight about. Boys at school always tussled over different things. Assigning them beds was already a brilliant move and would cut down on tension.

"Let me know if you need anything, Mr. Wyatt. There'll be a schoolwide assembly in an hour in the ballroom downstairs. Please be prompt."

"Thank you, Mr. Smythe," he said, meaning it.

The door closed and he sat on his bed, looking in the direction of the silent boy. He wondered why the boy had been sent to Turner Academy. Had he done something heinous? Or had he been a mere inconvenience and sent here in order to be out of the way.

"I'm Wyatt," he said.

The boy didn't answer.

Wyatt glanced up and saw *William Finchley* on the sign, identifying who the boy was.

"I'm ten," he added, thinking William Finchley looked to be close to his age.

Still no reply.

The door swung open and another new pupil appeared with a different servant carrying in his trunk.

"This is Mr. Hart," the servant announced. He tilted his head. "This is your place," he told the newcomer.

Wyatt saw the placard read *Aaron Hartfield*.

The servant rested the trunk on the ground at the foot of Hart's bed. "Don't forget the assembly I mentioned."

"I won't. Thank you."

Once the door closed, Wyatt took a step forward and stuck out his hand. "I'm Wyatt Stanton."

Shaking it, Aaron said, "Don't ever call me Aaron. I despite that name. The first thing I need to see about is having that changed." He pointed to the plaque. "I go by Hart. That's my name."

"Good to meet you, Hart," he said sincerely. He liked this boy.

"What about him?" Hart asked, curiosity written on his face as he stared at the silent boy.

"He hasn't said a word."

Wyatt sat on his bunk and Hart did the same. They talked for a few minutes, neither revealing much about his past. He wondered if they would all be wary and on their guard and prayed that, somehow, he could make friends with at least one of the boys who lived in this room.

Then another boy arrived with Mr. Smythe, who warned him not to be late to the assembly before he left the room.

Knowing this one was Miles since Smythe placed the trunk where *Miles Notley* would sleep, Wyatt strode toward him, offering him his hand.

"I'm Wyatt. Wyatt Stanton. They say I burned down our

stables and killed all our horses. I didn't. It was my idiot brother's fault."

There. It was out in the open. He'd talked a good fifteen minutes with Hart and knew whatever each had done hovered over their heads. Wyatt refused to spend the rest of his life dithering around. It felt good to announce what he was falsely accused of.

Miles looked at him with a bit of surprise and then determination filled him. Wyatt knew this boy would also speak his truth. Guilty of a crime or not, he decided he would accept this newcomer.

"I appreciate you being frank. My older brother shot and killed my younger brother. He's a marquess and my father's favorite. Ralph blamed me—and no one dared to question his version of the events."

Immediately, Hart joined them and offered Miles a hand.

"I'm Aaron Hartfield. My friends call me Hart." He studied Miles. "I hope we can be friends."

Miles asked why Hart was at Turner Academy, a topic Wyatt and Hart had avoided before this new boy's arrival.

Hart snorted. "It seems we three have something in common. My older brother, Reginald, pushed my baby brother into the water. Percy was scared. Always hated the water. Reg thought he'd force Percy to finally conquer his fear. Instead, Percy's neck was broken and he drowned before I could reach him. Guess who got the blame?" Hart shrugged. "It doesn't matter. I hate the lot of them anyway."

Wyatt took in the fact that both of these boys had lost their younger brothers and had been wrongly blamed for it. He sensed these two had been protective of their little brothers and carried a sense of having failed to keep them safe.

"Do they want you back?" Miles asked, glancing from Wyatt to Hart.

He wondered if Miles was in the same position and had been told he couldn't return to his home because of his misdeeds.

Wyatt swallowed hard and shook his head.

Hart jumped in. "You mean are we allowed to go home? Not me. My father, the Duke of Mansfield, washed his hands of me. He hasn't spoken a word to me since Percy died. His solicitor is the one who told me I would be attending school with a bunch of wayward, wicked boys. And that I am not welcomed at Deerfield ever again."

Though upset by Hart's familiar story, relief flooded Wyatt. "Thank God. I thought I was the only one who had been banished for good. I live—lived—at Amberwood, about ten miles southeast of Maidstone. Our family butler delivered me here. My parents have disowned me."

Wyatt went into an imitation of his father's final speech to him and his companions recognized what he did.

Then Miles glanced toward the silent boy and asked he if talked.

"Not yet," Hart replied.

Another pupil was shown in, making Donovan Martin the final arrival. He introduced himself. Hart and Miles did the same, and Miles asked the newcomer what he had done to be placed at Turner Academy.

"Nothing," Donovan said, belligerence in his voice.

"No one is sent here without doing something," Wyatt quietly said. "Or being accused of something they never did."

Hurt filled Donovan's face. Miles quickly assured the boy, telling him, "If you're ever ready, we're here to listen."

Donovan stepped away and went to his trunk, moving things about as they watched him.

"It was my mother."

As tears filled his eyes, the dark-haired boy explained how on one of their frequent walks through the forest, his mother had accidentally stepped into a poacher's trap. Donovan had gone for help but the duchess lost a good deal of blood. The doctor recommended amputation, which the duke had forbid.

"Infection set in. She ran a high fever and became delirious.

And then she died." Donovan paused. Wyatt felt the boy's hurt and wanted to comfort him.

"That's why I'm here. Father can't stand the sight of me."

As Donovan angrily wiped away his streaming tears, he said he never wanted to see his father and brother again. Wyatt understood—and in that moment, he knew not only would this boy be his friend, but the others would, as well.

"We're here for you," Hart told Donovan. "We've all been done wrong. We may not have our families anymore—but we have each other."

They all looked to the fifth boy in the room, who had remained silent throughout all they had revealed to one another.

"Won't you join us?" Miles asked.

Finally, the blond boy lifted his head. Wyatt recognized the immense pain that filled William Finchley as he came toward them and took a step back, welcoming what he hoped would no longer be a stranger to their circle.

"I'm Finch," the boy said after a long pause. "William Finchley. And I don't give a damn about what any of you did or didn't do." He stared hard, his eyes flicking over each of them. "I sure as hell won't ever tell you why I was sent here."

Donovan was the first to speak. "You don't need to. You're here. And you're with us. That's all that matters. We're all new here. That's what Mr. Smythe told me. I think we could all use a few friends."

"Whether you did anything or not, you're a part of us. We're all stuck here together. We might as well make the best of it," Miles told Finch. "Agreed?" he asked the others.

"Agreed," four voices echoed.

Miles thrust out his hand and Wyatt placed his atop it. The others did the same until all the boys were connected.

"To the Turner Terrors," Miles proclaimed.

"The Turner Terrors," they replied, warmth filling Wyatt as he spoke the new nickname bestowed upon the five standing here.

"To the Turner Terrors," Miles declared.

United as one, they made their way downstairs to the assembly. With Miles on his right and Finch on his left and Donovan and Hart just beyond them, Wyatt felt a trickle of hope run through him. Hope that he wouldn't be alone. That he now had brothers of his heart.

CHAPTER THREE

Sussex—February 1810

"YOU SHOULD PREPARE yourself, Lady Selfridge," Dr. Mobley said. "Your husband hasn't long to live."

Meadow fought to keep the nervous giggles from erupting. They had plagued her from the time she was a small child and always struck her at the most inappropriate time.

Husband.

That was laughable. Lord Selfridge was her husband in name only. They had been wed six years and had yet to consummate their marriage. With the physician's news, she would now become a widow—and still be a virgin.

She moved to the window and glanced out, trying to compose herself. She was known for her composure. Her serene, placid nature. She ran a peaceful household and visited their tenants frequently, nursing the sick among them, helping to deliver babies, and spending time with the women, especially new mothers. Something she had longed to be on that morning she had spoken her wedding vows.

Before her marriage, Meadow learned that she had been sold to Viscount Selfridge by her father, who perpetually was in debt, thanks to his love of gambling. Lord Selfridge was only too eager to acquire her but had no interest in her once he owned her. It was the same with other things he collected. Chess sets. First editions of books. Snuff boxes. He would pay for items and artfully arrange them for display—and immediately lose interest in them. Meadow had been one of the things he had collected and then pushed to the side, leaving her at his country estate for the entire length of their marriage, while he spent a majority of his time in London. When Selfridge did visit the country, he would spend hours locked in his study, a place even the servants weren't allowed to enter.

"My lady?"

She turned to face Doctor Mobley. "I quite understand. Do you have any special instructions for me, Doctor?"

"Only to make his lordship as comfortable as possible, my lady. Sit with him if you are up to it. He is already confused, which is one of the symptoms of the pneumonia in older patients."

"I have done everything I can to reduce his fever," she shared.

He shook his head, pity in his eyes. "I am afraid there is very little any of us can do at this point." The physician cleared his throat. "I will be back at this time tomorrow though I am not certain your husband will make it until then."

"I understand," she said solemnly, swallowing the giggle dancing in her throat.

"Good day, my lady."

Dr. Mobley left and Meadow hurried to a cushion sitting in the nearest chair. She buried her face in it, erupting in laughter. Finally, the fit subsided and she returned the pillow to its chair. Composing herself, she left the drawing room and made for the viscount's bedchamber.

Selfridge's valet sat by her husband's bedside and she told him, "Get some rest. I will call if I need you."

"Yes, my lady." The servant left without argument, his weariness apparent.

Meadow took the seat the valet vacated and studied the man in the bed. When they had wed, Selfridge had been thirty years her senior, handsome for a man approaching fifty, with beautiful, silver hair and a trim figure. The man she now observed had wasted away. His hair was dull and matted, his cheeks flushed with a high fever. Even in sleep, he trembled with chills though sweat poured from his body.

She placed her palm against his brow and found it scalding. Dipping a cloth into a basin of water next to the bed, she bathed his face and watched as he frowned. His lips had turned blue, as had his fingernails, one of the signs the pneumonia had reached its last stage before death occurred.

Selfridge opened his eyes and stared vacantly at her, as if trying to remember who she was. She remembered Dr. Mobley mentioning possible confusion.

"It is Meadow," she said and then corrected herself. "Lady Selfridge. Your wife."

The last time he had addressed her as Meadow had been when repeating their wedding vows. To the servants, he called her Lady Selfridge. The few times they were alone, he referred to her as Wife.

Misery filled his face. "What's wrong with me?" he asked feebly.

"It is the pneumonia, my lord. You have a high fever." She brushed the damp cloth across his brow again.

"Stop that," he ordered.

Meadow withdrew the cloth and rested it beside the bowl as he began coughing. She handed him a handkerchief. After the fit subsided, he passed it to her and she saw the dull green mucus mixed with blood.

"I'm dying?" he finally asked.

"Yes, my lord," she replied evenly.

His symptoms had only started three days ago and hadn't worsened until yesterday. Suddenly, Meadow realized that with her husband's passing, she might have nowhere to go. The heir to the viscountcy was a nephew she had met at her wedding and hadn't seen since then. Once he was notified that he was the new Viscount Selfridge, she most likely would be asked to leave. Her parents were dead, her mother dying after the last of half a dozen miscarriages when Meadow was twelve. Her father had passed two years ago. With no son, the earldom had gone to a cousin fifteen years older than she was, and she hadn't heard a word from him since that time.

Where would she go?

She chided herself silently for only thinking of herself when the man in the bed probably had less than a day to live. Still, he had presented her with no jewelry during their marriage. The thought would never have occurred to him. Everything in this house, beyond her clothes, would belong to the next Viscount Selfridge. Panic rose within her.

Then she relaxed. Tilda would take her in. Her cousin, only a year Meadow's senior, was now the Countess of Marshmore. They had been close growing up and even made their come-outs together though Meadow had only been to a handful of the Season's events before her father insisted she wed Lord Selfridge. The couple had retired from London society after their hasty marriage and never participated in a Season again. At least she hadn't. Selfridge had gone to town numerous times over the years without her for long stretches, always in search of new items to collect.

She and Tilda still exchanged letters, though, several times a year. Meadow knew her cousin would offer her a place to stay. Knowing Tilda, she would push for Meadow to re-enter Polite Society as quickly as possible and find another husband.

It wasn't a bad idea. This time, she was free and could make her own decision. Marry a man of her own choosing.

And finally have the children she so desperately desired.

"You're my wife, you said?" her husband asked, studying her closely.

"Yes, my lord. We have been wed six years."

"How old are you?"

"Twenty-four."

"Hmm."

Another round of coughing occurred, weakening him further.

She bathed his face again with fresh water, his skin blazing to the touch.

"Sell the collection," he mumbled.

"The collection, my lord?" she asked. "You have several. Everything you have accumulated will belong to the next Lord Selfridge."

"They like you, don't they? The servants. The tenants. I remember that. They always tell me so."

His words pleased her since she had devoted herself to those on his estate.

He began to shake violently and Meadow pulled the bedclothes up to his neck.

"Thank you," he wheezed.

"I am here for you, my lord. Let me know what you need."

"I wish I remembered you," he said sadly. "Are you my daughter?"

Sadness washed over her. "No, my lord. I am your wife."

"My wife." He mulled that over. "When I am gone, where will you go?"

She shook her head. "I have no idea. Probably to my cousin."

"Sell the collection," he repeated.

"You collect many things."

Including me.

"Sell it," he insisted. "In my study. The chest in the corner. The key is in the vase on the table by the window. Sell it—and you will have more than enough. Tell no one." He swallowed, clearly in pain. "Kibbard wants it."

Meadow couldn't imagine what he referred to or who Kibbard might be. She had never been inside the viscount's study during all the years of their marriage. He went there frequently after dinner and remained inside for hours anytime he was in the country. She had always wondered what he did behind closed doors.

"Rest now," she urged, watching as he closed his eyes.

Over the next several hours, his breathing grew more labored and his fever spiked. He murmured incoherently for several minutes before another coughing spell struck, exhausting him. When it finished, he gazed up at her with sad eyes.

"Who are you?"

Those were his last words.

His eyes closed and he took a single breath before he shuddered and grew still. She waited a moment and then touched her fingers to his throat. Finding no pulse, she placed them under his nose and found no air came out. She rose and pulled the rope, summoning their butler, who appeared with the viscount's valet.

"Lord Selfridge has passed," she announced to them. "Please send a message to Dr. Mobley to that effect and to the vicar. Ask that he come tomorrow morning and meet with me regarding his lordship's funeral service."

"Yes, my lady," the butler said. "We shall prepare the body. Might we do anything for you?"

Dry-eyed, she said, "No, thank you. I will leave you to your task."

Meadow left the bedchamber and roamed the halls for several minutes, stretching her legs and clearing her head. She had no appetite, despite not having eaten since early that morning. She decided she should go to bed. First thing tomorrow, she would write to the new Viscount Selfridge.

Returning to her bedchamber, she paused at the door, remembering her husband's words.

Sell the collection.

Curiosity overwhelmed her. She wondered what the viscount might have collected and pored over in his study all those many hours. Of course, she wouldn't think of selling it and keeping the profits. Whatever it was, it belonged to the heir since it had been purchased with estate funds. Still, she wanted to see what her husband referred to.

Heading downstairs, Meadow opened the study door for the first time and entered the chilly room that had been her husband's sanctuary, feeling guilty as she closed it behind her. She glanced about the room and spotted the table sitting by the window. Crossing the room, she picked up the vase, Grecian in style, and turned it upside down. A small key fell into her palm. Nervously, she turned and found a battered chest in the corner of the room, looking out of place among the rest of the room's elegant furnishings.

She went to it and dropped to her knees. Inserting the key in the lock, it turned easily. She lifted the lid and saw stacks of lithographs lying within it. Lifting the one on top of the first stack, her jaw dropped as she viewed it.

It was a picture of a couple doing something incredibly lewd, something so unfathomable that she blinked rapidly several times, trying to make sense of it. She set it aside and picked up another one. Then another. Each scene depicted naked people, sometimes a solitary figure but more often two people. Not all were English. Some of the lithographs portrayed couples from the Far East.

Embarrassed, she quickly replaced the lithographs and shut the trunk, locking it again.

This was what Selfridge had spent hours looking upon each night after they dined?

Meadow's face grew hot with embarrassment. Obviously, he had been collecting the lithographs for quite some time to have amassed so many of them. She guessed there must be hundreds within the ancient chest. If she left them for the next Selfridge, what would he think of her? Her husband? Would he go and blab what he had found to Polite Society? If he did, her reputation would be ruined. Thoughts of marrying again would be impossible. If any gentleman of the *ton* thought she had viewed this sordid collection with her husband, much less acted out the various scenes depicted, she would become a pariah.

No, no one must ever see these lithographs. Ever.

Should she call for a servant to light a fire so she could burn the assorted pictures?

Meadow rose to summon one and then caught herself.

Selfridge seemed to think the collection was worth a great deal. He said it would be more than enough. But how was she to go about finding Kibbard, whoever he might be? Was he the seller of such wicked goods? Or a collector as Selfridge was? Either way, it would be foolish to burn something that might be so valuable, though she couldn't imagine the kind of person who might enjoy looking at such things.

Pocketing the key, she left the study in search of a footman. When she found one, she brought him back to her husband's study and directed him to bring the trunk to her bedchamber, even waiting for him to lift it and escorting him there. She had him place it behind her dressing screen and then thanked him.

"I am sorry to hear his lordship is gone, my lady," the footman told her.

"Thank you," she said and showed him out the door.

As Meadow closed it, she leaned against it and took a deep breath, relaxing as she did. Though her future was uncertain, she was finally free of her husband. She had been isolated in the country for many years. Now, she would have a chance to return to society and make a match.

Freedom tasted sweet as she twirled and fell on her bed, allowing her laughter to finally be released.

CHAPTER FOUR

Amberwood—February 1811

WYATT ROSE, WASHED, and dressed in his captain's uniform because it was the only clothing he possessed.

He didn't *want* to be a bloody duke. He couldn't believe he had been forced back from the war, doing the king's business, just to claim a title he never wanted.

Going downstairs to the kitchens, several servants scurried from his path, averting their eyes as he stomped through the halls of Amberwood. He had loved this place once and been banished from it.

He wondered if he had it in him to love it again.

Entering the kitchens, he went to Cook, who gave him a genuine smile. Wyatt wondered when the last time that had occurred. Four years at war had seared his soul.

"Good morning, Your Grace," she said merrily. "We must decide how you will take your breakfast. In the breakfast room, I suppose. I can either have a buffet laid out for you or make whatever you wish each morning."

He sat at the table. "I'd rather eat here," he said sullenly.

Her eyes widened. She glanced around and said, "Leave us."

Quickly, the scullery maids vacated the room. Cook sat across from him and frowned.

"It doesn't do to have a duke eating in his kitchens, Your

Grace."

Wyatt sighed. "What if I don't wish to be Amesbury?"

She clucked her tongue. "That is neither here nor there. The fact is you *are* Amesbury now so you'd best make up your mind to be a good one. The last two certainly weren't," she added, her frankness bold for a servant but appreciated by him all the same.

"Can I be a good duke?" he asked, uncertainty filling him. "I've already sacked my butler and housekeeper."

"You did that with good reason," she assured him. "Both of them were judgmental coming out of the womb. Amberwood will be better off without the pair."

He raked a hand through his hair. "It was how they looked at me, Cook. As if they still blamed me for what happened to the horses in the stables all those years ago. I didn't cause the fire," he insisted.

She nodded. "Most of the servants realized that, Your Grace. Especially with Joan leaving and marrying that dairy farmer so quickly. It was obvious your brother was up to no good, as usual, and you were the wee boy who paid the ultimate price for his sins."

"How is Joan?" he asked. "I have thought of her often over the years."

"I'm sorry to say that she lost her husband a few weeks ago. She's a widow now."

A thought occurred to him. "Where is this dairy farm?" he asked, and Cook told him.

She rose. "Be off with you. Go to the breakfast room like a good duke should. I'll send a plate to you. And a slice of pie with it," she declared.

He chuckled. "You remembered?"

She beamed at him. "You always did like your pies, Your Grace. And now that you're a duke, I say you should celebrate and have a slice for breakfast. It's apple. I made it last night, once you'd arrived."

He stood and bent to kiss her cheek. "Thank you," he said

simply and retreated to dine in solitude.

As he ate, Wyatt determined to speak to Miles before he did anything at Amberwood. His friend had left the army the previous spring when he had unexpectedly become the Duke of Winslow. Wyatt knew Miles would have seized the reins at Wildwood and be someone who could give him advice he could trust.

But first, he would go and see Joan.

He had no butler to inform to have the carriage readied so he walked to the stables. The structure faced a different direction than the previous one. He closed his eyes a moment and could still see the fire blazing out of control. Hear the screams of the horses as they burned.

All because of Clive.

A groom emerged and Wyatt said, "Have my driver ready the carriage."

"Yes, Your Grace."

Minutes later, the horses had been harnessed and a man of about forty strode toward him.

"I'm Blevins, Your Grace. Your driver."

"Good to meet you, Blevins. We are headed to a local dairy farm first, where a Mr. Haskins and his family reside. Then it will be on to Maidstone. After that, we will call upon the Duke of Winslow at Wildwood. It's about ten miles north of Maidstone. We may stay a day or two there."

"Very good, Your Grace."

Wyatt climbed into the vehicle and watched the countryside pass for a few minutes. His emotions still jumbled inside of him, a constant turmoil ever since he had received the letter naming him the Duke of Amesbury. The carriage turned and he sat up, preparing himself to speak to Joan. Praying she would accept his offer.

A footman placed stairs down and Wyatt descended from the carriage. He saw a small house to his left and a large barn to his right. He decided to try the barn first, knowing Haskins was gone and figuring Joan now cared for their herd of cows.

As he entered the barn, he heard her voice, recognizing it after all these years.

"That's right, Philip. A gentle hand goes a long away. Keep to the lessons your father taught you and all will be well."

Wyatt followed her voice and found Joan sitting on a stool. A boy of about eleven or twelve sat on a second stool as they milked a cow.

Before he could make his presence known, she glanced up. He saw recognition in her eyes. She scrambled to her feet, drawing the boy up with her, and dropped a curtsey.

"Your Grace."

"Good morning, Joan. Or Mrs. Haskins, I'm told."

A shadow flickered across her face. "Yes, I am Mrs. Haskins. And this is my boy, Philip."

"Hello, Philip," he said pleasantly, noting the boy had his mother's golden hair and kind eyes. "I knew your mother when I was younger than you are now."

"Pleased to meet you, Your Grace," the boy said, nodding his head.

"Might we speak privately a moment?" he asked.

"Philip, continue with the milking. I will be back shortly." She indicated for Wyatt to follow her and they went to the entrance of the barn.

"I must offer you my condolences. I hear you are a recent widow," he said.

"Yes, we lost Mr. Haskins almost a month ago."

"Do you plan to keep the dairy farm?"

She shrugged. "What choice do I have? If I can keep it afloat, it will be Philip's legacy."

"What if you had a chance to do something different?" he proposed. "I would like you to return to Amberwood as my housekeeper."

"Your—what?"

"Housekeeper, Joan. I let go both my housekeeper and butler.

It was obvious to me they still believed the lies from all those years ago. I wasn't comfortable having them serve me at Amberwood." He sighed. "I will need massive help in running the estate. In running all the estates I have inherited. I need people around me I can trust. You are one of those people, Joan."

Her smile warmed him. "You are a good man, Your Grace. It would be a wonderful opportunity for me." She hesitated. "Still, Mr. Haskins would want Philip to have the dairy farm. My husband was a very independent man."

"I'll buy the bloody farm," he told her, not wanting anything to stand in her way of returning to Amberwood. "Have others take care of it for now. If Philip still wants it when he comes of age, I will gift it to him."

"You are serious," she said, clearly stunned by his proposal.

"Absolutely. In the meantime, you and Philip can come to Amberwood. The boy can train to be whatever you wish." He smiled ruefully. "I also let Clive's valet go. I had a feeling the first time he shaved me, he might slit my throat."

She laughed. "You have to admit that both the previous dukes are rolling in their graves at the thought of you as Amesbury." She sobered. "Yes, Philip would do well training as your valet. But for you to gift him with the farm if he chose that path in life? It is far too generous, Your Grace."

"Let us cross that bridge several years from now. Can you come today?"

"I would need to find someone to take over the milking of the cows. It must be done at least twice a day, but preferably thrice."

"Come along," he said, marching over to Blevins and the footman and motioning them over.

Blevins hurried down from his driver's seat. "Yes, Your Grace?"

"Mrs. Haskins has agreed to become my new housekeeper. She will start in the position immediately. Help her and her boy to pack. Someone must be found to milk her cows in the meantime and keep the dairy farm running."

The footman spoke up. "Our newest groom came from a dairy farm, Your Grace. He would know what to do."

"Very well. Walk back to Amberwood and fetch him. Bring back a cart for Mrs. Haskins' things. Blevins, convey her and Philip to the house in it."

"But what of the carriage, Your Grace?" asked the puzzled driver.

"I shall take it into Maidstone and on to Wildwood," he stated.

"You . . . a duke . . . driving a carriage?" Blevins sputtered.

"I know how to drive a bloody carriage," Wyatt shouted angrily. "Simply because I have become a duke overnight doesn't mean I don't remember how to dress myself or handle horses. Do as I say without question."

"Your Grace? A word?" Joan asked, steel in her voice.

"Yes?"

She walked away from the driver and footman until they couldn't be overheard.

"This is not like you, Your Grace. You have never spoken with such ill temper to anyone, least of all a servant."

"I shouldn't be questioned," he said, fury now flowing through him. "I am a duke."

"No, but you must admit the thought of a duke driving his own ducal carriage is something no servant might ever imagine. I understand that you are angry. You have been taken from the life you have known and sucked back into one that rejected you when you were still a small boy. You are a good man, Your Grace. You proved that when you came to my rescue and stood up for me against your brother all those years ago. Don't make the mistake of being an arrogant lord. Be respectful to your staff and you will earn their loyalty a hundredfold."

Wyatt took a calming breath. "I know you are right. It is just one of many reasons why I need you at Amberwood. Will you still come? Or have I already ruined everything?"

"Of course, I will come," she reassured him. "The opportunity to run a duke's country seat is something I would never refuse."

"Thank you, Joan. I'm sorry. Mrs. Haskins. I suppose we will have to be more formal now that our roles have changed."

"You will grow into your new role, Your Grace. I have faith that you will be the duke Amberwood has long cried out for."

He returned to his servants. "I am sorry for my earlier behavior. It was uncalled for."

Shock filled Blevins' face, while the footman looked as if he might faint at receiving an apology from a duke.

"Please take care of Mrs. Haskins and her son as I asked." He turned to her. "Mrs. Haskins, you have the authority to make any changes necessary. We can discuss more upon my return. I am off to see an old friend for a day or two and then I will return."

"Certainly, Your Grace," Joan said. To the servants, she added, "I will show you what will be moved but first, I must finish the milking." Glancing back at him, she said, "Have a safe trip, Your Grace."

Wyatt climbed into the driver's seat and took up the reins. Knowing the others looked at him, he prayed the team would cooperate. They did and he set out for Maidstone, another six miles away. Once he arrived, he headed to the hostler's and left the horses in his care, telling the hostler he would be gone an hour or two and asking that the horses be fed and watered.

That taken care of, Wyatt continued to the local tailor's shop that he remembered his family patronizing. He couldn't wear his captain's uniforms forever and needed something quickly. He had the tailor measure him for three coats and three pairs of trousers and half a dozen shirts. He decided he would accrue the bulk of his wardrobe in London before the Season began.

Thoughts of entering ballrooms and attending social events was the last thing Wyatt wanted to dwell upon but he determined he must find a bride and get an heir as quickly as possible. Clive apparently had thought he had all the time in the world—and look what had happened. Instead of Clive's son becoming

Amesbury as should have occurred, Clive died a bachelor, allowing the brother he despised to claim his title. Wyatt hadn't a clue as to who might be his heir apparent but if he were to be Amesbury now, he would be the best damned Amesbury he could be. He would train his son to be the same.

A son meant a wife—and finding the right kind of wife suitable to be a duchess meant traveling to London. The upcoming Season would allow him his choice. As a duke, he would have his pick of any number of lovely young women. He would find one as soon as possible and wed and bed her in order to get the heir he needed.

With that in mind, Wyatt reclaimed his carriage and set out for Wildwood, having asked the tailor its exact location and learning he could be at Miles' estate in less than an hour. It would be nice living so close to his old friend. Miles would probably have advice for Wyatt as he entered the Marriage Mart since Miles had wed shortly after he returned to England. It had surprised Wyatt when he had received the letter from Miles revealing he no longer was a bachelor. Perhaps the new duchess could help Wyatt make a match.

Determination filled him as he steered the carriage north.

He arrived at Wildwood, taking in its lush landscape, happy for his friend. Bringing the horses to a halt in front of the stately mansion, he exited the driver's seat, only to find a groom waiting him.

"Shall I take your horses and carriage to the stables, Captain?"

"Yes," he said. "I will be staying a day or so."

"They're a fine team," the lad said, climbing into the driver's seat and turning the carriage.

Wyatt went to the front door and knocked. A butler answered.

"I am here to see His Grace," he said, not recalling Miles' title. "I am not expected. I have no calling cards. But he'll want to see me all the same."

"Come in, Captain," the butler invited.

He entered the grand foyer and saw a woman of great beauty descending the stairs, curiosity on her face. This could be none other than Emery, Miles' duchess.

"A visit from a captain? Which Turner Terror might you be?" she mused.

"You know of us?" he asked, surprised.

"Of course," she said. "Finch officiated at my wedding ceremony."

"Your Grace," he said, bowing to her.

"You must be Wyatt Stanton," she continued. "It's your eyes. Miles said they were hazel. I like the mix of greens and browns in them. He will be so happy you've come to call." She looked at the butler. "Mr. Trottmann, please inform His Grace that Captain Stanton has arrived. Have tea sent to the drawing room, as well." She smiled, her eyes sparkling. "But wait a quarter-hour before you do so. I want to have the captain all to myself and see what wicked things I can learn about my husband."

"Of course, Your Grace," the butler said, not bothering to hide his smile as he left.

The duchess slipped her hand through Wyatt's arm. "Come with me, Captain. I am sure you have much you can tell me."

CHAPTER FIVE

W YATT ALLOWED MILES' wife to lead him up the staircase. As they reached the landing, she came to an abrupt halt and made an odd noise. Pulling away, she ran the few steps to a bowl sitting on a table and vomited into it. Quickly, she slipped a handkerchief from her sleeve and patted her mouth and then walked back to the stairs.

Calling down, she said, "I've done it again."

A maid appeared at the foot of the stairs. "I'll take care of it right away, Your Grace." She began hurrying toward them.

The duchess took his arm again and tugged him along, climbing the staircase.

"I do apologize, Captain," she said, her cheeks tinged with pink. "The nausea strikes me at the oddest times. My mother tells me it will eventually pass."

They reached the next floor and he paused. "You are with child."

"I am. It's early yet. Come the end of September—or possibly the beginning of October—Miles and I will be parents."

"My heartiest congratulations, Your Grace."

She frowned. "Oh, please. None of this Your Grace. Finch calls me Emery. I expect you should do the same."

"Then please call me Wyatt," he told her, already liking Miles' wife a great deal.

They went to the drawing room and made themselves comfortable and then she said, "Please, tell me about Miles as a boy. I am so curious."

He cleared his throat. "Well, none of the Turner Terrors were perfect angels, else we wouldn't have been sent there."

"Oh, none of you had done any of those terrible things," she insisted. "Miles has shared with me a little of each of your stories. He loves you more than brothers."

It took him aback that his friend had opened up about the pasts of each Terror, but then one look at Emery and Wyatt could understand. He could tell she was friendly and supportive. Naturally, Miles would have confided in her, especially because he had written to each Terror to tell them he'd made a love match and hoped they all found their own one day. Wyatt and Donovan had a good laugh about it at the time, knowing they both enjoyed the company of women far too much to ever become a husband to merely one woman.

Yet here he was only weeks later, disengaged from his army career and attempting to be a duke. *And find a bride*, he reminded himself.

"Do you have any friends, Emery? Ones who might wish to wed?"

She eyed him with interest. "Are you in the market for a bride, Captain?"

He sighed. "I must confess that I am no longer Captain Stanton. I have sold my commission."

"You've what?"

Miles came striding across the room and Emery said, "You aren't supposed to be here yet. I was ready to extract all kinds of information from Wyatt before you showed up."

The two men shook hands and then Miles hugged Wyatt tightly.

"It is good to see you, my friend. Now, what's this about selling out?" Miles took a seat next to Emery and threaded his fingers through hers as he tenderly kissed her cheek.

The gestures took Wyatt aback. He watched as the couple

smiled at one another, forgetting for a moment that they had a guest. It was a powerful few seconds, one that impressed him to no end.

He wanted what they had. Desperately.

Wyatt hadn't thought about marriage at any point in his life until recently and then only in vague terms simply because he desired an heir. The idea of love entering into the equation never occurred to him. Seeing the look in Miles' eyes as he gazed at his wife was like being struck with lightning, however. His friend, always so solid and practical, had an added layer to himself.

"Miles," Emery said gently when it looked as if her husband leaned forward to kiss her, "we do have company."

Miles blinked twice. "Yes. We do." He gave his wife a charming smile and then looked to Wyatt.

"Why have you left the army? Of all of us, you were the one who seemed to love war the most." He turned to Emery. "Wyatt wasn't a typical soldier. Now that he has left service, I can tell you that he acted upon numerous occasions as a spy for Wellington. Also a scout. Wyatt spent as much time in threadbare civilian clothes as he did his officer's uniform."

"Is this true?" Emery asked. "It sounds dangerous."

"It was," Wyatt confided. "When Miles and I last spoke, I was about to insert myself into a ring of men with French sympathies. I did so and built a case against them. Frankly, I despised having to leave the army because I had created a large network of spies who reported to me. It took months to build trust with them. Wellington was furious."

"Why did you leave then?" Miles asked. "Unless . . ." His voice trailed off. "No. Clive."

"Yes. Clive is dead. Apparently, my father died almost a decade ago and Clive spent most of his time either spending money or drinking it away. He was drunk at ten o'clock in the morning when he went to descend the stairs and tumbled down them. He broke his neck in the fall.

"I am the Duke of Amesbury now."

Emery reached out and placed a hand upon his. "I know the animosity that lay between you and your brother. I understand how becoming a duke was the last thing you envisioned. It will take time to sort out your feelings. Miles will be here to help you."

"Thank you. Yes, I have come to complain to my old friend." He shook his head. "How many men in England would prefer skulking about with treacherous traitors over becoming a duke and living a life of opulence?"

"Only you," Miles said, smiling. "Then again, you have always been a rebel at heart, Wyatt. The one good thing that will come of it is that you will be able to help your people. Your brother no doubt sorely neglected them."

"I am certain he did. I know I have an entire estate to learn about. More, actually. In truth, I have no idea the number of properties I now possess. A solicitor is coming at the end of the week to discuss my financial affairs." He paused. "I need help, Miles. You know what kind of student I was. I could barely tolerate sitting in the classroom. I always wanted to be out doing something. I have no idea how to read a ledger. I'm not a farmer and have no knowledge of the growing seasons or what crop yields are about. I came here today to plead with you to help me. I understand you are still new at this—but you've got to know more than I do."

Miles smiled. "Oh, I am still learning, my friend. But I have a most excellent teacher." He turned to his wife. "Emery is an expert at numbers and crop rotation and animal breeding."

Then Miles kissed her, shocking Wyatt to his core. The ever in control Miles Notley was besotted with his wife.

Breaking the kiss, Miles grinned. "I find I have to do that every so often or I might lose my sanity. Emery thinks I should practice more restraint."

She stroked her husband's cheek. "Only in front of others, darling." Her eyes turned mischievous and Wyatt decided the very proper-looking Duchess of Winslow might be a wanton in the bedroom.

Miles chuckled. "Emery's father served as Wildwood's steward for many years and then she took the job upon herself when his health took a turn for the worse. She can run an estate as well as any man. Better than most if I am allowed to brag upon her."

Miles lifted her hand and tenderly kissed her fingers. Again, the sweet, simple gesture told Wyatt that great love existed between these two.

"We would be happy to accompany you back to your country estate," Emery said, tearing her gaze from her husband. "I can spend a week with you, teaching you the most important things you need to know and what to look for." She stopped. "And I believe you mentioned something about finding a bride?"

Wyatt felt the color rise in his cheeks. "I figured a duke needs a duchess. Miles found one in record time. I thought if you knew of anyone—friends, acquaintances, cousins—who might be eager to wed, I am newly available and a much better catch as a duke than a spy."

Emery and Miles both laughed heartily.

"Shall we work on getting your estate in hand first, Wyatt?" Emery said. "Then we can think about a bride. I have lived all my life in the country. Miles has promised to take me to London for the first part of the Season. While we prefer country life, he wishes me to get a taste of Polite Society and introduce me about. I am positive I can help you find your duchess there. After all, there will be many young ladies to choose from."

Miles took her hand and brought it to his lips for a kiss. "Who knows, Wyatt? You might fall in love with the first woman you see."

He wanted to tell the pair love had nothing to do with marriage. That he only wanted a wife in order to get an heir and, hopefully, a spare. But he fought the desire that filled him to have the kind of marriage Miles and Emery had.

Could he possibly find love?

He doubted it.

CHAPTER SIX

London—Opening night of the Season

MEADOW DISMISSED THE maid who had helped her dress and arrange her hair. She gazed intently into the mirror, wondering how she would be received at tonight's ball, held by Lord and Lady Rockwell. She had been an acquaintance of Lady Rockwell during their come-out but Meadow had not seen her since her marriage. She hadn't seen anyone, having been left in the country while her husband made frequent trips to London, both during and after the Season.

She had never understood his fascination with collecting things. Especially her. Once he had claimed her and told her why he wed her, she had thought he would want to show off what he considered his prized possession. Instead, once purchased, she had been ignored.

She studied her image with a critical eye. Her hair, glossy brown, was what she considered her best feature. The maid had piled it high atop Meadow's head, helping give her a bit of height since she was but two inches over five feet. The peach gown suited her coloring. She only hoped her neckline wasn't too low. She hadn't worn a ball gown in years. Tilda assured her this was in style and that it showed off her figure well.

At least she had money to purchase gowns. Her father might have been a spendthrift and gambler but the wedding contracts he had negotiated with Viscount Selfridge had actually seen that Meadow was taken care of once she became a widow. The new Lord Selfridge and his solicitor had explained to her that for every year of marriage, the contracts had called for her to receive the sum of one thousand pounds upon the death of her husband. Since she had been wed to Selfridge for six years, she was issued six thousand pounds, a small fortune. Her husband had told her that he bought up markers that bore her father's name in the amount of five thousand pounds before their marriage, so she thought she had actually made a profit. It was a godsend, though, that her father was already dead, else he would have demanded the full sum from her, thinking it his own.

She could have rented a small place to live but her cousin had insisted that Meadow come live with her. Tilda had a generous soul and the past year, though spent in mourning, had been the best of Meadow's life. Tilda had two sons, three and five years of age, and being with the boys had made the year fly by. It only confirmed what she knew in her heart, that she was destined to be a mother.

Glancing in the mirror again, she wondered what it would be like competing against all the fresh-faced beauties making their come-outs. Would any gentleman bother to even look at her with so many new faces appearing on the Marriage Mart? She didn't need a handsome or wealthy man. She simply wanted a husband who would be kind and give her the children she longed for.

A soft knock sounded at the door and Tilda entered, closing the door behind her. Her cousin looked lovely in a lilac frock and matching gloves.

"Oh, my!" Tilda exclaimed. "You look heavenly, Meadow. The men will be falling over themselves when they see you."

"I don't know about that. I am five and twenty, Tilda. Many of them might consider me too old to pursue."

Tilda sighed. "I need to speak to you, Meadow. About tonight. And your expectations."

"Oh." She swallowed. "I suppose you're here to tell me that

many new young ladies will be at the Rockwells' ball tonight. I know I am no fresh flower to be plucked. If I could find an older gentleman, perhaps a widower who needs a mother for his children, I would be happy. I understand I cannot expect a young man close to my own age to express interest in me."

"On the contrary, many will." Tilda took her hands. "I need to have a frank conversation with you, Meadow. One that may prove to be a bit awkward but Marshmore and I have your best interests at heart—so hear me out."

"What is it?" she asked, concerned at how serious her cousin looked.

"You will gain quite a bit of attention tonight because you are a widow."

"I hope the night won't be full of sympathy for me simply because I lost a husband."

"No, that is not what I mean. There will be a group of men on the prowl, looking especially for widows." Tilda paused. "They will be interested in . . . sexual congress with you."

She wrinkled her nose. "I don't understand. What is that?"

Her cousin now squeezed Meadow's hands. "They are the rakes that we were warned about, Meadow. The ones whom you must never be alone with, else your reputation will be ruined. They are interested in affairs of the heart. Or body, more like it. These rogues seek out widows because they are experienced."

Her cheeks burned at what her cousin revealed. Tilda would think Meadow was embarrassed. In truth, she was humiliated because she was still a virgin and knew nothing of relations between a man and woman. With her mother passing when Meadow was but twelve, no one had tutored her about the wedding night and beyond. Even now, though she had delivered countless babies over the years, she understood nothing about the ways of lovemaking that got those babies here.

She supposed she could have looked at the hidden collection to try and figure things out but she had not opened that trunk since the night Selfridge died. It came with her and sat in a corner of her bedchamber now, waiting for her to do something with it.

"Marshmore and I wanted you to be warned. You only had a couple of weeks in your only Season, while I had my entire one and have participated in several beyond that. I know from gossip and innuendo about these rakes and the widows they target."

Tilda's face softened. "I am not saying I would prevent you from engaging in an affair. If you do so, however, you must be extremely discreet."

Her face now flaming, Meadow said, "I would never lie with a man outside the bonds of wedlock."

"Very well. Then Marshmore and I will steer you to the right kind of man."

"Do you think your husband has a friend that I might suit with?"

Tilda shrugged. "We haven't discussed that possibility. I just want you to be very careful, Meadow. As you were told before, never be alone with a man. It could lead to your ruin. Your goal is to wed by Season's end. If you are caught kissing one of these rakes—or worse—it would ruin your chances of making a respectable match. Others would gossip that you were free with your favors. So you must avoid those young bucks who merely want to bed you. Oh, eventually most of them settle down, especially those holding a title and desiring an heir."

Her cousin placed her hands on Meadow's shoulders. "What are you looking for in a husband? A title? Wealth?"

"Neither," she replied. "I would be happy with a man of plain looks and no title, as long as he was of good character and kind. Though I suppose if he has no title, he will be in search of a hefty dowry. What I have from Selfridge is quite adequate but I am certain the amount couldn't compete with many of the other ladies on the Marriage Mart and the dowries they possess."

Tilda cupped her cheek. "We will find a good man for you, Meadow. I simply wanted you to be warned about the rogues out there and how many of them prey upon widows."

"I wish you would have told me this before. Hearing it now,

as we are about to leave for the first event of the Season, has me flustered."

Tilda stepped away, chuckling. "It is because I knew you would fret that I did not share this information with you before. You would have worried yourself sick." She linked arms with Meadow. "Come, let us go downstairs. Marshmore will be waiting."

She accompanied her cousin downstairs and greeted the earl.

"Ready for tonight's ball?" he asked.

"If you are asking if Tilda has prepared me for the reputation widows have, yes, my lord. I am most ready. I will be circumspect with whom I dance and I know never to be alone with any man, gentleman or rake."

"If any wish to call upon you tomorrow, Meadow, only agree to the ones you think have potential," Tilda volunteered. "And no rides in Hyde Park or walks in a garden until we know more of a man's motives."

"I understand, Tilda. And thank you for explaining these unwritten rules of Polite Society to me. I fear there is so much I still don't know."

"Come along, Cousin," Tilda said happily. "I remember that you loved to dance. That will be appropriate tonight. It's a second come-out for you, shedding your widow's weeds and entering Polite Society again. We will have fun. I promise."

As they entered the carriage and made their way through the streets of London, nerves sprouted within Meadow. She had been trusting when she entered her first Season years ago. After being sold, in effect, by her father, she was not that naive girl anymore. She was strong. Resilient. Fortunately, she wouldn't have to risk her heart in order to find a man and bear him children. Love hadn't been a part of her parents' marriage and certainly not one of her own. Even Tilda and Marshmore seemed civil toward one another but showed no signs of affection.

Though her girlhood dreams had included finding love, Meadow had become pragmatic. If she could find a decent man who would treat her with respect and agree to give her children, she would agree to marry him and run his household with ease.

The carriage halted and a footman helped them descend the stairs.

Ready or not, Meadow moved toward the Rockwell mansion.

WYATT SAT OPPOSITE Miles and Emery as their driver started up the carriage. They were going to Lord and Lady Rockwell's ball, the first event of the Season. Nerves filled him, which he would never admit to his friends.

"You look especially lovely tonight, Emery," he said, reaching for her hand and kissing her fingers.

"If you plan to remain alive long enough to look for a duchess of your own, you'll release my wife's hand at once," Miles growled ill-temperedly.

He grinned at Emery and did as her husband asked, sitting back against the plush leather seat.

"I do enjoy this side of you, Miles," he drawled. "My stoic, steely friend, who now melts at the first sight of his wife and whose jealous streak runs wide. You have to know there will be many men who kiss her hand tonight."

"Not without me by her side," Miles said succinctly.

"Are you her jailor?" he teased.

"No," his friend said softly, gazing at his wife in utter devotion. "Her slave."

Miles leaned in and kissed Emery, something Wyatt had witnessed on more than one occasion. The couple had accompanied him back to Amberwood, where in two weeks' time, Emery had done her best to cram as much knowledge regarding estate affairs into Wyatt's head. He had been amazed that the beauty had such keen intelligence and he'd learned more about ledgers and running an estate than he thought possible.

During their time at Amberwood, he had witnessed the devotion between the pair. They could merely gaze at one another and seem to hold a silent conversation between them. They were open with their affection and Wyatt found himself envious of their love match.

He expected nothing of the kind. His own parents had been strangers to one another. Though he had been at war for years, he knew the *ton* didn't wed for love. Miles and Emery would be a bit of an oddity tonight.

They finally stopped kissing and Wyatt said, "You realize you won't be able to do that in the Rockwells' ballroom."

Miles played with Emery's fingers. "I fully understand that. We are here tonight to allow me to show the world my beautiful bride."

"I don't consider myself a bride anymore, Husband," Emery teased. "We have been wed for months now and have a baby on the way. I am merely a wife."

"You are my wife," Miles murmured, kissing her fingers. "My duchess. The one woman meant for me."

"Oh, don't start again," Wyatt said, half-teasing, half-serious.

Emery withdrew her fingers from her husband's and said, "We should talk about what qualities you are looking for in your wife, Wyatt. That way, I will have an idea who might be a good match for you."

"My duchess is a wonderful judge of character," Miles said. "So tell us, what do you believe is essential in the future Duchess of Amesbury?"

He shrugged. "I am not judging you. Far from it. I am delighted you have found one another and that you are in love. I don't need that. I don't even want it."

"You don't want to find love?" Emery asked, disappointment filling her face.

"*Ton* matches are usually made to strengthen families, love," Miles told his wife. "Unite powerful ones together. Bring wealth to coffers. Love isn't a part of the process."

"That sounds so cold," she remarked. "Wyatt can do better than that."

"I don't want to do better," he said flatly, knowing if he didn't expect to find love that he couldn't possibly be disappointed. "I need an heir. Plain and simple. A spare would be nice, considering my own case. Since I have decided to wed, I will search among the newcomers, the ones making their come-out. They will be malleable. They will do as I ask and leave me alone."

Emery's eyes flashed with anger. "You will not, Wyatt Stanton. In fact, you need to look among women who are older. More mature. Who might have seen a Season or more. You need a woman of intelligence and charm. One who will match you in every way and not give in to you like some simpering fool would." She snorted. "I will look among those women and I am certain I will bring a few suitable candidates to your attention."

He shook his head. "Suit yourself, Emery. I plan to look among the fresh-faced girls who have no opinions. My title alone will dazzle them."

"You should find a woman who doesn't care if you possess a title," Emery retorted.

Wyatt ran his fingers through his hair. "Why were we even invited tonight?" he asked. "Neither of us knows Lord Rockwell."

"We are dukes," Miles said. "That is reason enough. Rockwell will be able to brag that he was the first to introduce the Duke and Duchess of Winslow into Polite Society. I am sure the *ton* is curious about the man who came home from war to be a duke and wed a woman from outside society a short while later." He smiled at his wife. "We had planned to attend a few events last summer when we came to London briefly on our honeymoon but decided against it."

He thought the newlyweds had probably not left their bed long enough to even think about attend a Season affair.

"I know I must be prepared," Emery added. "Because I am not of Polite Society, I most likely will not be accepted by all. Oh, there would never be a cut direct because I am a duchess, but I suppose some who are fawning to my face will utter nonsense about me behind my back. Still, I hope to make a few friends while we are in London."

"Do you still plan to stay a month or two?" Wyatt asked.

"I think six or eight weeks will be enough," Miles said. "We will have gone to a variety of events. I will also show Emery more of London and we will enjoy ourselves that way. So most likely, we will leave town by mid-June at the latest. The heat will have set in by then and Emery will be growing heavier with child. Retreating to Wildwood will be our only choice."

"Well, I would like you at my wedding," he said. "That means I must find a young lady and offer for her quickly so you might be present at the ceremony."

Emery laughed. "Even I know that you cannot walk up to a stranger and offer for her, Wyatt. You must first court her."

"Court her? Court her?" he repeated.

"Yes. You need to find several women suitable to become your duchess and get to know them. Call on them. Take them on walks or rides in the park. Oh, and escort them to Gunter's. I am most eager for Miles to take me there. I long to try the ices they sell. Perhaps we could even accompany you on a few of these outings and give you our opinion on your future intended."

He crossed his arms. "This sounds like more trouble than I had anticipated. Perhaps I can return to Amberwood and find someone in the neighborhood there, just as Miles did."

"No," Emery said firmly. "You are to stay in town and look here first. Only if no one seems agreeable to you will I allow you to look elsewhere."

Wyatt chuckled. "When did you become my keeper, Emery?"

"When I accepted you as a brother," she replied. "I always regretted being an only child. I have already taken to Finch and consider him my brother." She reached out and took his hand. "I feel the same about you, Wyatt."

His throat grew thick with emotion. "Thank you," he said. "I feel the same toward you. I felt like an only child. Clive was nine years my senior. He had nothing to do with me. That's one thing I want to change. I want to have children as quickly as possible and many of them. I want them to be close and love one another."

"Yet you don't care if you love your wife?" Miles persisted.

"I will respect her. Hopefully, I will even like her. But love will have nothing to do with our arrangement," Wyatt said firmly.

"We'll see." Emery smiled.

"So, what do you plan to do tonight, Wyatt?" Miles asked. "Cull a few young ladies from the pack and give them your charming smile? Ask them to dance?"

"I may have not liked academic lessons but if you remember, I excelled at the ones involving dancing and horses." He gave Miles a brilliant smile. "Yes, I plan to smile and dance. Who knows? By this time tomorrow, I may already have made up my mind as to who will be the new Duchess of Amesbury."

The vehicle slowed and then came to a halt. A footman opened the door.

"This is as close as the driver says we can get, Your Grace," the servant apologized. "With it being the first event, the crowds are large and their carriages swell the streets."

"Quite all right," Miles said agreeably and descended the stairs.

Emery followed and as she reached the last step, she frowned.

"What's wrong, love?"

"I am irritated. That's all. I purchased new slippers for tonight and now they will get muddy by the time we reach the Rock-wells' townhouse."

"No, they won't," her husband said, scooping her from the stairs and walking away.

Wyatt shook his head and hurried to catch up with them. Already, couples were motioning to the Winslows and whispering behind gloved hands.

"You do know you are causing a spectacle, Miles?" he asked

cheerfully.

"Who cares?" said his friend, sounding carefree and light-hearted. "My duchess will be the only one in the ballroom not traipsing about with muddy slippers. That is reason enough to allow a few tongues to wag."

As they made their way toward the Rockwell townhouse, he marveled at the change in his somber, steadfast friend. Love had altered everything about Miles.

Wyatt liked himself the way he was, however. He saw no need to change for any woman, much less one who would become his wife. If anyone needed to change, it would be the female in his marriage. He was perfectly happy with who he was.

And dared any woman to try and make him someone he wasn't.

CHAPTER SEVEN

M EADOW WENT THROUGH the receiving line with her cousin and husband. Lady Rockwell paused a moment.

"I know you," she said, her brows knitting together as she tried to recall their connection.

"We made our come-out together, Lady Rockwell. I was—"

"Lady Meadow," the countess interrupted. "I remember you now. You were the most beautiful girl in our group. I must say, we were all a bit relieved when you were quickly taken off the Marriage Mart. Everyone thought you would wind up with a marquess—if not a duke. Where have you been all this time?"

"In the country. I lost my husband and am only now returning to society. This is the first ball I have attended since I wed. I am Lady Selfridge."

The woman looked at her shrewdly. "You will get your fair share of attention, my lady. A pretty widow always does. A beautiful one will have her choice of lovers."

Her cheeks heated. "I do not seek a lover, Lady Rockwell. I would like to find a husband. I long for children."

The countess snorted. "They are tiresome. And they ruin your figure." She eyed Meadow up and down. "It is obvious you have had none with your hourglass silhouette."

"It was nice to see you again, my lady," she said, moving away, embarrassed by their conversation.

"She's right you know," Tilda said, parting from Marshmore,

who made for the card room. "You always did have quite the figure. That gown shows off your attributes."

Her face flamed. "I am afraid all men will do is stare at my bosom tonight."

"Let them," Tilda said airily. "It is a lovely one. If you are to entice a husband, it doesn't hurt to display it. Come along. I will introduce you to some of my friends."

A few of the names sounded familiar to Meadow but many did not. As she spoke to the circle of women, she sensed eyes upon her and looked to her right. Several men in their own tightknit circle studied her as if she were fresh meat upon which they planned to dine.

A storm of emotions whirled within her. She had thought tonight would be one of fun. Where she would reenter society and possibly make a friend or two as she danced with eligible men. Instead, she felt like a sheep surrounded by wolves ready to drag her away and feast.

"Meadow? Take your dance card," Tilda said.

"Sorry. I was woolgathering," she said, fighting the urge to lift her skirts and dash from the ballroom.

"Ah, here they come," a woman said as a group of men descended upon them.

"Not the dark-haired one on the right," murmured Tilda in her ear. "Or his blond friend. They are well-known for their bedroom antics."

"Tilda," Meadow hissed.

"I told you I was here to warn you, didn't I? I won't let you fall into the wrong hands."

The two men bowed to her and Tilda introduced them. Then she said, "My cousin is not dancing just yet gentlemen. Seek a partner elsewhere."

"Ah, protective, are we, Lady Marshmore?"

Tilda's chin went up a notch. "If you don't want my husband to soundly box your ears, you will depart, gentlemen."

The pair bowed again and left.

"Marshmore is known for his boxing skills," Tilda explained. "Oh, these three are wholly acceptable."

Over the next few minutes, many of the slots on Meadow's dance card filled. A few of her partners were actually handsome. Tilda said two were widowers and that both had small children. Meadow would definitely consider them.

She had ignored most of the announcements made by the butler when guests arrived because she had been caught up in conversations around her. A brief lull had occurred and so when the butler called out the next guests, she happened to glance up.

"The Duke and Duchess of Winslow and the Duke of Amesbury."

A quiet descended upon the ballroom as the trio appeared and paused in the doorway.

The Duke of Winslow was tall, lean, and had golden brown hair. Meadow was close enough to see the scar standing white against his tanned cheek. The duchess was very tall for a woman, just a few inches shorter than her husband. Her raven hair was artfully piled atop her head. She had a glow about her.

But it was their companion who drew Meadow's eyes. The Duke of Amesbury. He scanned the ballroom as if assessing its inhabitants. His athletic build suited him, as did the chocolate brown hair. He wore confidence as if it were a frock coat designed solely for him. An air of danger seemed to surround him.

Suddenly, his gaze locked on hers. For a moment, time stood still. She felt her heart fiercely beating. Her palms broke out in sweat, dampening her gloves.

Then he looked away. Meadow didn't know whether she felt relief or disappointment.

"Winslow carried his wife from their carriage to the front door," the woman on her left said excitedly. "I saw the entire incident. He just swept her up and didn't put her down until they had reached the entrance."

"I heard she didn't want her slippers muddied and she forced him to carry her," another said.

"She must have him wound tightly around her finger," a third said. "I heard her mother is the duke's housekeeper."

A murmur rose in the circle, disapproval obvious.

"I think it is sweet that he didn't want her slippers ruined," Meadow said, surprising herself when she spoke up.

When she'd made her come-out, she had been shy, over-whelmed by the massive attention she had received. She had remained withdrawn until several months after her marriage. Left to her own devices, she had slowly emerged from her shell, accepting her responsibilities of running the household and taking on others, many dealing with matters involving their tenants.

"Her Grace must be a very special woman for His Grace to wed her," she continued. "I would hate to see others gossip about her when they have yet to meet her."

Guilt flashed in the eyes of many surrounding her and Meadow felt good for having spoken up for this duchess.

"The previous Duke of Amesbury drank far too much. I heard his so-called accidental death was a result of his drinking," one woman said. "This new duke left the army to return to England and take up the title."

Her eyes searched the ballroom and found the man they spoke of. Yes, his bearing was that of someone in the army, with the ramrod posture. The look in his eyes drew her in, though. It spoke of someone who was undisciplined. Their eyes met again and he nodded to her. Meadow glanced away, feeling her cheeks flush.

"He's coming this way," Tilda hissed. "He's looking at you."

She kept her lashes lowered, staring at the ground. Then she sensed his presence and it was as if he forced her to look up.

"I know it untoward of me," he began, his voice a deep rumble. "However, I have been on the Continent for several years and know no one to make the introductions. Since I am a duke—and we all know no one tells a duke what he can and cannot do—I will introduce myself."

His eyes on her, he said, "I am the Duke of Amesbury."

She and everyone in the circle curtseyed. Tilda's fingers tightened on her arm almost painfully.

Amesbury asked, "And who might you be, my lady?"

"I am Lady Selfridge, Your Grace." She indicated Tilda. "This is my cousin, Lady Marshmore."

"A pleasure," he said, taking Tilda's hand and kissing it and then capturing Meadow's and doing the same.

He held it a moment longer than he should have, asking, "Do you have any vacancies on your programme, Lady Selfridge?"

"I d-do," she stammered.

"May I?"

He lifted the dance card from where it was tied to her wrist and studied it carefully. Taking the pencil, he scrawled his name.

"There. I shall see you for the supper dance."

She curtseyed again. "Yes, Your Grace."

He walked away without having acknowledged any of the others. They all began to buzz.

Tilda stared at her. "I know nothing of him. Only he is a duke, recently come into his title, and that he is close friends with Winslow." Her cousin shook her head. "Oh, be very careful, Meadow. You might have caught a tiger by the tail."

The others gazed upon her with every kind of look, from curious to disdainful to jealous.

Just then, the musicians began tuning their instruments and Lord and Lady Rockwell moved to the middle of the dance floor. Meadow's partner joined her.

"The Rockwells like to dance the first measures alone," he told her. "Lady Rockwell seems to enjoy the attention."

She thought that unkind to say, especially since she didn't even recall this man's name. She glanced at her programme and saw he was Lord Naughton. Mentally, she crossed him off her list of potential husbands. Any man who would be so callous as to made a disparaging remark about his hostess to a woman he had just met was not the husband for her.

Meadow danced several times over the next two hours and Tilda introduced her to many people in-between sets. She grew more anxious, though, as the supper dance approached. She had caught glimpses of the duke dancing with numerous women, all young ladies who looked as though they were making their come-out. If he was interested in obtaining a wife, it was obvious he was looking to the new faces in the crowd tonight.

Then why had he asked her to dance?

She was a good seven or more years older than tonight's group of debutantes. A duke could have his pick of any unmarried lady in this ballroom. Why had he singled her out?

Marshmore joined them. "I am here as expected for the supper dance," he told his wife and then to Meadow, he said, "Have you a partner? If you don't, you are most welcome to join us at supper, my lady."

"Oh, she has a partner, Marshmore," Tilda said, pride evident in her voice. "The Duke of Amesbury has asked to be her partner."

"Amesbury? Oh, the one who died recently. Hmm. So, it's the new duke who'll partner with you? I can't recall who the heir might be."

Meadow spied the duke making his way toward them. "He's coming this way," she told Marshmore.

"Oh. Him."

She frowned at the earl, catching the disdain in his voice. "Do you know him?"

"I went to school with him for a while. He left after two or three years to attend another one."

"Tell me what you know of him," she urged. "You and Tilda have promised to look out for me."

He turned to her. "Rumor had it that he burned down his family's stables out of spite. Jealous of his older brother, the heir. Cost the family a fortune in horseflesh. I believe his father never spoke to him again."

"Lady Selfridge?"

Meadow turned and found the Duke of Amesbury before them.

"I believe this is our dance."

She placed her hand on his sleeve, her belly roiling, and he led her onto the dance floor.

CHAPTER EIGHT

B OREDOM FILLED WYATT. Being at a ball was worse than
conjugating Latin verbs. He had been smart but a terrible
student, always restless sitting while his Turner Academy tutors
tried to engage him in lessons. University hadn't been any better.
It was only when he went to war that he felt alive, taking risks for
the crown. Living for the danger.

Though he excelled at dancing and had almost looked forward to tonight, hoping to quickly find a bride, he now saw it
would be an arduous process. Every woman he had danced with
had seemed a mere child. They were either silly or tongue-tied
merely because he was a duke. A few remarked upon the weather
and two had mentioned the music being played.

It was like slowly roasting in Hell.

The only woman who had interested him was one he would
soon dance with. The brown-haired beauty with gray eyes he had
spotted upon his arrival. She was no chit out of the schoolroom.
Unfortunately, all he knew was her name. It occurred to him that
with his luck, she was most likely already wed.

As was his current partner. She could be no more than twenty
years of age and had a lively look about her, which had drawn
him to her in the first place. She constantly waggled her fingers in
the direction of her husband, who had to be seventy if he was a
day. She had told Wyatt they had been wed after last Season and
that her husband was too old to dance but enjoyed watching her

do so.

"My husband is wealthy, though. More than King Midas, or so he says." She smiled. "He gives me everything I ask him for. A new carriage with a gorgeous team of horses. Diamonds. All the clothes and shoes I desire. And he lets me dance with handsome men, such as you, Your Grace."

She batted her eyelashes prettily at him. "We could always do more than dance," she said huskily.

Wyatt was having none of it. She had chosen to wed an old goat. He had no interest in engaging in an affair with her. He was in town to find his duchess. Period.

He escorted his current partner back to her doting husband and then went and stood off to the side, not engaged for this dance and wishing to observe his surroundings. As he stood, he found Lady Selfridge, color high on her cheeks as she danced a country reel. Something about her appealed to him, not just the fact that she was one of the most beautiful women present tonight. Perhaps Emery was right and he needed a woman with a little substance, not a featherhead.

"That's her. Lady Selfridge."

Wyatt glanced to his right, where four men stood. All were in their late twenties.

"The widow is a beauty," one said.

So, she *was* available.

"That hourglass figure," another one marveled. "I am ready to dip my wick into her."

He bristled at the crass words.

"I have already danced with her," stated a third. "She is not for us. She is one who will demand a ring on her finger before she even gives up a kiss."

The last of the group laughed harshly. "Has that ever stopped us before? I say we wager which of us first beds the gorgeously endowed widow."

Anger seared through him. They sounded like cocky soldiers the night before a battle, ones who had never experienced a skirmish. Ones who wound up losing their bravado when the charge began and called for their mothers as they lay wounded, their blood running into the ground. For the likes of him, he had never understood why bedding women was a game to some men. He certainly had spent his fair share romping in women's beds during university but even the few whores he had paid he had treated with respect. These four supposed gentlemen spoke of Lady Selfridge in a manner that troubled him greatly. Why, he couldn't say. He had yet to even dance with her.

Still, he took two steps in their direction, inserting himself in their conversation.

"Lady Selfridge is a widow, you say?" he said.

"Who are you?" This came from the one who had urged them to wager.

"The Duke of Amesbury."

Immediately, they all stood a bit taller.

"You were in the war," said the one who had danced with Lady Selfridge.

"Yes. I was a captain. What of it?"

"N-nothing," the man said. "I had just heard you had served, along with your friend, Winslow."

"That is the Duke of Winslow to you," he said in clipped tones. "Do not pretend to be familiar when you are not."

The man looked as if Wyatt had slapped him.

"Of course, Your Grace," he apologized quickly.

"I am to dance with Lady Selfridge soon. I may be interested in pursuing her." He stared daggers, his eyes roaming the group. "I neither want nor expect any competition. All wagers are off regarding the lady." He paused. "Is that understood?"

"Yes, Your Grace," the four said in unison.

The music came to an end. Wyatt turned and left their company.

Why had he said he was interested in her?

Of course, he needed to be interested in someone. It might as well be her. It certainly wasn't any of the emptyheaded girls he'd spent time with so far. Perhaps Emery was correct and he needed to broaden his search. He refused to admit failure after one night. Surely, he could find a bride among the women present. He already thought Lady Selfridge beautiful and poised. If she didn't have a grating voice and she was able to carry on even the bare minimum of a conversation, she would do.

Besides, it would protect her from those rakehells he'd just left.

Wyatt didn't ask himself why he wanted to protect her.

Because he didn't think he would like the answer.

He scanned the ballroom and located her on the far side and headed in her direction. She was speaking to a man he hadn't yet met. A sudden flare of jealousy coursed through him.

Ridiculous. He didn't even know the chit.

The man bent and said something in her ear. Wyatt watched her stiffen. Whatever he said had upset her greatly.

As he reached them, he vaguely recognized something about the man. Since he hadn't attended Turner Academy, that could only mean he had been a former schoolmate of Wyatt's before he went to Turner.

Ignoring him, he said, "Lady Selfridge?"

She turned and looked at him, the color draining from her face.

Bloody hell. What had the bastard said to her?

Without bothering to introduce himself, Wyatt said, "I believe this is our dance."

With an unsteady hand, she placed her fingers upon his sleeve and he led her away. They stopped at the center of the ballroom and the music started. Panic filled her face.

"It's a waltz," she blurted out. "I . . . don't know it. I wasn't allowed to dance it when I made my come-out."

She bit her lip, causing heat to shoot through him.

"I haven't been to a ball in years. Until tonight," she added.

"I shall teach it to you," he said calmly, though his heart raced as he slipped his hand about her waist and took her gloved hand in his. "It's all about following your partner's lead, my lady. Trust me."

Couples around them had already begun to dance while they stood stock still, close to one another.

"All right," she said, reluctance in her eyes.

"One is the down beat," he shared. "The other two follow quickly. You will feel it," he promised her.

He began moving them with small steps at first. Because she concentrated so hard, he realized they would not be able to converse. He moved her along with ease, grateful to Emery for hiring a dance instructor when the three of them had arrived in London three weeks ago. Though Wyatt and Miles had learned to dance at Turner Academy, the waltz had crossed to England from the Continent after their school days. Emery knew it would be played at the balls they attended and so had engaged the services of a dance master for an afternoon. It was easy getting the steps down and she had practiced with both men for a short while each afternoon.

Wyatt felt Lady Selfridge began to relax in his arms. She still gripped his hand and shoulder but he didn't mind. He liked the feel of his arm about her waist and the fresh, clean scent of lemons that wafted from her.

"I'm doing it," she said, looking up at him in gratitude. "I am dancing the waltz."

"I told you. It isn't a complicated dance. Not like a Scotch reel."

"It was considered quite scandalous when I made my come-out. The patronesses at Almack's didn't allow it."

"Why did you stop attending balls?" he asked.

She licked her lips, making him want to do the same.

"I married shortly after my come-out. I have spent the last seven years in the country, first as a wife and then the past year as a widow. I live with my cousin and her husband, Lord Marshmore."

"Ah, I met Lady Marshmore with you earlier this evening.

She seems very nice."

"Oh, Tilda is like a sister to me. I am an only child and we were always close. She offered me a home once I lost Lord Selfridge."

He was curious. Had Selfridge been as old as his previous partner's husband? Or some young man who had died tragically young, leaving behind a beautiful widow.

The last strains of the song fell away and Wyatt forced himself to release her.

"You danced the waltz beautifully, Lady Selfridge."

She gave him a sweet smile. "I have you to thank, Your Grace, for teaching it to me so effortlessly." Then she frowned.

"Shall I escort you into supper now, my lady?" he asked.

"Oh. That was the supper dance. You wish to dine with me?" she asked nervously, once more skittish as she had been when they'd first set out.

"That is what you are expected to do with your partner for the supper dance. Unless you have a prior commitment."

"No. Marshmore had told me I could eat with Tilda and him if I didn't dance that number."

She waved and he saw Lady Marshmore smile at them. The man beside her had been the one standing with Lady Selfridge. The one who had told her something.

Wyatt believed he knew what.

He hadn't thought about it as a boy but surely there had been questions when he had not returned to his former school. Boys that age gossiped just as much as fishwives. He wondered what had been said about him. His gut told him Lord Marshmore had been one of his former classmates and had passed along an untruth to Lady Selfridge.

"I was planning to join my friends, the Duke and Duchess of Winslow," he said. "Is that agreeable to you?"

He wanted her to say yes. They had only spoken briefly after she felt confident in her dance steps. Taking supper with her would give him a chance to learn more about her. It wouldn't hurt that Emery would be present. He already relied on Miles' wife for advice in business matters and she had seemingly taken on the role of helping him find a match, as well. He would be curious as to her opinion of Lady Selfridge.

"Yes, Your Grace," she said demurely and then giggled.

He brought her hand to his sleeve and rested it there. "Then we should join them."

The giggle disappointed him. He had thought her better than those he had previously danced with. Wyatt sighed inwardly, now dreading the supper that awaited them.

They were among the last to leave the ballroom. By the time they reached the space where supper was to be held, the room teemed with guests.

Wyatt searched it and saw Miles had risen, waving them over. They approached the table, with seating for four only. Relief swept through him. He wouldn't have to be sociable with anyone else. Already, he was tired of smiling.

"Lady Selfridge, may I introduce to you the Duke and Duchess of Winslow?"

Greetings were exchanged and then Miles said, "Why don't we allow the ladies to rest and you and I go through the buffet line for them?"

"Oh, would you, darling?" Emery said. "And no fish." She wrinkled her nose.

Miles captured his wife's hand and kissed her fingers. "No fish at the entire table," he proclaimed and then looked at Lady Selfridge. "I hope that is agreeable with you, my lady?"

"Of course."

Wyatt seated her. "Any requests?"

"No. I am not very picky."

With that, he and Miles excused themselves.

Wyatt was grateful to leave Lady Selfridge behind.

CHAPTER NINE

M EADOW SWALLOWED, IN awe that she would be dining with two dukes and a duchess. She was also a bit flustered, having witnessed the duke kiss his wife's hand so tenderly. Such a public display of affection—especially with the look the duke had given his duchess—was something she had never witnessed before.

"Thank you for abstaining from fish tonight," the duchess said.

"Are you not fond of it?" she asked politely, in awe of the woman's beauty.

"I adore fish. It simply doesn't agree with me these days. At least the smell." She paused. "I am enceinte. Our child is due in the autumn."

"No wonder you have such a glow about you," Meadow said. "My best wishes to you and His Grace."

The duchess placed a palm against her belly. "I am almost four months along. From what I gather, most women of the *ton* wouldn't attend a ball in my condition, but Miles insisted we come to London for the first part of the Season."

"Do you attend every year?"

The duchess laughed merrily. "This is my first time. We wed last summer. My father was a fourth son and so he had to make his own way in the world. He married a local doctor's daughter and eventually became the steward for the Duke of Winslow's country seat, north of Maidstone. When the duke passed, Miles came home from the war." She sighed, a dreamy expression on her face. "And we fell in love."

Tears brimmed in Meadow's eyes. Once, she had hoped for a love match. Then her father demanded she wed Viscount Selfridge when the Season was in its infancy. The years had been lonely ones, more lonely than she had realized.

"Miles wanted to show me London and introduce me to Polite Society. We will stay several weeks and then make our way back to Kent. We both love the country and are happiest there. But I am dominating our conversation. Tell me about yourself, Lady Selfridge."

Flustered, she said, "I really don't have much to say, Your Grace. I am a widow. I lost my husband a year ago February last."

"I am so sorry to hear that. Was it hard for you and your children?"

Meadow blinked rapidly, her eyes filling with tears. "We weren't blessed with children, Your Grace. I do love them, though. I have been staying with my cousin, Lady Marshmore. She has two sons. I play with them each afternoon. They are such little loves."

"Would you like children of your own one day?"

"More than anything," she admitted. "It is the only reason I chose to enter society again."

"So, you are in need of a husband?"

"Yes. I realize I am much older than those on the Marriage Mart so I shan't be choosy."

The duchess took Meadow's hand. "On the contrary, my dear, you should be most selective. You have a mature beauty and you radiate kindness. I am telling you now, do not settle. Listen to your heart."

"I understand that this time it will be my choice and not my father's. He arranged my first marriage." She bit her lip.

"I assume it was not a happy one."

She gasped. "I did not say that, Your Grace."

The duchess squeezed her hand. "You didn't have to, my lady. Women understand other women. Sometimes, no words are necessary." The duchess removed her hand.

"You will be courted by many, Lady Selfridge. Don't let fancy titles and false compliments sway you. Looks fade. Fortunes can be lost. Find a man you have something in common with. One you respect. One that makes your heart pound. One whose kiss you cannot live without."

The duchess' recommendations floored Meadow. "How can I do that? Kiss a man before we are wed?"

The duchess smiled. "I have a feeling you will find one that will make you want to try."

She felt her face go hot.

"I would also like to put in a word for our friend, the Duke of Amesbury. He has recently returned from the war. He was a second son and not expecting to claim the ducal title. Amesbury is a good man. He has had a hard life, from the time he was young. He is eager to start a family."

Her mind whirled. Marshmore had told her Amesbury was horrible and destructive as a child, causing a good number of horses to be destroyed. Perhaps he had matured from that spoiled, destructive child. The duke had displayed elegant manners with her. He was a close friend of the Winslows. Already, Meadow liked the Duchess of Winslow quite a bit and didn't think she would be taken in by an unprincipled man.

Worse, Meadow sensed the attraction between them. The waltz had been even more intimate a dance than she had been told. Dancing it with the duke, feeling the heat of his body so close to hers, had caused her to grow dizzy. Yet they had moved as one, swept up in the beat of the music, until she felt she had always danced with him.

Would she consider kissing him?

Only time would tell.

She saw the two dukes approaching and the duchess said, "We shall keep this little talk between us. I do hope you will consider Amesbury."

"Thank you for the recommendation, Your Grace," Meadow said as the pair arrived with plates loaded with food.

Amesbury seated himself, placing a plate before her. "I hope I found some of your favorites, my lady."

She looked at all the food on the plate. "This would be enough to feed an army," she declared.

"Ah, that is where you are wrong," he said, a twinkle in his eyes. "For I have been in the army. A soldier would inhale this and be ready for four more plates of this size. Especially after a battle."

Meadow realized she knew nothing of this man, other than he danced superbly and had been patient enough to teach her the waltz. The little she thought she knew was merely a rumor Marshmore had shared with her. She hoped it wasn't true.

"Amesbury and I both served in His Majesty's army," the Duke of Winslow said. "I sold out last spring when I learned of the deaths of my father and brother."

"You were the second son?" she asked.

"I was, as was Amesbury. We met at school and attended university together, along with three of our other friends."

"Are they here tonight?"

"No," Amesbury said. "Two of them are still on the Continent. Career soldiers. The fifth in our group is a vicar in Kent."

She took a bite of the puffed pastry. "Delicious," she proclaimed, vowing to simply enjoy the rest of this night. Most likely, she would never dance with a duke again, nor dine with two. Whether what Marshmore had told her was true or not, it was no concern of hers. The Duke of Amesbury would forget about their encounter by the time he arrived at his carriage tonight.

WYATT STUDIED LADY Selfridge, marking her as unforgettable in the sea of faces he had encountered this evening. The giggles hadn't returned, which relieved him greatly. She wasn't shy about expressing her opinion and she and Emery got along splendidly. Considering he lived but a few hours from Wildwood and had every intention of seeing Miles and Emery often over the years, Wyatt decided that he need look no further for candidates.

It was settled. Lady Selfridge would be the next Duchess of Amesbury.

It didn't hurt that he found her quite desirable, what with her tiny waist and ample bosom. It would make the producing of his heir and other children pleasurable. Of course, that would be the last test. It was important before they parted tonight that he ask her about children. She might already have one or more, having been wed for several years. It didn't matter to him. He would happily welcome the lady and any of her offspring to Amberwood.

As long as she was willing to provide more children so that the dukedom would be secured.

He listened to her and Emery discussing tenants on their estates. It seemed Lady Selfridge had spent a good deal of her time with her husband's tenants and had missed doing so while she lived with her cousin. Idly, he glanced in the direction of Lady Marshmore and found Lord Marshmore glaring at him. Wyatt determined to find out who Marshmore had been before he inherited his title. He still believed the earl had said something to Lady Selfridge about Wyatt's troubled past. He had paid enough for Clive's sins and his father's inability to see the truth.

He wouldn't lose this woman over the incident that had changed his life.

Emery yawned. "I am so sorry," she apologized. "I fear I am beginning to tire."

Miles touched her cheek tenderly. "You have experienced enough for one night, love. You have been to a *ton* ball. Met a good number of lords and ladies. Had a delicious buffet supper. I think it is high time I take you home." He turned to Wyatt. "I hate to cut your evening short."

"Don't worry. I have what I came for. Why don't you call for the carriage while I say my goodbyes to Lady Selfridge? I will meet you outside."

Emery gave Wyatt a knowing look. "Have a care," she cautioned.

He rose and helped her to her feet, saying in her ear, "It's not as if I will offer for her here and now. I will wait until tomorrow." Wyatt straightened. "I will see you shortly."

"It was a pleasure to meet you, Your Graces," Lady Selfridge said.

"We must have you to tea soon," Emery told her. "I feel we are already old friends."

"I would like that very much."

Wyatt waited until Miles escorted Emery away and then seated himself again. Turning to his companion, he asked, "Might I call upon you tomorrow afternoon, Lady Selfridge?"

Color bloomed in her cheeks. "Why would you wish to do so, Your Grace?"

He couldn't very well tell her he planned to offer for her then so he said, "I have enjoyed your company tonight. Surely, you wouldn't deny me more of it?"

She studied him. "If I did so, I suppose it would be the first time you have been told no."

He laughed heartily. "Believe it or not, I have heard the word *no* often over the years. I wasn't born a duke. You heard what Winslow said—he and I both were second sons, never expecting to come into these lofty titles we now bear."

"Still, you seem to be a man who is determined to get his way."

"You aren't comfortable with that?" he asked lightly.

"Not if it clashes with what I want," she said frankly.

"What is it you do want, my lady? I am curious. You have already been wed once. Does marriage still hold a fascination for you? Or do your children keep you occupied when you are not attending society events?"

She seemed to wilt. Immediately, Wyatt grew anxious.

"I have no children, Your Grace. That is the very reason I am at this ball tonight. I am an only child. One who played make believe and created siblings of my own. My mother suffered numerous miscarriages and had little to do with me before her death, always trying to provide my father with an heir."

She swallowed, pain flickering across her delicate features. "I would very much like to have children of my own. It is the only reason I accompanied my cousin and her husband to London for the Season. They have been invited to numerous affairs over the next few weeks and most likely will receive other invitations. Hosts are very generously including me in those invitations. I plan to take advantage of every event I attend because I know that, somewhere, I will find a man who is honorable and caring. One who wishes to have children as much as I do."

Relief flooded him. At least they were on the same page regarding children. She was beautiful. He would be the envy of many men when she became his wife. She easily carried on a conversation with strangers at supper, letting him know she would be comfortable in social situations. He resolved that tomorrow he would make his intentions known to her.

"What are you looking for in a husband?" he asked, wanting to satisfy his curiosity.

"Besides finding a man who wants children, I wish for him to be involved with those children. Too many in Polite Society, be they male or female, ignore their children once they come into the world. My husband will need to be actively involved in raising them. In addition, I would want him to be kind to me and respectful to others, especially his staff and tenants."

"That is all? Surely, you wish for more, my lady."

"What more is there, Your Grace? To me, that is what is important." She paused, a knowing look entering her gray eyes. "Oh, simply because you hold a revered title, you think all women want to marry a duke? I suppose a good majority of them do. Titles. Wealth. Looks. Land. There are scores of young ladies who value those things. I cherish goodness and kindness instead."

"How will you judge a man and see if he possesses those qualities?"

"Frankly, I believe I am a decent judge of character. I was quite naïve when I made my come-out years ago but I have matured over the years. I know my mind, Your Grace, and am determined to find exactly who I am looking for."

"Then I wish you the best in your search, Lady Selfridge." He paused. "I would warn you off of a few gentlemen, however. And I use that term quite loosely."

"What do you mean?" she asked, her eyes clouding with some unnamed emotion.

"I know widows sometimes are preyed upon by rogues of the *ton*. I might have heard your name come up in a certain wager."

"A wager?" She looked more angry than fearful.

"Yes." His eyes searched the room. "I do not know their names. Only that you have already danced with one of them."

One by one, he pointed out the four who had stood next to him as they gossiped about her.

"I do recognize one of them. He did not impress me in the least. He couldn't even dance well."

"Oh, is being a good dancer another thing you should add to your list?" he teased.

"It is not a requirement in a husband. Perhaps I spoke too quickly. However, I did not find anything about this man to cause me to remember his name."

"Good," he said firmly. "You shouldn't. He—and the other three I pointed out to you—have a bet to see which of them can entice you into his bed first."

"What?" she gasped, her face and neck coloring quickly. "You cannot say things like that in public, Your Grace. It's . . . uncivil."

He gave her a wry smile. "I think it is uncivil for men to be publicly speaking about such a wager so that anyone might overhear their uncouth conversation."

"Well, of course it is," she said quickly. "But you . . . you shouldn't . . . that is . . . telling a lady she is the subject of such a ghastly wager is . . . highly inappropriate."

"Be that as it may, you are now sufficiently warned about them."

She nodded. "I am sorry I took affront and attacked the messenger, Your Grace. Thank you for providing me with this information. I will see that none of the lot dances with me. If they even attempt to speak to me, I will reject any advances."

"See that you do," he said.

Wyatt saw that others were finishing with supper and beginning to leave the room. He asked, "Might I escort you back to the ballroom, my lady?"

"Yes. That would be most agreeable."

He did so, returning her to her cousin's side. Lord Marshmore was nowhere in sight.

"It was lovely meeting you, Lady Marshmore," he said pleasantly. "And your charming cousin."

He took Lady Selfridge's hand and brought it to his lips. "I will see you soon," he told her. "Good evening."

Wyatt left the pair and went in search of Miles and Emery. As he reached them, he realized he hadn't gotten permission from Lady Selfridge to call upon her tomorrow.

It didn't matter. He knew she was the one he would make his duchess.

Their carriage pulled up and they entered it. Once again, he sat across from the pair.

"I hope you aren't breaking any hearts by leaving the ball early," Miles said.

"Most of the young ladies present tonight don't even know if they possess a heart," he replied. "All they know is that they are on the hunt for a husband. I gather the higher the title, the more they think they will have met with success."

"You did have your share of beautiful women around you

tonight," his friend noted.

"It doesn't matter. I have decided upon my duchess."

"Lady Selfridge?" Emery asked, a knowing look in her eyes.

"Who else?" he asked, surprised Emery even had to ask. "No one present tonight could hold a candle to her beauty and charm."

"Then I hope you will begin your courtship of her starting tomorrow," Emery told him.

"Courtship?" His brows knit together, puzzled. "Why is that necessary? I am a duke. She is in need of a husband. One who wishes to have children. I long for a large family. I see no reason to dally and court her when I can simply offer for her."

"I advise against that, Wyatt," she said.

He studied her. "You're serious, aren't you?"

"I am. She is a lovely young woman and many men will be vying for her hand."

"But I am a duke," he stated. "It's the only good thing about being one. You snap your fingers. You get your way."

"This new title of yours seems to have gone to your head," Emery fired back. "For a man who never thought he would one day be a duke, you are certainly acting as haughty as any duke Polite Society has ever seen." She paused. "And it is wrong, Wyatt. You are a better man than this. Although I have not known you long, I have not seen such arrogance in you as I do now. As your friend, I am saying this in private for your own good. You must remain the man you have always been and bring *that* to the title. The good man and experienced army captain you are has much to offer to others. Be the best Duke of Amesbury that you can be. Do not imitate your father or brother or act pompous and overbearing because that is what you think a duke should do. Do not make harsh demands and expect everyone to acquiesce to your every whim.

"Be yourself, Wyatt. Bring a dignity and grace to being Amesbury. The best duke is not one who lords over others but is a man who is kind and charitable." Emery gazed at him intensely.

"Lady Selfridge is looking for a good man. Not a title. You are going to have to compete with others and show her you are the best match for her. Woo her, Wyatt. Don't offer for her immediately, I beg you."

"That's a ridiculous waste of my time," he said, his head and heart warring with each other over her words. "I am a duke, Emery, and not subject to being dressed down by you."

Fire lit her eyes. "As your friend, I will do as I please. I don't want you to make a huge mistake, Wyatt. Do not rush Lady Selfridge. As a woman, I know of what I speak."

Miles spoke up. "I agree with my wife. You are acting out of character, Wyatt. Don't forget that I have known you for far too long to believe you would change simply because of a lofty title. Emery is the wisest person I know. Listen to her if you truly want to win Lady Selfridge's hand."

"Since you point out we have known each other for many years, you know I have always been one to know my mind and act quickly, whether I was a duke or not. What does it matter if I wish to quickly make Lady Selfridge my duchess?" Wyatt demanded. "She should be grateful that a duke is interested in her."

"Do you love her?" Miles asked quietly.

"What has love got to do with anything?" he demanded. "I've only met her tonight."

"Love is everything," his friend told him. "Do not offer for her if you don't love her."

Frustration filled him. "Miles, I will speak plainly here. You are a besotted fool over your wife. I can understand why because Emery is a very special woman. But I neither need nor want love. I merely require a woman I find agreeable because I will be faithful to her. We will make our children and then pursue our own interests."

His glared at his friends, who looked back at him with pity in their eyes.

Crossing his arms, he said, "I will do this my way. The ducal way. I may not have been a duke for long but I know when a duke offers for a woman, she accepts. There is no other choice."

Emery cocked an eyebrow. "We'll see."

CHAPTER TEN

M EADOW LEFT HER bedchamber and made her way to the drawing room. She had changed gowns three times before deciding upon the rose-colored one. The maid assisting her reassured her the color was striking upon her. Normally, she didn't think twice about what gown she put on. Today was different, however. She had several men who had asked to call upon her today.

Including the Duke of Amesbury. At least, she hoped he would call.

She had not outright rejected his request to visit with her. Instead, they had verbally sparred over whether she should allow him to call or not. Then he had made the shocking revelation regarding the group of rakes who had wagered among themselves about whose bed she would first grace. The outlandish and improper conversation had kept them from the earlier topic. Meadow had no idea whether the duke would show up this afternoon or not.

She feared that was the reason she had gone through several gowns, which was ridiculous. She wasn't truly interested in him. Even if he was sinfully handsome and flirted with her with ease. Dukes were a law unto themselves. She wanted a man who would be faithful to her.

Oh. She hadn't thought about that before. Fidelity would be important to her. Too many in the *ton* wed and then went their separate ways after an heir had been provided. That wasn't for her. She worried that her growing list of characteristics she desired in a husband might limit her choices. Meadow told herself it didn't matter. If it was like the biblical Sodom and Gomorrah and she only found one good man in the midst of Polite Society who would suit her, so be it.

It wouldn't be the Duke of Amesbury.

As she entered the drawing room, the overwhelming scent of flowers assailed her. She gazed about the room at the multitude of bouquets.

"Finally, you can see the results of last night!" proclaimed Tilda. "Look at all these lovely flower arrangements you have received."

"These . . . are all for me?"

Long ago, she had been the recipient of numerous bouquets. It had lasted a scant two weeks and then her father had told her she would be the instrument by which he would pay his gambling markers. Meadow had wed Lord Selfridge three days later, using a special license the viscount had procured. She had forgotten what it was like to feel special and sought after. That she still was at her age surprised her.

"Here are the cards," her cousin said, handing Meadow a stack. "I saved them all. I couldn't help but look through them. You have gathered quite the collection of titled lords." Tilda frowned. "I was disappointed that nothing came from the Duke of Amesbury, though."

Amesbury was all Tilda had spoken of as they had ridden home from the Rockwells' ball. She had peppered Meadow with questions about what he was like, especially since they had not only danced but supped together. The fact that Meadow had dined with two dukes had left Tilda flustered, as if her cousin had been the one to do so.

"Did he ask to call upon you, Meadow?"

He had—but she was not going to explain to her cousin how that conversation had gone astray, especially since Lord Marshmore was also present, though he read a book and seemed unbothered by their conversation.

Tilda saw Meadow's gaze land upon her husband and said, "Marshmore has agreed to help chaperone you for these first few days. We know—or know of—everyone in the *ton*. With our guidance, it will only be a matter of time before a match has been arranged."

"Do I truly need a chaperone, Tilda? I am a widow. I thought widows were given a bit of leeway."

"They are but Marshmore and I agree that you have been gone far too long from Polite Society. We insist upon giving you some advice."

Since the couple had been kind enough to open their home to her for the past year, Meadow felt it would be churlish to refuse to allow them to sit in their own drawing room while she entertained suitors.

"I appreciate all your efforts," she told her cousin.

The butler entered. "Lord Swarthmore and Lord Villiers."

"Show them in," Marshmore said, closing his book and setting it aside.

Within minutes, a flurry of new arrivals were announced. Meadow's head swam from being the center of so much attention. Then she heard a new name announced.

"Excuse me," she said, marching toward the door as the butler ducked out and the latest arrival started to step into the room. He was quite good-looking, with fair hair and deep blue eyes.

And happened to be one of the infamous four rakes the Duke of Amesbury had pointed out.

Meadow hadn't thought to provide the four names to the Marshmore butler. She moved close, keeping the newcomer in the frame of the door.

"You are not welcomed here, Lord Chambers," she said firmly.

"Why, you know my name, Lady Selfridge." He gave her a ready smile. "I am flattered since we were never properly introduced last night."

"We need no introduction, my lord, because I have no intentions of getting to know you."

He frowned. "Why would that be?"

"Perhaps it is related to the atrocious wager you made last night with your friends." She named them, having asked Tilda to provide the names of all the gentlemen Amesbury had pointed out in order to be prepared.

Lord Chambers looked dumbfounded. "You know?"

"I may be a widow, my lord, but I am no featherhead. Kindly remove yourself from Lord Marshmore's residence and make certain you never call here again."

Meadow whirled and crossed the room to rejoin those she had abandoned. She only hoped the rakehell would leave as she requested.

WYATT TIED HIS cravat with care. He knew it was time to get a valet, even if he loathed the idea of someone doing things that he could easily do for himself. He had allowed young Philip Haskins to remain at Amberwood instead of coming to London with him. The boy was sweet but had shown no interest or aptitude in what it took to become a valet. Instead, Philip had begged for Wyatt to put him in the stables. He had loved the cows at his former home and had even a greater love for horses. Wyatt had agreed once he discussed the matter with the boy's mother. Joan thought Philip would be happier in a job that allowed him to remain outdoors most of the day—leaving Wyatt without a valet again.

Miles shared that he, too, hadn't liked the idea of hiring a valet but explained that a duke was expected to maintain a certain number of servants within his household. It would also give a job to someone in need of one. Wyatt supposed the best thing to do was find a valet while he was here in London. One who knew his stuff but wouldn't mind retreating to the country for most of the year.

He hoped Lady Selfridge liked the country. From what she revealed, she had spent very little time in London. While they would always go for the Season and make an appearance for a few weeks, much as Miles and Emery intended to do, he would prefer the peace and quiet of country life, especially after the noise of war. He had always loved Amberwood. The estate and not his family. That would change with his marriage. He yearned for a large family. He wanted to teach his sons to hunt and his daughters to ride. He would read to them. Play with them. Walk the land with them.

Everything his own parents hadn't done.

As he called for his carriage, he wondered what his and Lady Selfridge's children would look like. With both of them having dark hair, he assumed their children would, as well. He thought her gray eyes one of her best features and hoped at least one or two of their children would have them. He chuckled, thinking Emery would scold him for being so confident. He couldn't help it. He had found his duchess in a single night. All he had to do was inform her she was his choice and he would purchase the special license. Though he would rather leave London sooner than later, he knew she deserved to enjoy a bit of the attention she would receive, becoming the first bride of the Season—and wedding a duke, as well. If she wished, they would remain until the Season ended in August and then return to Amberwood. Or perhaps go on a honeymoon. She might like to see some of his various estates. He certainly would.

He rode the short distance to the Marshmore townhouse, Miles' valet having discovered its location for him. As he exited the vehicle, he saw two gentlemen leaving the entrance. Jealousy flared within him. That was both good and bad. He had never experienced it before and wasn't at all sure he liked the feeling now but it let him know that he did have a physical attraction to his chosen bride and was feeling a bit possessive. Having already been wed, she would know what to expect in the bedroom, but he still felt a bit of relief that he wouldn't be initiating a virgin into the ways of lovemaking. He only hoped he could rein in this jealousy and not make an arse of himself in front of others. Not that he thought Miles did so. It was different with his friend. Emery was a wonderful woman. It was understandable that Miles loved her so much.

Love had never been any part of Wyatt's life, though. His priggish mother never hugged him once that he could remember. His demanding father had ignored Wyatt for the most part. Clive was more stranger than brother, being so much older. He determined to break the mold and love his children with all his heart and soul. In Lady Selfridge, he would have a wife he could respect and be kind toward, one of the attributes she insisted upon. And naturally, he was a good dancer. He would enjoy partnering with her at future balls.

He presented his card to the butler, whose eyebrows rose a tad before settling back down.

"Please follow me, Your Grace," the servant said.

Wyatt did so and they arrived at the drawing room door, which was open. He gazed in and saw a sea of bouquets and kicked himself for not thinking to send one himself.

Then he heard Lady Selfridge's voice. "Perhaps it is related to the atrocious wager you made last night with your friends."

Wyatt heard the frost in her tone and realized one of the idiots he'd warned off last night had the audacity to call upon her today.

"You know?" a voice asked.

"I may be a widow, my lord, but I am no featherhead. Kindly remove yourself from Lord Marshmore's residence and make certain you never call here again."

Wyatt grinned. Beauty, intelligence—and a spitfire. He had thought the lady calm and charming but found himself even more attracted to her seeing this side. To tell off a nobleman took gumption and courage. Pride surged through him at knowing his future duchess was no retiring wallflower.

Lord Chambers stormed past him. He almost stopped the man to ask if he truly understood how the object of his false affections felt but decided that would simply be rubbing salt into an open wound.

"I apologize for that, Your Grace. Lady Selfridge had not warned me that she would not be at home to Lord Chambers. Let me announce you now."

"Wait," he said, stepping back and motioning for the butler to do the same. "Would you send a footman to the garden to cut a single bloom for me? I was remiss and did not send Lady Selfridge flowers this morning. I would like to give her a small token. Do you have roses?"

The butler smiled. "We do, Your Grace. I will see it taken care of at once."

The servant vanished and Wyatt paced the corridor, seeing three other gentlemen leave before the butler returned with a single red rose, perfectly shaped.

"Ah, this will do rather nicely," he praised. "Thank you."

"Of course, Your Grace."

The butler entered the drawing room and announced him. Wyatt stepped inside and spied Lady Selfridge immediately, crossing the room to speak with her. Everyone rose and she curtseyed to him. He, in turn, took her hand and kissed it, enjoying the blush that spread across her porcelain cheeks.

"Thank you for receiving me, my lady." He brought up his left hand, which had been by his side. "Please accept this simple token of my affection."

"Oh!" she took it and brought it to her nose, inhaling deeply. Then she gave him a sweet smile. "Thank you, Your Grace. I did not realize you would be calling this afternoon."

Ah, the little minx.

"I do believe I inquired about it, my lady," he said, not letting her off the hook.

"Thank you for coming," she said politely. "I must see to my other guests, however."

She seated herself again and he quickly took the place next to her. Then she proceeded to ignore him for the next half-hour.

Though she did play with his rose, twirling it in her hands.

One by one, her suitors left until only he remained, along with Lord and Lady Marshmore.

Lady Selfridge bid the last gentleman goodbye and then turned. "Oh, I did not realize you were still here, Your Grace."

"It is quite all right, my lady. I understand that you needed to dance attendance upon those you were expecting. Now, though, perhaps we might have a chat. Or a stroll through the gardens would be preferable."

He glanced to the earl. "Would that be agreeable with you, Lord Marshmore?"

Marshmore's face darkened. "Not a chance in Hell, Amesbury. You might be a duke now—but you are not welcomed in my household."

CHAPTER ELEVEN

MEADOW GASPED ALOUD. "Marshmore!" she chided, in unison with Tilda.

Her gaze turned to the Duke of Amesbury. His hazel eyes, usually a light green mixed with brown, now flared hot green. It was the only thing that revealed his anger. The rest of him appeared composed as he flicked a piece of lint from the sleeve of his coat.

Then he studied Marshmore a long moment. Tension hung heavily as silence ruled.

"You are Morrow," the duke finally said. "I should have realized it sooner. You have changed quite a bit since our school days. Are you still a bully?"

The earl huffed. "Now, see here, Amesbury."

"It is Your Grace," the duke said sharply. "We are not even acquaintances, much less bosom friends." He stared daggers at Marshmore. "I was the runt of my class. The smallest boy when I arrived at school. You were a year ahead of me and the tallest boy in yours. I remember how you tormented me for weeks. First with taunts. Then physical blows. You made my life miserable."

Meadow marveled at how calmly the duke stated all of this, despite the fire in his eyes.

"You finally left me alone and moved on to other boys. I began to grow and sprouted like a weed during that summer break. When we returned to school, I came across you. Pinning a new boy to the ground. Mashing his face and forcing him to eat the dirt there. I soundly thrashed you and warned you never to lord over another boy again. You listened then. Do so now."

"Listen to what?" Marshmore demanded. "The rumors were rampant when you did not return to school. I know what you did."

"Do you?" Amesbury asked, his tone so cold and deadly that Meadow shivered. "Were you there? Did you witness the event that changed lives?"

Flustered, the earl said, "No, but you must understand—"

"I understand that you are trying to ruin my reputation. Well, I am no longer a scrawny, scared boy, Marshmore. I am a duke. If you proceed to continue spreading rumors about me, I will destroy you."

Tilda gasped. Meadow dug her fingernails into her palms, shocked at the enmity between the two men.

"Please, Marshmore. Please," Tilda begged her husband. "Apologize to His Grace at once and be done with it."

"Why should I?" he asked her as Tilda trembled from head to toe. "There is always a grain of truth to even the most outlandish of rumors. Why should Polite Society dance attendance upon this man merely because he is now a duke?"

Meadow could no longer remain silent. "Because he is far more powerful than you could ever dream of being, Marshmore. If the Duke of Amesbury gives you and Tilda the cut direct, your time in the *ton* will be done. Not for a night. Not for this Season. Forever. Quit preening like a proud peacock and think of your family. You have two sons. Do you want them ostracized at school, having only each other as friends? Two decades from now, when they wish to wed, would you have them have no choice because they are shunned by Polite Society—because their father thought to take down a duke over a rumor that was circulated during their boyhoods?"

Marshmore swallowed, worry now wrinkling his brow.

"You know it is true," Tilda said quietly. "We would become

no ones. So would our boys. Please, Marshmore, please. I beg you."

"Very well," the earl said. "I shall keep quiet about your rumored transgressions." He paused. "But I cannot keep the rest of Polite Society from gossiping about you, Your Grace."

"Thank you," the duke said. Turning to her, he added, "I believe we were to chat while walking the gardens, Lady Selfridge. If you will excuse us, Lady Marshmore. Thank you again for hosting me this afternoon. I have heard how well you have treated your cousin, both when you were girls and again after she lost her husband."

Wide-eyed, Tilda said, "I adore Meadow, Your Grace. There is nothing I wouldn't do for her."

Before Meadow could speak, the duke had taken her hand and slipped it through the crook of his arm. He ushered her from the drawing room and along the corridor.

"Please show me Marshmore's gardens, my lady. I think the fresh air will do both of us some good."

Her head spinning, she brought them to Tilda's sitting room, where they exited from a set of French doors. The gardens lay only a few steps away and the duke led her to the entrance and down the path.

They strolled for a few minutes, no words between them. She didn't know what kind of conversation he expected after the dramatic scene in the drawing room. As for her, she was overwhelmed by his sheer size. He was tall and broad and smelled marvelous. Her body brushed against his slightly as they moved, causing her belly to do continuous flipflops, keeping her off-balance.

She finally stopped their motion. "Why did you wish to speak with me, Your Grace?"

"I believe we have a great deal to say to one another, Meadow."

The use of her name coming from his sensual lips caused an explosion of butterflies to flap their wings inside her.

"I did not give you leave to call me by my Christian name, Your Grace. We are not and never will be that familiar with one another."

"I totally disagree," he said, his voice a low rumble. "I think we will become very familiar with one another, Meadow." His tone had turned flirtatious.

She realized he was a rogue. Just like the very ones he had warned her against last night.

"If you think I will be lured to your bed like the rakes you cautioned me about, you are mistaken, Your Grace. No man will tempt me enough to behave as a wanton. I may be a widow but I have my pride and reputation to consider. I neither want nor need to have an affair with you."

He placed his hands upon her shoulders, sending a rush of heat through her.

"Oh, I am not interested in an affair, Meadow."

With that, he lowered his head. She started to protest. Then his lips touched hers.

He was . . . kissing her . . .

She had never been kissed.

Meadow had been out in society for such a short time before her marriage. She had also been warned of rogues who tried to steal kisses from pretty debutantes. She had never been alone with a man during those two weeks attending *ton* events. Even when she became engaged, her father had been present along with Viscount Selfridge, both men telling her of the upcoming ceremony. When it concluded, her new husband had merely brushed his lips against her cheek for a brief moment—and then never attempted to physically touch her again.

Her head began to spin as new sensations filled her. She grasped the duke's shoulders to steady herself. His hands left her shoulders, one cupping her nape, the other palm splayed against the small of her back, drawing her to him.

His lips were soft and yet somehow firm as he kissed her. The intimacy of being so close to another person overwhelmed her.

He angled his mouth over hers, the pressure increasing as did the fierce pounding of her heart as it slammed against her ribs. She began kneading his shoulder as a kitten might and a low growl sounded within him, causing a shiver to dance through her. He pulled her closer until her breasts pressed against the hard wall of his muscled chest.

Meadow grew lightheaded and clung to him. Then he pulled his mouth from hers, only to run his tongue along her bottom lip. Slowly, back and forth, causing delicious sensations to run through her. Her breath quickened, as did her pulse. He ran his tongue along the seam of her lips, startling her. As she gasped, it slipped inside, stroking her own tongue, the velvet smoothness like a siren's song.

Her fingers tightened on his shoulders. His arms now encased her. Instead of feeling imprisoned, she felt incredibly safe as his warmth engulfed her. Tentatively, she moved her tongue against his, wishing to explore him as much as he did her. He groaned.

Emboldened by his response, she continued the action, even as something startled her, a throbbing between her legs. She only touched there to wash, moving the cloth quickly over her privates. Now, she wanted to touch there. No.

She wanted him to touch there.

The wicked thought caused her to realize that the duke was seducing her. She had always wondered why women became so wanton and would go to a man's bed unwed. Now, she had a glimmer of why. His mouth and tongue promised her things that were wrong. Like in the pictures from Selfridge's collection.

Meadow had to put a stop to this.

She pulled her tongue from his mouth and shook her head, breaking the contact between them.

Panting, she said, "Please release me, Your Grace. Now."

His eyes gleamed with what she realized was desire. A part of her thrilled, knowing this handsome, powerful man wanted her. Still, she shook her head again, trying to clear it. It angered her that she wanted him to want her.

Without thinking, she slapped him.

Her action startled her. She had never struck anyone before. Her palm felt as if she had dipped it in fire. Already, she could see the mark she had left on his cheek. Her apology froze in her throat as she realized she had not just slapped any man.

She had struck the Duke of Amesbury.

"I do not want a clandestine affair with you, Meadow."

"Quit calling me that," she ordered, trying to get control of her feelings. "We have nothing to say to one another. After all, you have threatened to destroy the man who has taken me in."

"And a good man—a kind man—like the one you seek, would never do that."

"Exactly." She pushed hard against his chest and to her surprise—and relief—he released her. "Do not call here again, Your Grace. Marshmore might have to cave and welcome you with open arms in order to keep from being punished by you. I, on the other hand, will not be at home to you."

Blinking back tears, she lifted her skirts and rushed away.

"Meadow, wait," he called after her.

She didn't slow. Temptation of the worst sort awaited her if she did. If she hesitated but a moment, she would turn and run back to him. Back into the arms that made her feel warm and safe. Back to the lips that had awakened a fire within her.

Back to chaos and what could only result in doom.

Meadow entered the house again through the same French doors, closing and locking them. She took a minute to compose herself and then retreated up the stairs to her bedchamber, thankful she had seen no one.

Falling onto her bed, she wept. Whether tears of relief or regret, she couldn't say.

"Hell and damnation," Wyatt muttered under his breath as he

dressed for the musicale to be held at Lord and Lady Martindale's townhouse tonight.

"Hold still, Your Grace," said Winkle, his London butler.

He sighed inwardly, knowing his impatience was only prolonging the process of dressing for the evening.

"Have you thought about hiring a valet, Your Grace?" Winkle asked diplomatically.

"I have thought about it. I have done nothing about it, however," he admitted. "What do you suggest? Should I go through an employment agency? How do I go about finding a valet that won't irritate me?"

Winkle finished tying Wyatt's cravat and stepped back. "That will do nicely," he proclaimed. "As for a valet, an employment agency is the usual route. However, my cousin, Frame, has served as a valet until recently. His employer passed away last week and the heir already had a valet of his own. Poor Frame was let go. He has decent references, Your Grace, and would do an excellent job in the position."

"Hire him," Wyatt said.

"His salary, Your Grace?"

"What do you think is fair?"

Winkle named a figure and Wyatt nodded. "Have him start immediately. Who pays my London staff?"

"Usually, that would be your secretary, Your Grace. Since you have none, your solicitor handles the matter at the moment."

He sighed. "Do I also need a secretary?"

"It is not unheard of for a duke to go without one. It is rare, though," the butler revealed.

"Bloody hell," he murmured. "I'll think about it."

"Anything else, Your Grace?"

"No. Thank you. But have the carriage brought around if you would."

Winkle nodded and left, leaving Wyatt to his thoughts.

All of which revolved around Meadow.

He liked the name. Meadow. It rolled pleasantly off his

tongue. The thought of tongues had him immediately thinking about their kiss. Or cavalcade of kisses, he supposed.

One thing had been obvious. She hadn't known how to kiss. Not that it mattered. She was a bright woman and caught on quickly. Eagerly. Even now, he could taste her as he imagined her tongue teasing his. His thoughts lingered over their short time in the gardens and he smiled.

He was going to enjoy making love to this woman.

Wyatt chuckled, thinking how she believed him to be as much a rakehell as the ones he had warned her of. He also enjoyed that Meadow had depth to her. She wasn't just beautiful. She was goodhearted and intelligent. And she was a spitfire. The way she had first stood up to Marshmore, demanding that her cousin's husband push aside thoughts of himself and place his sons' interests above his own. Then again, how fiery she had become when she thought he only wanted to bed her. She had slapped and then chastised Wyatt before she flounced off, not waiting around to hear his offer of marriage.

He grinned. Having Meadow as a wife might even be fun. He hadn't dwelled on the relationship he would have with his duchess. He merely had focused on finding a suitable woman who desired children as much as he did. He had concentrated on the results of their lovemaking, the children that wife would bear, and not the wife—or the lovemaking.

Physically, he knew they would be a perfect match in bed. His loins already ached, wanting to be inside her. His hands longed to stroke her every curve. His lips desired her kiss and also wanted to kiss every inch of her beautiful flesh. He believed they would have both fun and passion in their marriage bed. Outside it, she would most likely prove to be a good companion. It would be nice to wed a woman he actually liked.

He just had to offer for her.

Wyatt wondered if she would be present at tonight's musicale. Emery had told him the guest list was much smaller than last night's ball. If he arrived and found Meadow wasn't in attendance, he would stay a short while and then leave. He only knew he needed to confirm their engagement soon. She was far too beautiful to be left running about, men falling over themselves to be near her. The number of flower arrangements she had received spoke to her popularity after only a single *ton* event.

He went downstairs and found the carriage waiting for him. He instructed his driver to call first at the Duke and Duchess of Winslow's residence before continuing on to the Martindales' affair.

When his friends joined him, he said, "You look lovely tonight, Emery."

Miles slipped an arm possessively about his wife's waist and smiled at her. "She does, doesn't she?"

"You seem to be in excellent spirits," Miles noted. "Might that be because you called upon a certain lady this afternoon?"

"I did," he revealed.

"I hope you weren't foolish enough to offer for her," Emery said.

"I wanted to," Wyatt admitted. "She left rather abruptly, though, and I wasn't able to do so."

"What did you do?" she asked, suspicion in her eyes.

"Why do you accuse me of committing some faux pas?" he asked.

"Women do not abruptly leave their guests," she said.

"I may have kissed her," he admitted.

"Wyatt!" Emery chided. "*May* have?"

"All right. I did kiss her. And it was quite good if you are curious."

"I'm not," Miles said drolly.

"Well, I am," his wife said. "Did kissing her cause her to leave?"

"In a way. We were in Lord Marshmore's gardens. We kissed. I can tell we suit in that area."

"Still not interested," Miles interjected, his tone teasing.

"And then she slapped me."

"Good for her," remarked Emery.

"Whose side are you on?" he asked. "I thought you wanted me to find a bride that was bit more mature than the younger women making their come-outs. Meadow is perfect for me. She is closer to my age. She is poised and beautiful. She can carry on a conversation with ease. I thought you approved of her, based upon your behavior toward her last night."

"I do like her, Wyatt. A great deal," Emery said. "I will not have you take advantage of her, though."

"That's what she suspected. Or accused me of. She thought I was only interested in luring her to my bed. That is why she slapped me."

Emery blew out a long breath, shaking her head. "Oh, Wyatt," she said, sympathy in her eyes.

"She ran off before I could correct her assumption. I will remedy that during our next encounter."

"You better," Emery warned. "And no kissing during it."

"Why not?" he asked.

"I am staying out of this," Miles uttered, glancing out the window.

"Wyatt, a man shouldn't offer for a woman after meeting her once."

"It's been twice," he corrected.

"Twice," she said through gritted teeth. "Lady Selfridge is a sweet, delightful woman. From what I gathered last night, she hasn't enjoyed much of society. She should be able to enjoy it—and that includes meeting various gentlemen. Only after you ask permission to court her and you have gotten to know one another should you even think of offering marriage to her."

"Why would I waste all that time?" he asked. "Worse, what if some other blockhead muscles in?"

"Lady Selfridge should be given a choice in the matter of who courts her and who seeks to wed her. I beg you, Wyatt, don't try to force her hand. If you do, you will be disappointed—and you might lose out on her forever."

Though Emery had a point, stubbornness filled him. He was a duke. Of course she would accept him. He would prove Emery wrong.

The first time he came upon Meadow, he would state his case and they would become engaged. In fact, they could announce their betrothal tonight.

"We're here," Miles said. "Thank goodness." He stepped from the carriage and helped his wife down before turning to Wyatt. "You would do well to listen to my duchess. She has a way with people and understands their nature, especially when it comes to women." Then he frowned. "No, I can tell. You are going to be your usual reckless self and plunge ahead, not bothering to heed her advice."

Miles shook his head. "I hope you are prepared for when Emery says, 'I told you so.' Because she will when you act like a dunderhead and ruin everything."

Wyatt didn't bother to respond as he followed Miles and Emery into the Martindales' townhouse.

CHAPTER TWELVE

M EADOW LIKED THAT this second event of the Season would be a much smaller gathering. While she loved to dance, she also enjoyed music. Listening to it. Not playing. She had taken pianoforte lessons as a child and had been abominable at the instrument. The one time her mother asked her to play for her, Meadow had only gotten through a few measures of the Bach piece before she was ordered to stop. After that, her lessons ceased. Though it relieved her not to have to practice for endless hours, she had walked away from those lessons with an appreciation for music, which was why she looked forward to tonight's musicale.

No receiving line meant she, Tilda, and Marshmore could simply enter the townhouse and wander about, greeting other guests in a more casual, relaxed atmosphere. The earl immediately abandoned them to go speak with friends. She thought of how Amesbury had accused her cousin's husband of being a bully during their school days. Marshmore hadn't denied it. She wondered if men changed. Marshmore didn't seem like a bully now. Of course, she knew very little about him. He rarely spent time in her and Tilda's company. She saw him at meals sometimes but he had little to say. Meadow couldn't help but wonder what kind of marriage they had. Probably the same as most of the *ton*, one of convenience.

Still, if Marshmore had changed for the better as he had matured, couldn't the Duke of Amesbury have done so, as well? She had thought on Marshmore's words, the rumor of how the duke had been jealous of his brother and caused the death of an entire stable of horses. Was he that same man today, callous and cold? Or had he changed?

She remembered he had told Marshmore that he would destroy him if the earl insisted in spreading rumors about him. Though she didn't think Amesbury a man to care for the opinion of others, she had no doubt he would have made good on his threat to ruin her cousin's husband.

This constant thinking about the duke had to cease. Whether or not he had behaved so criminally as a boy or he acted the reprobate now, it was none of her concern.

Even if he had kissed her.

Even if she had liked it.

Immensely.

What she didn't like was his insufferable behavior. If she were to compose of a list of eligible men from which to wed, the Duke of Amesbury would be at the bottom of the list. Or totally stricken from the page. He wasn't in the least bit close to the kind of man she wished to wed. She needed someone gentle. Kind. Faithful. Consumed by family. Not a haughty, conceited man.

Even if he kissed remarkably well.

Oh, how was she to know? He might simply be competent at kissing. There could be a hundred men better at it. She wouldn't know because she'd only kissed him.

Meadow knew she lied to herself. The Duke of Amesbury had been a marvelous kisser. He was the kind of man who was good at everything he did, whether it was ruining people or kissing them.

"Quit thinking about him," she muttered under her breath.

Tilda turned to her. "Are you quite all right? You have been quiet ever since Amesbury's visit."

"You do not have to worry about him visiting again," she told her cousin. "I made that quite clear."

Disappointment flickered in Tilda's eyes. "I see. Is there any specific reason why you would do such a thing?"

"Isn't it enough that he spoke so casually about ruining your husband?"

Tilda shrugged. "Amesbury is a duke. They have it within their power to do such things." She sighed. "Frankly, it wouldn't surprise me if Marshmore had been the bully the duke accused him of being."

"Why do you say that?" Meadow asked anxiously. "Has he ever hurt you?"

"No. He would have to care about me to do so."

That one sentence told her everything she needed to know about Tilda's marriage.

She took Tilda's hands in hers. "I am so sorry, Cousin."

Tilda pulled away. "Don't be. I went into the marriage with few expectations. He had a title. Wealth to ensure I would never want for anything. He has given me two sons. He no longer comes to my bed. I am fine with that. It wasn't something I enjoyed anyway. I am sure you felt the same about Selfridge bedding you. It's a pity, though, he never gave you any children."

Meadow swallowed, wanting to immediately change the topic. It was too personal. They were in public. Worse, all she could think about was Amesbury coming to her bed. Kissing her. Touching her.

Meadow cleared her throat. "I think I see Lady Charlotte. We should go say hello to her."

The two women went to visit with Tilda's friend and neighbor. Meadow tried to follow the conversation as she scanned the room. She told herself she was merely looking to see which guests had been invited.

It was definitely not to see if the Duke of Amesbury was in attendance.

Then she heard her name and turned. "Good evening, Your Grace." Though she was happy to see the Duchess of Winslow, she thought that would mean Amesbury might have accompanied the duchess and her husband to tonight's event.

"Did you have many callers this afternoon?" the duchess asked, pulling her aside from Tilda and Lady Charlotte.

"Yes, quite a few."

"If you are free tomorrow afternoon, I would be happy for you to come and take tea with me and His Grace."

Warmth filled her. "I would like that very much."

"I am delighted to hear that. Of all the women I met last night, I felt the most comfortable with you. I do hope we can be friends, Lady Selfridge."

"I would like that, as well, Your Grace."

"Please. I hate to stand on formality. Especially with the one woman whom I have befriended. Would you call me Emery?"

Surprise filled her. "Yes, I would be happy to do so. You must address me as Meadow, in return."

"Meadow. What a lovely name."

She smiled. "I was thinking the same of Emery. I don't believe I have ever heard that before."

"It was my mother's maiden name. She was an only child. That meant no one was left to carry on the family name. She did so in honor of her beloved father, who was a country doctor."

"You mentioned last night that she was once the duke's housekeeper?"

Emery laughed. "Oh, she still is. Miles wanted her to live a life of luxury when we wed but Mama was determined to keep the household running. She likes keeping busy."

"It must make it nice for you to have someone you trust in that position."

"It is nice but I will admit that others most likely find it to be odd. I don't care. That is what I like about my husband. He hasn't tried to change me. He accepts me and my family for who we are."

"He seems to love you very much," she commented.

"We love each other wholeheartedly," Emery said. "Might I be so bold as to ask if you loved your husband?"

"No," Meadow said. "Not in the least. Our marriage was arranged by my father less than two weeks into my first Season. We wed quickly. It was a marriage of convenience, one in which the viscount paid off my father's gambling debts in exchange for me."

Emery touched her arm. "I am so sorry, Meadow."

"Don't be. It is over and done. I am free after serving my years in his prison. It will be my choice this time. I don't expect a love match but I do have certain ideas about what I want in a husband."

"I had asked you to keep my friend, Amesbury in mind. I know he called upon you today. Did he offend you?"

"Why do you ask?" she asked, worry filling her.

"He admitted that he kissed you," the duchess said.

Meadow felt the heat of embarrassment sting her cheeks. "I do not think your friend will suit me," she said quickly.

"I will admit that he is brash. It helped make him a good spy."

"He was a spy?"

"Yes, during some of his time abroad. He will have to tell you about his adventures sometime."

"I don't think that would be wise," she said. "I don't wish to spend time with His Grace. If I do, others might believe there is an understanding between us. I want to be free to find the right husband for me, one who is gentle and kind."

Emery nodded. "Believe it or not, Amesbury can be those things."

"We will have to agree to disagree on this matter," she said firmly. Looking around, Meadow added, "It looks as though people are beginning to take their places. I have heard it will be an Italian soprano who sings for us tonight."

"Oh, dear," Emery said. "I know next to nothing about music. Is that good?"

She slipped her arm around her new friend's. "She will be divine."

Meadow led them to a row three from the front and stepped

into it. "Should we save a seat for His Grace?"

"I am here," Winslow said, joining them. "Someone said the soloist will be singing arias." He grimaced.

His wife chuckled as they took their seats. "We are more interested in history than music," she told Meadow.

Suddenly, she felt someone jostle her and she turned.

The Duke of Amesbury had taken the seat next to her.

"I don't think you wish to sit here, Your Grace," she told him.

"I am sure you can ignore me as you did when I sat beside you yesterday. You have practice at that, Meadow."

"Stop doing that," she hissed.

He leaned close. "Stop calling you Meadow?"

"You know that is what I mean. You are doing it to irritate me."

"Actually, I am doing it because I enjoy saying your name. Meadow," he said softly. "I quite like it."

"I am warning you, Your Grace."

"What? Are you going to slap me again?"

Her cheeks burned. "No. I do apologize for that. I quite lost my temper. I never do that. I have never behaved remotely in a way that would make me ashamed. That did. Please accept my apologies. I don't wish to be rude to you."

"That's a good start, don't you think?" he said lightly.

"To what?"

Before he could answer, a voice said, "Welcome. Thank you for coming this evening."

She turned and saw it was Lord Martindale addressing the room. She concentrated on him.

Not the warm shoulder that pressed against hers. Not the scent of bergamot that drifted from him. Not the feel of his wool coat that rested along her bare upper arm. Thank heavens she wore gloves that went slightly above her elbow else her arm would be singed with his heat.

He shifted slightly, his hip and thigh now brushing against hers. Why did she want to claw his eyes out and yet, at the same time, wish to grab hold of him and kiss him?

A woman moved to the front of the room and the guests applauded politely. A pianist began to play. Meadow focused on the music. Or at least she tried to. Each time a song began, she swore to herself she would do nothing but follow along with the music. By a few measures into the piece, she already had lost her focus. When the song ended and the guests clapped with enthusiasm, she did the same, irritated that she was missing the entire concert because of the man sitting next to her. It was so unfair. Her irritability grew with each song performed—and missed by her.

Lord Martindale rose again. "We are going to allow our little songbird a chance to rest her voice. Lady Martindale has prepared a cold buffet for your enjoyment. We will commence again in one hour. Enjoy!"

"Will you—"

"I will not dine with you," Meadow snapped at the duke.

He bit back a smile and she felt her neck and face grow hot, as the couple in front of them turned to stare.

She swallowed, tamping down her roiling feelings. It wasn't his fault that she was put out with him. He had merely sat next to her. He hadn't distracted her in any way. Unless you counted how much room he took up and parts of him resting against her.

"Forgive me, Your Grace. I am feeling a bit out of sorts," she apologized to him yet again. "Please excuse me. I need to visit the retiring room."

Meadow stood and followed the Duke and Duchess of Winslow from the row. Once in the aisle, she went directly to the retiring room. She asked for a hand towel and accepted one from the attendant before dipping its end in the water and wringing it out. Running the dampened cloth across her face, she breathed in and out deeply several times.

It was absurd to allow herself to be obsessed with Amesbury. He toyed with her—but she was no plaything. She wouldn't risk her chances of making a good match by going to his bed. The idea she even contemplated that was ludicrous. She was not that kind of woman.

Yet his kiss seemed to have her thinking things she never had. Feeling things she'd never dreamed existed. She had lain in her bed last night, reliving every moment of it. Wishing he had touched her in places too intimate to mention.

She bathed her face a second time and then dried it. Checking her reflection in the mirror, she saw the heightened color on her cheeks and how her eyes, usually a light gray, had darkened considerably.

"Enough!" she declared aloud, startling the maid in the corner, who almost fell from the stool she perched upon.

She would return to the other guests. She would force something down. Then she would find another seat for the remainder of the concert. Sitting beside Amesbury had proved disastrous. She wasn't going to have the rest of the evening she had so looked forward to ruined for her.

Another maid opened the door for her and Meadow stepped from the room.

Waiting for her was the Duke of Amesbury.

CHAPTER THIRTEEN

"W HAT ARE YOU doing here?" Meadow asked, exasperation filling her.

Along with a bit of excitement that he had come all this way, seeking her out.

"I told you I needed to speak with you urgently," he said, his eyes roaming her face, causing her body to tingle.

"I believe I have made it quite clear, Your Grace, that I—"

"Wyatt," he interrupted.

"What?" she asked.

"Wyatt. When we are alone, I wish you to address me as Wyatt."

She snorted. "There is *no* when we are alone, Your Grace."

"Wyatt," he insisted.

Meadow made a sound that had never come from her before, hoping it conveyed her annoyance.

"Quit trying to vex me," she demanded, her temper flaring.

"I wouldn't be vexing you at all if you would merely be quiet for a moment and listen to what I have to say," he pointed out calmly, causing her irritation to soar.

"I have no intention of listening to your words of seduction, Your Grace. I may be a widow but I am not the kind of woman you are looking for."

"You know me well enough to know the kind of woman I seek?" he asked, his voice low and playful.

"Stop flirting with me!" she cried, throwing her hands in the air. "It won't work. I will not come to your bed. It simply will not happen. Leave me alone. I do not want to be seen with you. You will chase off any respectable gentleman that might actually be interested in me. In marrying me."

He took a step toward her, causing her heart to race.

"I am interested in you, Meadow."

The man was impossible. He would never listen to her. She should save her breath and return as quickly as possible to the supper room. It wouldn't do for others to realize both she and Amesbury were missing at the same time.

She took two strides away from him, only to have him capture her wrist, impeding her progress. He pulled her toward him and the scent of bergamot wafted toward her.

"Please, Your Grace, release me. I must return to supper. I don't want Lord Martindale's guests to think . . . that is . . . I wouldn't want them . . ." Her voice trailed off, too embarrassed to voice her thoughts.

"You don't want them to think we planned a tryst during this short break?" he asked, his thumb stroking the underside of her wrist, causing her knees to go weak.

"Yes," she admitted, her voice but a whisper.

He continued massaging her wrist and she found looking into his eyes caused her to somehow fall under his spell. She blinked rapidly, trying to break it.

"I do want you in my bed, Meadow."

His words caused her blood to fire. To be desired by a man as sinfully handsome as the Duke of Amesbury was a heady thing. She played with fire, though. At any moment, someone could choose to come to the retiring room and see them together, his hand encircling her wrist, his eyes dark with passion.

"No," she said, her voice faint.

"I think you want to be there," he said. "I know how we both can be satisfied."

Meadow jerked away from him and took off, too afraid to

stay any longer. She didn't make it far, though. His hands caught her, spinning her around, clasping her by her elbows. He moved her toward the closest room and closed the door behind them.

"You are stubborn. I suppose that is one of the reasons I find you so attractive. You aren't making this easy for me."

She knew her very reputation was on the line and knew she had to stand up to this man. He might be a duke but she hoped he would be a gentleman.

"I do not want to have an affair with you, Your Grace."

"Wyatt," he insisted.

She glared at him. "You are a duke. You can have any woman in Polite Society, married or unmarried. I beg of you, Your Grace, to focus on someone else."

"But I want you," he said simply. "You are the most beautiful woman I have ever seen. The most spirited."

"Think of me as forbidden fruit," she snapped. "I am not available to you. Find someone else and use your charms on her."

His eyebrows rose. "You think I am charming?"

"Not particularly."

He sighed. "I have been away from England too long, Meadow. War changes a man. I thought I would spend my entire life in the army. A twist of fate occurred and I suddenly became something I never thought I would. A duke. Forgive me if I have seemed uncouth in manners. You are a bit exasperating, though. You keep interrupting me before I can spit out—"

"Spit out what?" she demanded.

He chucked, low and deep. "There you go again." He placed his hands on her shoulders. "What I have tried to say several times now is this.

"I wish to make you my duchess."

His words flabbergasted her. Her jaw dropped but no words came out.

"I would like us to wed as quickly as possible. I can arrange to purchase a special license. I don't know what kind of ceremony you wish to have, especially since you been through one before. I don't mind if it is small or large though I would ask that Miles and Emery be present. They are family to me."

"What?" she said, her head still swirling at his unexpected declaration.

"I thought I made myself clear." He dropped to one knee, capturing her hands in his. "I suppose this is what men are supposed to do."

He paused and, for a moment, she thought he looked extremely vulnerable and boyish.

"Meadow, I would like us to wed. I hope you are agreeable to the idea."

"But we have only just met," she protested. "At last night's ball. You know nothing about me."

He rose, still keeping her hands in his. "I am a good judge of character. I believe we will suit. You want children. So do I."

Surprised by his admission, nevertheless she said, "I know nothing about you. How can I commit myself to you?"

He frowned. "What is there to know? I am a duke. I possess more wealth than almost any man in England. You would want for nothing. There really is no decision."

His arrogance irked her. "You are saying that because you are a handsome, wealthy duke that I should say yes."

He grinned, looking boyish. "You think me handsome?"

"Irritatingly so," she told him. "But you are not listening to me. I don't know you."

Her words seem to baffle him. "What is there to know? You are in need of a husband. I am seeking a wife. Wedding me would make you one of the most exalted ladies in the land."

"That isn't important to me," she insisted.

"It should be. I can give you everything, Meadow. Including those children you have spoken of." He squeezed her hands. "I will purchase the special license tomorrow morning. I am certain Emery will want to host the wedding breakfast but if you would rather your cousin do so—"

"Stop!"

He ceased speaking and stared at her. "What?"

"I haven't agreed to marry you."

He frowned.

"You have assumed I will because of your looks. Your wealth. Your title. That is not enough, Your Grace."

"It isn't?"

She wriggled, trying to free her hands from his but he held fast. Giving up, she said, "I had a little more than two weeks of my come-out when my father told me I would be marrying Viscount Selfridge. I had no say in the matter. I was, in effect, sold to Selfridge because he didn't receive my dowry—which I found out my father had gambled away. No, I paid the price and was forced to wed a man I knew nothing about, simply to pay my father's gambling markers. Selfridge did that in order to have me. He had never even danced with me once. Never spoken to me. I went to the household of a stranger.

"I won't do it again," she said, resolve filling her.

Some would think her crazy for turning down a duke's proposal. No, probably all of Polite Society would think so. Meadow didn't care. She did want to wed, desperately, in order to have the children she sought.

"I will wed the man of my choice," she told Amesbury.

He searched her face. "You wish to be courted," he said softly.

"I do. I don't care if I have one or one hundred and one suitors. I will not be rushed into anything. I will take my time. Learn about any man who expresses interest in me. Get to know his likes and dislikes and hope he would do the same for me. It is my decision this time. No one else's. If you think I am mad for turning down a duke's proposal, so be it."

A slow smile spread across his handsome face. "No, I do not find it odd at all. Maddening—because I want you for myself now. But if it is your wish, Meadow, I will jump into the fray and woo you."

"It is," she said, her throat tightening with emotion. "I am surprised that you would take the time to bother with me when you could have any woman you wished with a mere snap of your fingers."

His eyes gleamed. "Yet I don't want just any woman. I want *you* to be my duchess." He threaded his fingers through hers. "May I take you for a drive in the park tomorrow? I believe I have been told that five o'clock is the fashionable hour."

"You may," she said primly, secretly thrilled that he was going along with her wishes so willingly.

"Then to make certain you understand, I am courting you," he said.

"I understand."

His eyes darkened. "And understand this, Meadow. I plan to win your hand. I would risk all to have you."

He lowered his mouth to hers and brushed his lips softly against hers. His fingers tightened around hers but he kept the kiss sweet.

Breaking it, he said, "Why don't you return to the supper room now?"

"All right," she said, her voice shaking.

"I will skip supper this evening and return to the hall. If any-one asks, I will let them assume I remained there instead of supping with the other guests."

He lifted her hands and brushed his lips against her fingers, then kissed them tenderly.

"I will be waiting for you in the hall."

Releasing her hands, he stepped away and opened the door. He looked out and nodded.

"It is safe for you to leave."

"Thank you."

Meadow found the supper room and joined the table where Tilda and Marshmore sat.

"Where have you been?" her cousin asked quietly.

She placed her palm against her belly, which still fluttered with unknown feelings she refused to categorize.

"I have been in the retiring room."

"Are you ill?" Tilda asked. "Do you have a fever? Your color is high."

"I don't think so."

"We should leave," Tilda decided. "Tomorrow is the Lattimore ball. We mustn't miss it." She turned to her husband. "Marshmore, have the carriage brought round. We are leaving."

"Very well," he said. "You know I am not much for opera. The singer has grated upon my every nerve this evening."

"We will join you outside shortly," Tilda said. She turned back to Meadow. "Do you think you can eat anything or is your stomach too upset?"

"I would rather not," she said.

"Stay here. I will make our excuses to Lady Martindale."

Meadow sat silently as others conversed around her. Soon, Tilda joined her and they left the townhouse and entered the carriage. She remained quiet during the ride home, knowing if she spoke she might blurt out that the Duke of Amesbury had asked for her hand in marriage.

No, she must keep this to herself. If she shared it, Tilda would immediately want to know all the details and begin planning their wedding. Meadow wasn't certain she wanted to wed the duke, even though she had given him permission to court her. He stirred too many wild feelings within her, things that frightened her. She had thought to choose a husband who would be easy to live with. Something told her that a life with Wyatt would be anything but.

Wyatt . . .

The name suited him well. He was dashing. Arrogant. Confrontational. Intelligent.

She promised herself that she would give him a chance. She wanted to know more about him. What his life had been like in the army. The things he had seen and done.

Meadow also wanted to know the truth about the event Marshmore had revealed to her. If Wyatt would tell her what had happened, she might trust him enough to think about a future with him.

CHAPTER FOURTEEN

MEADOW WENT DOWNSTAIRS to breakfast. Marshmore sat engrossed in his newspaper, not speaking as usual. Once again, she pitied Tilda for the kind of marriage her cousin had made and vowed to have one much different.

Last night, she had fallen into a restless sleep, awaking before dawn, her body tense, taut as a string drawn too tight, at its breaking point. She rose and splashed water on her face, rolling her shoulders and then her neck, trying to erase the tension. Thoughts of Wyatt's long fingers kneading her nape came to her. She closed her eyes and pretended he did so, his fingers easing the tense muscles, sliding along her shoulders, cupping her breasts.

What?

No one had ever touched her breasts except her. That was always for a brief moment as she slid a washcloth over them. Why would she be thinking of Wyatt's hands on them?

Why was she even thinking of him at all?

And why was she now thinking of him as Wyatt?

She let out a growl of frustration. Amesbury had inserted himself into her life only a few days ago and yet her every waking thought seem to revolve around him. She wanted him. She would admit that, whatever wanting a man meant. She wanted him to kiss her the way he had in the garden. The thought of his lips on hers had her body on edge, thinking of other places he might put them.

Preposterous!

Meadow admitted that even though she knew nothing of him, she was besotted with him. Oh, wouldn't he love to know that. He wasn't anything she wanted in a husband. He was conceited. Blunt. Too handsome by far. If she married him, she would forever be worried about him going astray. Wyatt was the kind of man who would take what he wanted, when he wanted, wherever he wanted. And that would include women.

A fit of jealousy possessed her, thinking of him in the company of another woman. She hadn't known she had a jealous bone in her body yet if she saw him even dancing with someone else, it would break her heart. These thoughts should be warning enough to her. The Duke of Amesbury wasn't for her. She must put as much distance between them as possible. She would honor her commitment and go for a drive with him today but that would be the end of it. It would be important for her to continue her search for a husband elsewhere. The duke could look for a wife from all the many young beauties on the Marriage Mart. Being a duke, he traveled in far loftier circles than she ever would. She would find herself a nice viscount or lowly baron and settle into a domestic life in the country, far from town. She wouldn't need any more Seasons after this one. She would retire to the country and be content with the children her new husband would give her.

That made her think again about wedding a widower. She was a widow. It would be natural to be drawn to a man who found himself in similar circumstances as herself, especially if he already had a child or two. She could become a mother immediately and then wait to find herself with child. That would be best. No more looking at men who had never wed.

Beyond her obligation today with Wyatt. Amesbury.

Meadow went to the buffet and served herself, not putting much on her plate since she found she had no appetite. She joined Tilda, who began talking about tonight's ball.

"I believe you should wear the blue," her cousin advised.

"The pale blue rather than the darker shade."

She frowned. "I don't know. That neckline is a bit low, don't you think?"

"I have told you that is the fashion, Meadow. If you want to attract a husband, you must display your assets adequately."

"In other words, show enough bosom to lure in a man," she said drily.

Tilda sniffed. "You are sometimes impossible, do you know that? Yes, show your bosom. It is a beautiful one." She paused. "Perhaps even the Duke of Amesbury might ask you to dance then. He did before. He also sat with you at last night's musicale."

She decided she better break the news now. "He is coming to call today." Her eyes cut to Marshmore, still reading his newspaper. "I hope that won't bring about trouble."

Tilda sniffed. "Marshmore doesn't even have to see the duke. I will make certain he is in his study. What time will Amesbury call? For tea?"

"Oh!"

"What's wrong?"

"I just remembered that I had promised the Duchess of Winslow that I would take tea with her this afternoon."

She shuffled through the letters next to her plate, having thought to eat first before she bothered with them. Finding what she believed to be a note from Emery, she opened it. It confirmed their teatime of four o'clock this afternoon.

Dismayed, she said, "I am invited for tea at four—but I agreed to go riding in the park with His Grace at five o'clock."

"You mustn't let His Grace down. Write to Her Grace and say you have a prior commitment which you had forgotten about."

"But I promised her first," Meadow said.

"Although I will admit going to tea with a duchess is out of the ordinary, you simply cannot keep a duke waiting, Meadow. Write to Her Grace. I am sure she will invite you for another day."

She supposed it would be better to write to Emery than to be bold enough to write to Wyatt. No, Amesbury. He needed to remain Amesbury in her thoughts from now on.

Excusing herself, she went to her bedchamber. As she sat at the small escritoire, she changed her mind. Emery had asked first. She would honor that commitment.

Taking out a piece of parchment, she dipped the quill into the inkwell. How would she address him? Amesbury? My dear duke? She decided not to bother with a salutation.

I regret that I must inform you that I cannot go driving in Hyde Park with you today. I had forgotten my previous commitment to take tea at four o'clock with the Duchess of Winslow. I believe it is important to honor my commitments, especially since I had promised the duchess a visit before I agreed to plans with you.

Perhaps we might take our drive on another day if that is convenient for you.

Sincerely,
Lady Selfridge

Meadow read over it three times. Was it too daring to suggest a different day? She chuckled. Writing a duke she barely knew was bold enough. Before she could change her mind, she folded and dribbled sealing wax to seal it. Taking the note downstairs, she found a footman and asked that he deliver it. When she told him the recipient, his eyes bugged out somewhat.

"Do you know where His Grace resides?"

The footman nodded. "It's one of the grandest townhouses in London, my lady. Lord Marshmore has a friend that lives across the street. I take letters there frequently."

"Good. Please see that it is delivered now if you would."

"Yes, my lady."

Meadow returned to her room and lay upon the bed. With the lack of sleep from last night, she was weary. She decided to take a short nap. She had plenty of time to do so before this afternoon's tea.

WYATT SAT AT breakfast, turning the pages of the newspaper but not really reading any of them. Articles of the war and the economy held no interest for him. His thoughts were reserved for Meadow.

She hadn't returned for the second half of the concert last night. He had eagerly awaited her appearance but she never showed up. He had scanned the room and found he couldn't locate Lord and Lady Marshmore and decided the trio had left. Others might think it odd if they left and so did he so Wyatt remained for the rest of the musicale. He had never thought of the opinion of others but it seemed important to Meadow so he must make it a priority, as well. He remembered how she had talked to Marshmore about how his children would be received in society if he alienated Wyatt. It would be important that he stay on the good side of those in the *ton* in order for his own children to be accepted.

Emery had quizzed him on the carriage ride home, where he admitted that he had offered for Meadow—and that she had turned him down. He explained that she thought it too soon to announce an engagement because they barely knew one another. Emery had nodded knowingly but hadn't rubbed it in that she had been right all along. It seemed Meadow did want to be courted. Wyatt also realized that she had only attended a handful of events before her reprobate father had used her to excuse his debts.

Meadow deserved a bit of fun and attention. She should attend balls and routs and garden parties. He would make sure he was at every event she was, dancing attendance upon her. She had put up a bit of a wall between them but he knew he could wear it down simply because of how she had responded to his kiss. Besides, he rather liked the challenge. He also liked the fact that she was making him work for her. No one in Polite Society told a duke no.

Except Meadow.

She might be saying no to him now but he knew in the long run that she would become his duchess.

"The post, Your Grace," Winkle said, bearing a silver tray with a stack full of letters. Probably more invitations. It might be worth hiring a secretary so he wouldn't have to wade through such nonsense.

He thumbed through them, opening a few, then paused. The handwriting attracted him. It was perfect. Instinct told him it was from Meadow.

Wyatt tore it opened and scanned the few lines, frowning. He supposed he couldn't fault her. Obviously, Emery had asked her to tea before he had suggested they drive through the park together. He hadn't known about the invitation to tea because Emery didn't mention it in the carriage on the way home last night.

He folded the note and thought a moment. And decided exactly what he would do.

Hours later, shortly before four o'clock, he was talking with his driver.

"The curricle will be out in a moment, Your Grace," Blevins told him. "The grooms are readying the horses now."

Wyatt had sought out his coachman after breakfast, having the servant show what vehicles were here in London, and explaining that he would be driving a young lady through the park today and that he needed a suitable bit of transportation.

They had settled on an ebony curricle with a matched pair of horses of the same color. A groom appeared, leading the team of two.

Wyatt whistled low. "They are beauties."

"They are indeed, Your Grace," the driver replied. "I hope you have a pleasant outing in the park."

He climbed into the driver's seat, happy to see that while there was room for two passengers, it would be a cozy fit.

With a jaunty wave, he set off for Miles' townhouse, turning the corner just before four. He saw Meadow emerging from a carriage. She headed to the front door. He held back the pair of blacks until she entered and then pulled up behind her carriage. A footman standing on the porch hurried over.

"Good afternoon, Your Grace. We weren't expecting you."

"I hope I won't be turned away. Please watch my curricle if you would."

"Certainly, Your Grace," the servant said with a cheeky grin.

Wyatt went to the vehicle in front of him. "Are you from the Earl of Marshmore?"

"Aye, I am, my lord."

"Is Lady Selfridge the only passenger you conveyed here today?"

The driver frowned, puzzled by the question. "Yes, my lord."

"It is Your Grace," he corrected this time, wanting the weight of his title to sink in. Then he added, "Lady Selfridge is to go driving with me in Hyde Park after tea. You may return to Marshmore's. I will see her home."

"Of course, Your Grace," the driver said, taking up the reins without question.

The carriage pulled away and Wyatt watched it a moment before going to the front door and ringing the bell. The butler answered and welcomed him.

"Good afternoon, Your Grace. Have you come to take tea?"

"I have. I will see my way up. No need to announce me."

Wyatt took the stairs two at a time, in high spirits because he would now get to see Meadow.

And the look on her face.

At the first landing, he heard his name and came to a halt. Turning, he saw Miles at the foot of the stairs.

"What the devil are you doing here?" his friend asked. "Oh, wait. I know."

Miles joined him. "You are here to take tea, I believe. Is that correct?"

"It is, Your Grace," Wyatt said, grinning.

His friend threw an arm about his shoulders. "Come along, you scamp. Let's surprise the ladies."

They entered the drawing room together and Emery glanced up first. Her eyes widened a bit and then she smiled.

"Good afternoon," she said as they crossed the room.

Meadow glanced up, her eyes as round as saucers. "Good afternoon," she echoed.

"I hope you have plenty," Miles said easily. "I ran across Wyatt and invited him to tea. I am sorry, I did not remember that you had a guest coming. Do you mind if we join you?"

He went and kissed his wife's cheek.

Emery looked to Meadow for the answer to his question and she said, "I would not keep you from tea in your own home, Your Grace. Or your guest," she added.

"Ring for two more cups, darling," Emery told her husband.

Miles did so as Wyatt went and sat next to Meadow.

"I have dismissed your driver," he told her. "I came in my curricle. We can still manage our drive once we leave here."

"Do you always get your way?" she asked, so low only he could hear her.

"I manage to do so as often as I can," he replied, a twinkle in his eyes.

CHAPTER FIFTEEN

MEADOW DIDN'T KNOW whether to kiss Wyatt or soundly box his ears after a remark like that. Fortunately for him, they were in the Duke and Duchess of Winslow's company. That kept her from acting upon either choice.

The next hour passed pleasantly and she wished the tea could go on indefinitely. She felt a closeness to Emery, despite the fact that she was a duchess. Perhaps it was because Emery hadn't come from the world of Polite Society and was an unlikely candidate to marry into the higher echelons of the *ton*, especially landing a duke as her husband. She seemed so unpretentious and was easy to talk with. The two women also had a love for their tenants and both had spent many hours out on their estates interacting with its people.

It surprised her how much she liked Emery's husband. The duke was quick-witted and entertaining. He and Wyatt talked about their school days, with the duke calling the two of them and their friends Terrors. She laughed at their antics and was moved by how deep the connection seemed between the two men. They spoke fondly of Hart and Donovan, two boys from their school days who stilled served in the army, as well as Finch, who was a vicar and had performed the marriage ceremony for Emery and her husband.

The clock struck five and Wyatt said, "I hate to break up this happy teatime but I have promised Lady Selfridge that I would drive her through Hyde Park now. I have heard this is the fashionable hour to do so."

"I so enjoyed having you for tea," Emery told Meadow.

"I would love to return the favor," she said. "Might you come for tea at my cousin's house tomorrow?"

Emery shook her head. "Not tomorrow. After tonight's ball, you will have a bevy of new suitors, as well as the ones from before, wishing to call upon you. You should be available to them. Why don't we plan for one day next week?"

"How about we all go to Gunter's?" Wyatt interjected. "I know you have longed to do so, Emery. The four of us could do so after calling hours tomorrow."

Her friend's face lit up. "Oh, I have been eager to try one of their ices. What a splendid idea, Wyatt."

He turned to Meadow. "Is that agreeable, my lady? Say, four o'clock tomorrow?"

"Yes, I would very much like to go on that outing," she said, thrilled he would ask and aware of his thoughtfulness, as well.

"Good. I will call here with my carriage at a quarter-till and then we will go on to Marshmore's."

Wyatt rose and offered her his hand. She took it, feeling the electricity crackle between them with the touch.

The duke and duchess walked them downstairs and Emery kissed Meadow's cheek. "I will see you tonight," she promised.

Once outside, Meadow saw a shining black curricle with two coal-black horses to lead it.

"Let me get settled first," Wyatt suggested. "It will be easier to help you up that way."

As he climbed into the vehicle, she had an excellent view of his muscular thighs and perfectly shaped calves, thanks to his tight fawn breeches. It caused her pulse to race, this glimpse of masculine beauty.

He held out his hands to her and she stepped closer, allowing him to capture her waist, his large hands easily spanning it. He placed her upon the seat and then sat next to her. As before, he took up more of it than most men. Instead of being irritated at him, as she had been at the musicale, she rather liked the feel of his entire side pressed against hers.

Wyatt took up the reins and, with a flick of his wrists, they set out for Hyde Park. Meadow was determined to learn more about him. Though they would be surrounded by dozens of other carriages filled with passengers, she hoped they could have a decent conversation since, in effect, they would be alone.

"Your horses are beautiful creatures," she began, knowing he was accused of killing an entire stable of them.

"I have always loved horses," he told her. "I wasn't much for sitting at a desk in my younger days, doing sums or conjugating verbs. I enjoyed being outdoors and especially riding. Perhaps you and I might ride in Rotten Row some morning." He paused. "Do you ride?"

"I didn't before my marriage," she admitted. "I had no one to teach me. Once I realized it was the best way to get about and visit with tenants, I had one of the grooms teach me. I am quite comfortable on a horse."

"Tell me about your tenants," he urged. "From what you and Emery spoke of, you must have been very involved in affairs on Lord Selfridge's estate."

Meadow did so, sharing all kinds of stories as they passed and nodded at others once they reached the park. While some stopped their carriages to chat, Wyatt didn't do so, telling her everyone they passed was boring and he'd rather not waste any time with them. Soon, she saw they were at the end of the park. As he turned the vehicle around, she realized she had talked far too much.

"I have dominated our conversation," she told him. "You should get equal time now and tell me about yourself. I know the duke referred to you and your friends as Terrors. Were you all so very bad?"

"Boys sent to Turner Academy were ones who were troubled—or ones who had caused trouble. It was a place for families to rid themselves of problems."

"Which were you?" she asked. "Troubled? Or one who caused trouble?"

"Neither," he said frankly. "I was a good boy at both school and home, though I was mostly ignored at the latter. When I found myself sent to Turner Academy, I landed in the company of four other boys that first day. We had been assigned to sleep in the same dormitory room. One by one—except for Finch—we told our stories of why we were there. I realized that we all had been falsely accused of an act none of us would have committed. That day, I bonded with those boys. It has led to the lasting friendships we have to this day. I attended class with them each day and slept in their company each night, from the time I arrived at the academy until we graduated from university years later."

"Except for holidays, of course," she said.

His jaw tightened. "There were no holidays at home for any of us."

Meadow sucked in a breath. "No holidays? You mean you remained at school for . . . years? You never saw your families?"

"No. My family became the staff at the academy, a group of adults who cared more about me and spent more time with me than my blood relatives ever did. As for the Turner Terrors, we became brothers. Miles christened our group as the Turner Terrors that first day and the sobriquet remains to this day. We all think of ourselves as Terrors."

Wyatt told her more about Turner Academy and the routine there, including who his favorite teachers were. He also talked about a Lord and Lady Marksby, a childless couple who had taken in the Terrors each summer for a short holiday.

By now, they had left the park and had pulled up in front of Marshmore's residence. Her heart ached for the five young boys who had been exiled from their homes, never to see their families again. At least they had had each other and still remained close.

Wyatt leaped to the ground and held out his hands, once again lifting her by her waist and placing Meadow on the ground.

His hands remained there a moment longer than necessary, causing her pulse to leap. Then he released her and escorted her to the front door.

"Thank you for the drive. The park is lovely this time of year," she told him.

"Not nearly as lovely as you," he said, taking her hands and raising them to his lips. He pressed a fervent kiss against them and then lowered them again. "I will see you at tonight's ball."

"Yes," she said, moved by the tender kiss.

"Will you reserve the supper dance for me?" he asked softly.

"I will," she promised.

A slow smile spread across his face and she couldn't help but think how handsome he was.

Bringing her hands up again, he kissed them once more. "I look forward to it."

"I do, too," Meadow said honestly, eager to spend more time in this man's company.

🢒🢒🢒🢐🢐🢐

MEADOW READIED HERSELF for the Lattimore ball, choosing the pale blue gown that Tilda had suggested. She still felt a bit exposed in it but it did create a beautiful silhouette. She couldn't help but wonder what Wyatt would think of her in it.

She had decided it would be all right to think of him as Wyatt. Of course, in public she would always refer to him as Your Grace. Even if they did manage a private moment alone, she doubted she would be so forward as to call him by his given name. She would no longer chide him, though, when he called her Meadow. She liked hearing him say her name. Probably more than she should.

Though she now believed him innocent of the accusation Marshmore had made, she still thought Wyatt an unsuitable husband for her. True, he did say he yearned for children. She wondered why and decided that could be a future conversation, along with more about his boyhood. After today's conversations at tea and during their carriage ride, she was starting to gain a clearer picture of him. Though he was intelligent and incredibly loyal to his friends, he still possessed an air of danger about him. He also seemed too quick to use the power he held as a duke. A more gentle man was her idea of an ideal husband. One who was a bit plainer. Wyatt was too handsome for her and would attract the attention of scores of women, young and old, wed and unwed. She didn't want or need to worry about a husband who strayed.

Meadow also knew she had absolutely no experience in the bedroom. It would take a lot to please a man as virile and sensual as Wyatt. She wouldn't possibly be up to the task.

Her eyes went to the trunk in the corner of her room. She hadn't opened it since the night of her husband's death, bringing it with her when she vacated her home upon the new viscount's arrival. No one had questioned her bringing the battered trunk with her nor had anyone seemed interested in its contents. She had told the maid who had helped her unpack when she first arrived at Tilda's that it contained sentimental treasures from her childhood which could be left inside it.

Curiosity filled her, though. How many of those lustful acts had Wyatt participated in? She shuddered, thinking back on a few of the lithographs and what they had depicted. When she had looked at them over a year ago, she had thought some of them vulgar. Now, having finally kissed a man, she wondered at some of them and how she would feel if Wyatt did those things to her.

"Pish-posh!" she declared aloud.

She was not going to find herself in that situation with him. She was not going to compromise her reputation for a few stolen minutes of pleasure with a dangerous man who would most likely laugh at her inexperience. He thought her a married lady who had been to her husband's bed many times, not the virgin she was.

Still, he was courting her. He wouldn't be the only man who did so. Meadow hoped for at least one more time when she could kiss Wyatt. Just to see if it was as wonderful as she remembered. That way, she could compare his kiss to others.

Oh, what was she thinking? She hadn't kissed any of the men who'd come around when she first made her come-out. Why would this time be different? She needed to heed Tilda's warnings of not being the widow with the fast and loose reputation. She had no business going about kissing any of her suitors.

Yet the thought of marrying a man without having kissed him bothered her more than she wanted to admit. Meadow wondered if men were born knowing how to kiss or if they learned to do it so well with practice. If so, Wyatt must have had legions of kisses with many women because his lips and tongue did the most delicious, unimaginable things. And if he had kissed them, most likely he had bedded them. He didn't seem the kind of man who would stop at mere kisses.

"Bloody hell," she murmured to herself, cursing for the first time in her life.

That is what this man did to her. Make her curse. Make her want to come to his bed. Make her want to forget everything and throw caution to the wind. Well, she wasn't having any of it. She needed to think with her head—and not her heart. Find an appropriate gentleman and settle down with him. Why, she might have already met him. Or he might be among those she danced with at the Lattimore ball tonight.

Meadow stared at her reflection in the mirror once more, satisfied that she looked her best, and collected her reticule before going downstairs. She and Tilda talked about the boys on the way to the ball, Meadow feeling guilty because she had spent so little time with them since the Season began.

When they arrived, they joined the receiving line and then entered the ballroom. It was even grander than the Rockwells' ballroom had been. She looked forward to the evening.

And tried not to think about the supper dance.

A footman distributed programmes and she claimed one, deciding to pencil in Wyatt's name before someone placed his name beside the space he had asked to claim. She was glad she did so because she was quickly surrounded by a large group of men who passed the programme from one to the next, returning it to her when it was filled.

"I told you so," Tilda said at her elbow. "You were the most beautiful girl in our come-out Season and you are still the most beautiful this time around. Mark my words, you will start receiving marriage proposals by the end of the week."

Meadow's cheeks heated, knowing she already had her first from Wyatt.

Her first partner claimed her. Lord Airedale told her he was twenty-eight years of age and a viscount, though he would become an earl upon his father's death. While handsome, he had an air about him that told her he would not be ready to settle down anytime soon, probably not until his father passed and Airedale was the new earl. He also focused more on her neckline than looking her in the face, which bothered her. When the viscount asked if he could call upon her the next afternoon, she told him no. He seemed surprised but also took it in stride.

"I am looking for a husband, my lord," she confided to him. "I am eager for children."

"Ah. I see. Thank you for being frank with me, Lady Selfridge." He bowed. "It was a pleasure to make your acquaintance."

Of the other men she partnered with, Meadow found herself interested in two, in particular. Lord Pomeroy was a widower who looked to be in his mid-thirties. He had a son and daughter and had lost his wife in childbirth two years ago when his daughter was born. He seemed a bit dull until he spoke of his children and then his eyes lit up. She thought he showed potential and agreed to his request to call upon her tomorrow.

The other, Lord Gimble, shared that he had just come into his title as he turned thirty. He spoke of how close he had been to his father and how he hoped to have the same relationship with his future sons. She thought Lord Gimble showed a bit of depth in revealing this because most men spoke of nothing personal at these events. He, too, asked if he might stop by tomorrow afternoon and she readily agreed.

All the while as she danced, she knew the supper dance approached. She had spotted Wyatt dancing twice and they had even briefly passed one another during a reel. Meadow could have sworn he winked at her but it had happened so quickly she couldn't be certain.

She bid Lord Gimble farewell and saw Wyatt striding toward her, determination in his step. He reached her, his hazel eyes also showing appreciation for her appearance.

"You saved this dance for me?" he asked.

"I did, Your Grace," she replied, her heart pounding so hard that she was afraid he would see her gown move in a steady beat.

"Good." He smiled at her, his even, white teeth gleaming, and led her onto the dance floor.

As she had expected, it was a waltz. Meadow had practiced the steps in her bedchamber prior to leaving and believed she would be fine. Until he slipped an arm about her and took her hand, his body so close to hers that her breasts grazed his chest. Suddenly, all thoughts of how to move fled.

The music began, though, and Wyatt swept her away, leading her effortlessly. She found it wasn't necessary to think about the steps or count the beat in her head. Instead, she allowed her body to merely react and let him play puppet master, moving her about the dance floor.

When the final note occurred, he brought them to a halt, his gaze mesmerizing. She realized they hadn't said a word throughout the entire dance. They hadn't needed to. Their bodies had done the talking for them.

"You are a marvelous dancer," she praised as he relaxed his hold and slipped her hand through his arm.

"It is because I have such a graceful partner," he replied glibly.

"I don't know about that. After all, it was only the second waltz I have attempted."

He smiled. "I hope you will dance all your waltzes with me, Meadow."

His words caused a frisson of desire to trickle through her.

"Shall we go into supper?" he asked when she remained mute.

"Yes," she managed to respond.

They were the last couple to leave the ballroom. Wyatt slowed their pace until all the other guests were far ahead of them. As they passed an alcove, he stepped into it. His arms went about her.

"I find I am hungry for something not on Lady Lattimore's menu," he said huskily and he lowered his mouth to hers.

CHAPTER SIXTEEN

M EADOW KNEW SHE shouldn't kiss Wyatt but her lips refused to deny him—or her.

All thoughts of being discovered in the alcove dissipated as his mouth brushed against hers. Her body sprang to life, her nipples hardening, a ripple of excitement running through her. Her arms went about his neck and she pressed her body against his, reveling in the hard wall of muscle.

She opened her mouth in invitation and his tongue slipped inside, gliding along her teeth, teasing the roof of her mouth, and then mating with her tongue. She made a contented sound and his arms tightened about her. He deepened the kiss, showing her just how hungry he was for her. Meadow's body throbbed in need. Her fingers pushed into his thick hair.

His hands moved to her waist, his thumbs stroking just under her ribcage. Her breasts ached for his touch.

"Touch me," she murmured against his mouth, not caring if it was wrong, only needed his hands on her.

Wyatt broke the kiss and looked at her. "Are you—"

"Touch my breasts," she ordered, swallowing, not recognizing the person she was becoming.

His response was to kiss her again, hard, deliberate, as his hands moved up and cupped her breasts.

"Yes," she said into his mouth. "Yes."

Wyatt continued kissing her deeply as his hands kneaded her

breasts. They seemed to swell at his touch. Then his thumbs brushed across her nipples, sending tingles shooting through her. He rubbed back and forth as her fingers clutched his hair. Then his nails swept back and forth against the raised buds, almost bringing her to her knees. She cried out into his mouth. He played with her nipples, tweaking them and then running his fingers along them, driving her to the point of madness. The pulsing between her legs grew stronger. He shifted and his leg went between the two of hers. She pushed her core against his leg, moving up and down it restlessly, uncertain why she did so but only knowing she had to.

"Let me," she thought he said and Wyatt shifted again, slipping his hand under her skirts and skimming it along her calf. It moved higher, his fingers brushing against her inner thigh, and her core pulsated with need.

He pulled his mouth from hers. "I will take care of you, Meadow. Trust me."

His lips pressed against her throat as his fingers danced up her leg and along the seam of her sex. Then he pushed one inside her and her back arched. She moaned as he moved it, stroking her deeply. Another one joined it and she gasped.

His mouth traveled back to hers and he began kissing her again as his fingers worked some kind of spell upon her. A pressure began to build inside her, threatening to erupt at any moment.

Then it did, her core exploding. Meadow saw colors pop as she clung to Wyatt, her moans swallowed by him. She strained against his hand, bucking wildly, riding a tidal wave of pure feeling. It finally calmed and he slipped his fingers from her, breaking their kiss as he brought them to his mouth and licked them.

"You taste divine," he told her huskily.

She felt her blush spring all the way to her roots.

Wyatt kissed her again, so softly it was almost as if air brushed against her lips.

"We must go into supper," he warned, "else we will be missed."

Meadow couldn't even put a coherent thought together and merely nodded as Wyatt smoothed her gown and then kissed her hand.

They stepped from the alcove. Thankfully, no one was in sight. He bent to the floor and raised her gown slightly above her ankle. Without warning, he ripped the bow from her slipper.

Holding it up, he said, "This is what we were looking for. We found it near the table by the punch bowl."

Her slipper was now loose on her foot since the ornamental bow had had ties which held the slipper in place. She limped along, holding his arm for support.

They entered the supper room, buzzing with conversation and guests flitting about. Fortunately, Emery waved to them from a table seating eight. It wasn't far from the doorway and they quickly joined the other couples.

"Where have you been?" someone inquired.

Wyatt reached into his pocket and brought out the ragged bow. "Lady Selfridge lost the flower from her slipper during our dance. It must have been kicked around as others waltzed about. It took forever but we found it."

"Near the punch bowl," Meadow piped up. "I hope it can be repaired. I can barely walk without the slipper wanting to fall from my foot."

"That has happened to me before," one woman said. She motioned for a servant and a footman came rushing over.

"Give him the bow, Your Grace," the woman ordered. "And Lady Selfridge, your slipper, please."

She handed over both to the footman and the woman said, "Take these to the retiring room. There should be a seamstress there—or at least a maid who sews. Have them repair Lady Selfridge's slipper the best they can. And be quick about it. She must have it before the dancing commences again else she will disappoint her many partners."

The footman scurried away.

"Thank you, my lady," Meadow said. "I do not believe we have met before."

"We haven't," the older woman said. "Everyone knows you, however. A beautiful widow is hard to miss." She looked at Meadow pointedly and she worried the woman knew exactly what Meadow had been up to with Wyatt.

"I am Lady Narson. This is my husband."

Introductions were made around the table and then Wyatt offered to get them something to eat.

The rest of supper passed quickly, especially since they had missed part of it. As they finished eating, the footman returned.

"This is the best that she could do, my lady," he told Meadow, handing the slipper to her. "The seamstress said your gown will cover the slipper."

"Thank you," she said.

"Here. I can help you," Wyatt said, taking it from her and leaning down.

He eased her foot inside the slipper and then tied it securely. His thumbs stroked her ankle a moment and then he sat up. "Good as new," he announced. "At least it should get you through the rest of the evening. I don't believe you'll be wearing it beyond tonight, though."

"I have others," she said, the feel of his hands on her ankle still burning her flesh.

"I am sorry if I am the one who stepped on it and tore it," he apologized.

"I don't know if you did or did not, Your Grace," she said. "All that matters is that I can finish the night now."

Couples began returning to the ballroom and he helped her to her feet.

"You didn't eat much," he said quietly.

"You ate enough for the both of us," she said lightly.

Wyatt leaned toward her ear. "I wish I could have had more of you."

She quickly lowered her face as the color rose in it. She wished the same.

"May I escort you back to the ballroom, Lady Selfridge?" he asked.

"Yes, Your Grace."

He did so and then took her hand and kissed it. "We will be there at four tomorrow afternoon. You will like Gunter's. I will count the minutes until I see you again, my lady."

⊰⊱

WYATT ALLOWED FRAME, his new valet, to shave him. He still felt ridiculous having so many people to wait on him but he did understand that because he did so, many were gainfully employed, both in London and across his various estates.

He had met with his solicitor for two hours this morning, reviewing all his properties. He now was in possession of documents that outlined the names of every estate, where they were located, and a listing of both servants and tenants on the properties. He had requested this compilation when he had first become the Duke of Amesbury and it had taken until now to complete the report. It also listed what crops were grown, the animals bred, and names and descriptions of every horse in the stables of each property.

Reviewing it this afternoon, he had decided that he and Meadow would enjoy visiting three of the estates when they honeymooned after their wedding. He knew she hadn't agreed to the match yet but it was only a matter of time.

Especially after last night's ball.

He was known for his spontaneity among his friends. When he had seen an opportunity to kiss Meadow again, he knew he had to take it. The alcove gave them a few private moments alone.

And had changed everything for him.

Before last night, Wyatt knew he had been strongly attracted to Meadow. He felt thankful that the woman who was suitable to be his duchess had looks, charm, and intelligence. What had taken place between them, though, had ignited a fire within him, one that he knew might never be extinguished. His desire for her flamed into the night sky like a bonfire raging out of control.

Worse, not only did his feelings extend to passion. He feared that they might involve love.

Love was such a foreign concept to him. He had felt no love for his parents or brother. They certainly hadn't bestowed any upon him, chastising and ignoring Wyatt until he was banished from Amberwood. He had felt respect and even admiration for tutors at Turner Academy but certainly not love. He had developed deep, abiding feelings of loyalty for his fellow Terrors and supposed that he did love them. He certainly would do anything for those four men. Even die for them if need be.

The idea of romantic love had never entered his mind until he had been exposed to Miles and Emery's relationship. With his friends, he saw passion in its purest form. Wyatt had even been jealous of what existed between the pair and had thought he wanted it for himself. Yet now, when the idea of loving Meadow was a distinct possibility, he feared it. He feared the unknown. The vulnerability it would lead to. Yes, he felt passion for her, as well as possession. He wanted her to be in his arms and no other man's. He wanted to spend every waking moment with her and when they were apart, all he did was think about her.

Was *that* love?

Wyatt couldn't say. Perhaps it was merely obsession. Fixating on her. Being fascinated by her. Craving her. Infatuated by her.

He shook his head. It couldn't possibly be love.

Yet the more he denied the feelings, the more they seemed to grow.

Could he truly be in love with her? They had known each other for such a short time. Did love take a set amount of time before it blossomed between a couple? Or could an instant attraction lead to a deep connection? Could the all-consuming feelings that engulfed him be love?

He couldn't say. All Wyatt knew was that he desired Meadow more than any woman he had ever known. That he wanted her by his side and in his bed from now on. Hopefully, the intimacies they had shared last night would lead her to capitulate and accept his offer of marriage sooner rather than later.

From her reactions, not only had she not known how to kiss but it was obvious her husband had brought her no pleasure. Wyatt knew Lord Selfridge had been much older than Meadow. That didn't excuse his selfishness, though. He had wed a young, beautiful girl on the verge of womanhood and taught her nothing about the marriage bed. In a way, that pleased Wyatt. He would be the one to introduce Meadow into the ways of pleasure. He would show her what it was like to be worshipped. To reach the heights of ecstasy each time she coupled with him.

He realized that he wanted to do those things for her in every way. It didn't matter what he experienced. He simply wanted every time they came together to be about her. Her comfort. Her pleasure. Her desire being sated.

Maybe he was in love with her, after all.

Frame wiped the shaving cream from Wyatt's face and re-moved the towel protecting his clothing.

"Shall I assist you into your coat, Your Grace?"

"Yes, please."

The valet did so and Wyatt said, "I hope you are happy in your new position, Frame."

The servant looked nonplussed at his employer's comment. Recovering, he said, "I am most happy, Your Grace. I hope you are happy with me."

"Very much so, Frame. Are you attached to London? I ask because I don't plan to spend much time here. I prefer the country."

Frame smiled. "I have always preferred the fresh air of the country, Your Grace. I will be happy to serve you wherever you wish to spend your time."

"I am off," he announced. "Going to Gunter's for the first time."

"Enjoy yourself, Your Grace."

He grinned. "I shall, Frame, for I am taking a beautiful woman to enjoy the ices with me."

The valet chuckled. "The ices are certain to taste even better with company."

"My thoughts exactly."

He had his butler ask for the carriage to be brought around and told Blevins, "First, to Winslow's residence and then Marshmore's. From there, to Gunter's at Berkeley Square."

"Very good, Your Grace," the driver replied.

They collected Miles and Emery and then Wyatt went up to Marshmore's door and rang the bell.

"Ah, Your Grace, good afternoon," the butler said. "If you will wait here, I will tell Lady Selfridge you have arrived. She said you were going to Gunter's today and seemed most pleased by it," the butler revealed, causing Wyatt to preen a bit since it had been his idea for them to go.

Meadow appeared in the foyer a few minutes later, wearing a gown of lilac that set off her perfect figure. Wyatt couldn't help but glance at her rounded breasts, wishing he could put his hands and lips on them.

"Good afternoon, my lady. I hope you aren't weary from your many callers this afternoon."

"I am happy to make time for you and our outing, Your Grace," Her gray eyes shone with a bit of mischief, making him wish Miles and Emery weren't waiting in the carriage so they might have it to themselves. He would have instructed Blevins to drive for hours so that Wyatt might kiss Meadow the entire time.

"Come along," he said, offering her his arm. "We want to make sure we can find a spot close on the square."

He helped her into the carriage, where she greeted his companions, and then the women began talking about the different flavors they would be able to choose from. Both seemed like young girls in their enthusiasm. It took everything he had not to hold Meadow's hand.

Then he decided there was no reason to refrain from doing so. Miles already had his fingers entwined with that of his wife's. No one else was present.

Boldly, he reached for Meadow's hand and threaded his fingers through hers. She stopped speaking and looked at him with wide eyes.

"We are inside a carriage with friends," he said. "If we were in my curricle or a barouche, it would be different because we could be seen then." He paused and then said, "I want to hold your hand, Meadow. I need to."

Her eyes lit up. She gave him a radiant smile. Her fingers squeezed his.

Wyatt's heart began to race.

Emery continued speaking as if it were the most natural thing for Wyatt to be holding Meadow's hand. Meadow chimed in and, once more, they began debating flavors and whether they would order ices or sorbets.

His eyes met Miles' and his friend nodded in approval.

They reached Berkeley Square, which was packed with carriages. Wyatt had learned that many of the *ton* remained inside their carriages, while waiters raced across the square to take their orders. Since there didn't seem to be any room in front of the establishment, he tapped once on the roof of the carriage and moments later, it came to a halt.

"Do you mind if we go inside?" he asked.

"Not at all," Emery answered for them all. "It is much too crowded outdoors today."

Stairs appeared and Wyatt went out first, followed by Miles, who helped his wife down. Wyatt noticed her rounded belly beginning to show more and thought of how Meadow would look when she carried their child. She appeared in the doorway and he grinned.

As he helped her descend, she asked, "What are you thinking of?"

"I am not sure you want to know," he said cryptically, seeing the blush stain her cheeks.

They crossed the street and went inside Gunter's, where they were quickly seated. A waiter appeared and presented them with a sheet listing that day's flavors. After much debate, the two women both decided upon lavender as their choice. Miles went with maple, while Wyatt selected a rich custard.

"That sounds lovely," Meadow said as the waiter left to place their orders.

"You may try a bite of mine if you'd like," he said.

She giggled and tried to compose herself as Emery said, "Oh, I see Lady Charlotte. We must go say hello to her, Miles."

Once they left, Meadow giggled again and apologized. "I am sorry. I seem to giggle at inappropriate times. Usually, when I am nervous," she explained.

"You are nervous to try an ice?"

"No. But the thought of trying yours has me thinking things I shouldn't," she admitted.

"Ah. The spoon in my mouth. Then yours. Sharing the treat."

Her cheeks filled with color. "Yes."

Wyatt leaned closer. "And perhaps thoughts of what we shared last night came to mind?" he said in a low voice.

"Yes," she said, turning redder. "Please stop."

"Stop talking about it? Or thinking about it?" he said flirtatiously.

Her lips parted and then she licked them nervously, causing desire to flare within him.

"Have you thought about it much?"

He grinned. "The entire time we have been apart. Even more, now that I am in your company again." He watched her eyes go dark. "I hope the opportunity presents itself again very soon."

She squeaked and her hand flew to her mouth. He decided

she was suppressing another giggle. What had irritated him before only delighted him now. He longed to reach for her hand but knew she would refuse him since they were now in public.

A shadow appeared and he glanced up, seeing a man he was unfamiliar with.

"I was told you were Lady Selfridge," the man said, smiling benignly. "I am Lord Kibbard, a very dear friend of your late husband."

Wyatt glanced to Meadow and saw the color draining from her face.

CHAPTER SEVENTEEN

T HIS WAS THE man Selfridge had told her about on his deathbed. The one who would buy the lithograph collection. He looked so ordinary. In his mid-forties with gray at his temples and streaks of it running through his full head of hair. The only thing that distinguished him was his coat and cravat, both a bright color, as opposed to the more subdued tones most men in Polite Society wore. To think Kibbard collected pictures like that and yet seemed so unremarkable shook her to her core.

Did he think she had also looked at them? Well, she had briefly and certainly not all of Selfridge's collection, but she hadn't studied them at length, as she suspected her husband and Kibbard had done.

Meadow quickly tried to compose herself and said, "Good afternoon, my lord. Have you met His Grace, the Duke of Amesbury?"

"No, I have not. Your Grace."

Wyatt rose and shook Kibbard's hand. "How did you know Lord Selfridge?" he asked.

"We were both collectors," Kibbard said, his gaze turning back to Meadow.

A chill ran through her.

"Did you know of your husband's collection, my lady?"

She clasped her hands together tightly. "Oh, Selfridge had many items he enjoyed assembling, my lord. He collected snuff boxes. Walking canes. Eyeglasses. First editions of rare books. Backgammon sets." She managed a weak laugh. "I think I lost count of the items he collected. All are now in the possession of his heir."

"Are they?" Kibbard asked, looking at her pointedly.

She licked her lips. "Yes, of course. They were bought with estate funds and so now belong to the new Selfridge."

"I see. I shall have to ask him about it."

"Are you looking to purchase something for one of your own collections?" Wyatt asked.

"I am," Kibbard confirmed. He smiled again. "It was a pleasure to meet you, Lady Selfridge. Your husband spoke so fondly of you. Might you be staying at the Selfridge townhouse while you are in town?"

"No, my lord. Since my husband's death, I have been living with my cousin, the Countess of Marshmore."

Meadow knew why he asked. She suspected he would soon be calling upon her.

To ask about the lithograph collection.

"I bid you good day." Kibbard tipped his hat and left them.

She felt Wyatt staring at her and drew in a deep breath as Emery and her husband rejoined them. They began talking of other matters and then the waiter brought their desserts. She no longer had an appetite for hers but determined to eat every bite, not wanting Wyatt anymore suspicious than he already seemed. He kept throwing glances at her, which she ignored.

"Would you care for a bite of mine?" he asked.

"No. I have changed my mind, Your Grace. Thank you, though. It is very thoughtful of you to ask."

"This is everything I was told it would be," Emery said, spooning the final bite into her mouth and sighing.

"I shall have to bring you here once a week until we depart for Kent," her husband said.

"When will you return to Wildwood?" Meadow asked, hoping to draw Wyatt's attention away from her.

"That is up to Emery," the duke said. "I wanted her to get a taste of Polite Society and see some of the sights in London. I do not want her exposed to the stench of the city in summer."

"We planned to stay six to eight weeks," her friend said, glancing in Wyatt's direction.

Meadow wondered what that look was for but politely refrained from asking.

"Are you going to the Ferricks' ball tonight?" Wyatt suddenly asked her.

"Yes, we plan to," she said, suddenly feeling in no mood to be gay and dance the night away.

"I think we are all done," Winslow said. "Shall we return home? I know how long it can take a lady to prepare for a ball," he joked.

The men rose and helped the ladies to their feet. Wyatt's ducal carriage returned her to Marshmore's townhouse and he walked her to the front door.

He took her hand. "I look forward to seeing you tonight, Meadow."

Ignoring his comment because she wasn't certain at this point if she would attend, she said, "Thank you for taking me to Gunter's. It was a treat to go." She mustered a smile and pushed open the door.

Retreating to her bedchamber, she locked her door and took the key secreted in an old boot and used it to unlock the battered trunk. With trepidation, she dropped to her knees and raised the lid. Her hand shaking, she lifted the lithograph sitting on top and stared at it.

It depicted a couple without clothes on. The woman lay on her back, a look of ecstasy on her face. The man's face was buried between her legs. Meadow didn't quite know what he did but still felt her face grow hot nonetheless. Embarrassed, she dropped the lithograph as if it burned her and quickly shut the trunk, locking it again and replacing the key in its hiding place.

She thought of Wyatt's fingers parting her folds last night and slipping inside her. Did the man in the picture kiss the woman there? Or . . .

She couldn't even fathom completing her thought. Her entire body had now gone hot thinking about it. Thinking about what Wyatt would do to her in that position.

Meadow returned to the boot and removed the key once more. She opened the trunk again and sat next to it, taking out a stack of pictures and thumbing through them. Some were erotic in nature and caused a stirring within her. She could actually see herself wanting to do some of these acts with Wyatt. Others, though, were offensive or downright disgusting.

She dug deeper and grew more horrified, as scenes of bondage were portrayed, with women being whipped, burned, and beaten. As she progressed, a majority of the couples were of the male and female variety but several lithographs featured either two men or two women together, touching one another and performing acts she didn't comprehend.

Then shock overwhelmed her. Quickly, she flipped through dozens of lithographs portraying men with children.

Children . . .

Her belly roiled as she thought of grown men abusing children in such a manner. She hadn't known men possessed such foul urges. Surely, not all men.

Closing the trunk again, she once more hid the key and then sat on her bed. She didn't want to be in possession of this horrific collection anymore. There were too many lithographs to burn, especially since the only fires being lit inside the townhouse were cook fires in the kitchens. If she went there numerous times with stacks of lithographs, it would cause too many questions. Perhaps she could have a footman bury the trunk somewhere. If he thought it valuable, though, he might dig it up without her knowing. She could only imagine the scandal that would break if a servant gossiped about what he'd found. Gossip spread like wildfire among servants in a household and then from house to house. It would paint her as a very depraved person.

Should she tear each one up? They were thick and it might prove difficult to do so. Meadow slammed her fists against the bed, worried about how to dispose of the trunk's contents without anyone being the wiser.

A knock sounded and she scrambled from the bed and hurried to the door, quietly turning the lock. Opening it, she found Tilda there.

"How was your outing with the two dukes and Her Grace?" her cousin asked as she sailed into the room. "My, you are traveling in high circles, Meadow."

"Gunter's is quite nice. I chose lavender for my ice."

"Who cares what you ate?" Tilda said. "Do you think His Grace will offer for you?" Without waiting for an answer, she mused, "He must think highly of you to have you accompany him with the Winslows. I hear they are thick as thieves. I only wish Amesbury had called this afternoon and seen how crowded our drawing room was with your suitors. It might spur him to action."

"He did send flowers," Meadow said, defending Wyatt.

It had surprised her when she went through the cards that Wyatt had sent a bouquet. It was of medium size, nothing too gaudy or overwhelming. Frankly, she had liked the single red rose he had presented her more than any other flowers she had received this Season.

"He did," Tilda agreed. "Did he ask you to reserve any dances for him?"

"No, he didn't." Probably because she had put him off and hurried inside the townhouse.

"Well, don't give away the supper dance to just anyone. He has danced it with you at both balls. People have noticed, you know, and are talking about that. Coupling your name with his. I hope that pleases you."

She had thought to deflect Wyatt since he seemed fixated in her direction. After last night, though, she found herself wanting to be the object of his affections. He still seemed wrong for her in ways too numerous to count but she was drawn to him like a magnet. To his looks. His charisma. His intelligence. His charm. Last night had been about seduction, as he lured her into a web of physical desire. She knew he wasn't a rake who tried to seduce and would then leave her dangling after he got what he wanted. No, Wyatt had made his intentions clear. He wanted to wed her—and tried to persuade her using all the tools he could. His hands. His tongue. His smile.

It had worked. Meadow could see herself with no other man but Wyatt. She wanted to go to his bed. Feel his touch. Bear his children. However, she didn't want to bend too soon. He'd said he wanted her.

He was going to have to work to earn her as his bride.

She smiled to herself. They both could enjoy the fruits of his labors.

"Yes, it does please me," she told Tilda. "If Amesbury were to offer for me now, I would certainly consider his proposal."

Tilda embraced her. "It is just a matter of time before he does so, Cousin. And he will be getting the most marvelous woman to be his duchess."

If he asked again—and she prayed he would—Meadow would say yes this time.

And think herself the lucky one to spend the rest of her life with Wyatt.

CHAPTER EIGHTEEN

T HE NEXT THREE weeks passed swiftly. Meadow had attended *ton* events every night and many that were held in the afternoons when she wasn't at home receiving guests.

Wyatt called upon her along with other suitors. She actually had met a few men that would have made for good husbands— but they paled in comparison to the Duke of Amesbury.

When he had asked her to reserve the supper dance for him, she had told him no, delighting in seeing the flare of annoyance in his eyes. Meadow told him he would have to wait in line and sign her programme as other gentlemen did. He had taken that as a challenge and was the first to arrive at her side most evenings when a ball was being held. Then he began toying with her, signing her dance card—but not for the supper dance. Instead, he would scribble his name next to two separate dances. Everyone in Polite Society knew a gentleman was only supposed to dance once an evening with a lady. Twice meant he was most taken with her.

So the whispers became louder, linking her name with his.

Meadow didn't mind that at all.

A few gentlemen took it as a challenge and began pursuing her aggressively, flooding Marshmore's townhouse with flowers and complimenting her to no end. Wyatt remained steadfast, still sending his own bouquets, simple ones that weren't ostentatious. As for compliments, he gave them only when deserved.

ALEXA ASTON

What she hated was that they had not been alone again during this entire time. No privacy meant no more kisses bestowed upon her. Meadow now craved Wyatt's kiss and touch. She was certain he knew that and was deliberately withholding them from her, though she realized it was rare to ever be alone with any man during the Season unless you were related to him. Still, she had hoped Wyatt would try a little harder.

As for other men, Meadow hadn't kissed any of them. Not when she strolled on a balcony with them during a ball, the excuse being that she might need fresh air. She hadn't agreed to any walks through the gardens with another man or drives through the park.

Her mind was made up—it would be Wyatt and no other.

A month had passed since they had met. He hadn't offered for her again. She wondered what was taking so long. Should she send her other suitors away? She didn't think him especially jealous of those who paid attention to her. Meadow hoped she hadn't pushed him too hard.

At least Lord Kibbard hadn't approached her again. She had been on pins and needles for the first few days after their encounter and wondered if the earl had gone to the country to see the new Viscount Selfridge, who had remained there because his wife was expecting their first child during the Season. If so, Kibbard had returned because Meadow saw him at two different events. He nodded politely to her but made no move to speak to her. She hoped he believed that the new Selfridge had found the obscene collection and gotten rid of it.

She decided to go to the nursery this morning, where she could read and play with Tilda's boys. It surprised her how little her cousin saw her own children. When Meadow had ones of her own, she planned to spend a good deal of time in their company.

After she had been there an hour, she told the nursery governess to go have a cup of tea. The servant had only been gone a few minutes when the Marshmore butler appeared in the doorway. She looked up from where she sat on the floor.

"His Grace, the Duke of Amesbury, is here to see you, my lady."

"Oh!"

That surprised her. The only morning she had seen Wyatt was two days prior, when he had taken her riding early in Rotten Row.

A hand went to smooth her hair. "I wasn't expecting His Grace," she said. "Tell him—"

Wyatt suddenly appeared in the doorway. "You can tell me yourself," he said, dismissing the butler and entering the nursery.

Immediately, he dropped to his knees, where the older boy stacked blocks. "What are you making?" he asked.

"A tower."

"Splendid. I am very good at making towers."

Wyatt took a block and begin to add to the stack, talking all the while as he did so, explaining why he put each block a certain way.

The younger boy climbed from her lap and plopped into Wyatt's. He continued building the tower and when it was over two feet high, both boys growled and knocked it down. Meadow was horrified and started to correct them but Wyatt burst out laughing.

"So, that's how it's to be?" he asked the boys.

Picking up another block, he started over. The game continued in that manner several times, the blocks being expertly laid until they reached a certain height and then the boys tearing them down. Even Wyatt got in on the action, slapping at blocks and laughing at his antics. He appeared so boyish and mischievous. She could see why he was a Turner Terror.

Tired of the game, the boys begged him to read to them. He settled with his back against the wall and one boy on each side of him as he read from a storybook Meadow handed to him. She spent the entire story watching him, his face animated as he changed his voice for the different characters, his fingers long as they turned the pages. She loved the low rumble of his voice and the noises he made, bringing the pages to life.

This would be what it would be like when he played and read to his children. Their children.

If the bloody fool would ask her to marry him, that is.

As he finished the story and closed the book, he lifted his eyes and their gazes met. Meadow could have sworn he knew exactly what she was thinking by the grin that appeared on his face.

The nursery governess entered, looking a bit startled to find both her and a duke on the floor.

"How was your cup of tea, Nanny?" she asked.

"A welcomed respite, my lady. I am ready to take charge again, though."

Wyatt easily got to his feet and then held out his hands. She took them and he pulled her to her feet. He thanked the boys for playing with him and they extracted a promise from him to return.

Exiting the nursery, he closed the door behind them. He glanced both ways and finding the corridor empty, his fingers encircled her wrist. Heat shot through her.

He took a few steps to the door directly across from the nursery and opened it, pulling her along and shutting it once they were both inside the room. Meadow had never been here before but could tell it had been used as a schoolroom for older children because of the slates lying on the tables and the chalk resting in the middle.

"Those are your cousin's only children?" Wyatt murmured, his fingers touching her cheek lightly.

"Yes," she said breathlessly.

"No one else should have a reason to be here then."

"No."

"Good."

His hands went to her waist, steering her backward until her back found the door. He was so close. So large. Her heart slammed against her ribs.

Wyatt released her and placed his palms flat on either side of her as he stepped forward, his body now grazing hers. She was caged by him. Her heart beat faster.

"What are you doing?" she asked, swallowing hard.

Heat filled his eyes. "What would you like me to do, Meadow?"

Why did her name on his lips thrill her so?

"I remember the last time we were alone," he told her, his head moving down until his lips hovered above hers. "You asked me to touch you."

"Yes," she said, her body thrumming in anticipation.

"Would you like me to touch you again?" he asked, his breath so near it feathered across her mouth.

Her cheeks burned. "Yes."

His lips finally met hers though he left his hands where they were, trapping her between them.

Wyatt took his time with the kiss, slowing brushing his mouth against hers, back and forth, hypnotizing her. Then his tongue came out to play, outlining the shape of her mouth, over and over. Her breath hitched. Her hands went to his back, where she grabbed a fistful of his coat in each. He teased her lips open and plunged inside, ruthlessly taking what he wanted.

And she reveled in it.

His hands captured her wrists, raising them over her head as he continued to plunder her mouth. Then he caught both in his left hand, pinning them to the door. He broke the kiss and gazed at her, a wicked look dancing in his eyes. She swallowed again, unsure of what he was about to do. Meadow squirmed against him and tried to free her hands.

"No," he told her firmly. "I am the one who will do the touching."

The place between her legs pulsed at the roughness in his voice.

He began kissing her again but this time, his right hand started stroking her. First her jaw. Then her throat. Then his fingers moved lower, trailing down her throat to the neckline of her dress. Since it was daytime, she had a fichu tucked into it.

Wyatt slowly pulled it from her, dropping it on the floor.

His mouth left hers, following his fingers from her jaw to her throat to the top curve of her breast. His tongue outlined the curve, sending a jolt of need through her. Meadow whimpered, wriggling again, trying to free her hands.

"No," he said again. "I want to be free to taste and touch."

His tongue found the other breast and licked along it, causing her to tremble. His hand began kneading one breast, then tweaking it, causing her to whimper. Her core pounded as loud as her heart. His fingers pulled her gown down until one breast was freed. Immediately, his mouth went to it, his teeth grazing her nipple, causing shoots of desire to run through her. He sucked and nipped and then blew on it. Meadow shuddered when the cool air touched her and continued to squirm, pushing against him.

Wyatt kissed her hard then, a kiss full of possession and longing. He released his hold on her wrists and her arms fell, her hands grasping his shoulders as she matched him, kiss for kiss. Suddenly, she was moving again and realized he clasped her elbows, steering her a few feet away. The back of her thighs nudged the table and he pushed her so she sat on it. His eyes gleamed at her as he eased her back onto the table, her legs dangling from it.

Dropping to his knees, his hands went under her skirts, massaging her calves and moving higher. Tickling her inner thighs. Moving higher. Blood rushed in her ears as he moved back down her legs and lifted her skirts, his head disappearing under them.

"What are you—"

She gasped.

His mouth pressed against her core. She remembered the lithograph and now understood what it had depicted as Wyatt continued to kiss her there. Then his fingers parted her folds and his tongue slipped inside her. Stroking her.

Meadow nearly came off the table.

He raised her gown and stuck out his head. "I want you to stay. Understood. No matter what. Do you trust me?"

She nodded simply because she had no voice.

He disappeared again. This time, his hands remained on her hips, anchoring her. His mouth and tongue began to make love to her. She moaned and writhed beneath his touch, bucking against him as she went back to that familiar place.

A wave of pleasure engulfed her and her body shuddered under the spasms as she rocked back and forth. His fingers tightened on her hips and hers fisted as she was carried away by something deliciously carnal. Finally, she stilled, feeling limp as a cloth wrung to dry.

Wyatt showed his face again, smoothing her gown and lifting her from the table until she was once more on her feet. He kissed her tenderly and she realized she tasted herself on his lips.

Breaking the kiss, he smiled at her. "Am I finally pulling away in the war of suitors?"

"There is no war," she said. "There never was."

"You have dangled several before me. Did you think I might become jealous?"

Meadow licked her lips. "Perhaps a little."

"I am the only one who will ever touch you like this," he boldly stated. "Say it."

Meadow looked deep into his hazel eyes, now afire, glowing like emeralds. "You are the only one."

"Ever."

"Ever," she repeated.

"Would you like to go to a bookstore with me?" he asked.

"A bookstore?" The sudden turn in the conversation perplexed her.

"Yes. I thought we might find something for your cousin's boys for when I come next to read to them."

"You don't have to do that, Wyatt."

"I want to, Meadow. I told you. I like children. I want to have many of them. So, will you accompany me to the bookstore?"

She arched her brows. "Yes, I will go to the bookstore with you," she said primly, as if he hadn't been between her legs, driving her wild moments ago.

Wyatt laughed easily, seeming to know her very thoughts.

Meadow vowed to say nothing to him about children—their children—until he had offered for her again.

CHAPTER NINETEEN

M EADOW ACCOMPANIED WYATT to his waiting carriage, the footman eagerly opening the vehicle's door for her and helping to hand her up. She sat in the middle of the seat, thinking that Wyatt would sit opposite her. Instead, he crowded next to her, forcing her to scoot over. She couldn't move as far as she liked, however, because he was sitting on the folds of part of her gown.

"Think you're trying to escape me?" he teased as he threaded his fingers through hers. She hated that she'd had to don her gloves and bonnet for this outing. She would much rather have had his skin next to hers.

"I simply wanted to make certain you had enough room."

"Oh, I can remedy that."

With a quick movement, he had scooped her up and placed her onto his lap.

"Wyatt!" she protested.

"No one can see. The curtains are drawn." His gaze fell to her mouth. "The curtains are drawn," he repeated softly and then brought his hand to cup the back of her neck, bringing her slowly toward him.

He kissed her softly, his scent filling her, desire for him filling her. She might not know anything about making love with a man but she knew that she wanted to with him.

Soon.

When would he ask her to marry him?

Wyatt continued the soft kisses and warm caresses of her body until the carriage began to slow. He broke the kiss and set her in the seat beside him again.

Moments later, the footman opened the door and Wyatt sprang from the carriage, offering his hand to aid her as she descended from it.

"My footman looks a bit put out, not getting to help you," he remarked.

"You are being silly," she chided.

"I can't help it. I think every man looks at you. And at me, with a bit of jealousy, because I am the one accompanying you."

He escorted her into the Mayfair bookstore, asking what kind of stories the boys liked to read.

"They are so young, it really doesn't matter," she told him. "They like the attention of being read to as much as the actual stories they hear." She paused. "It was very sweet of you to read to them today."

"I enjoyed it. I may not have liked school much but I have always enjoyed reading. Going to other worlds. Exploring them. Having new adventures."

She laughed. "I wish I could have seen you as a little boy."

A shadow crossed his face and she realized he thought back to his childhood and having to leave his home. She still wanted that tale from him.

"Is that why you became a spy?" she asked as they began walking down an aisle. "Because of what you read as a boy?"

"I don't think any boy grows up thinking he wants to be a spy. It is dangerous work. Unpredictable. Boring even, some-times. I did enjoy it though I only did it every now and then, whenever Wellington asked for me. I was up to more of it at the end, just before I was called home to Amberwood."

"Was it hard returning to a place you had been gone from for so long?"

He thought a moment. "Yes . . . and no. I always loved the house and surrounding property. I roamed it far and wide in my youth. To find it was suddenly mine was a bit overwhelming, especially thinking of the title and responsibilities that came along with it. I enjoyed the short time I spent there before the Season began. Miles and Emery came for two weeks and helped me settle in. Emery was acting as Wildwood's estate manager when Miles became the Duke of Winslow so she was able to help me sort through things and explain them to me in a way I could readily understand. I know I still have much to learn but at least I feel I have a solid foundation under my feet now."

They were interrupted then. First, by a clerk who wanted to see if they needed any assistance. Then, a parade of book buyers made their way to them, all wanting a moment to speak to a duke.

When a break came in the long line that had formed in front of them she said, "You may go to the children's section and look for books. If we are seen together there picking out something, the rumors will fly that I am enceinte and we are choosing books for our coming child."

He laughed. "Very well. Are you going to go hide from everyone and leave me to fend for myself?"

She nodded. "I think I will look for a book on arranging flowers. Tilda loves flowers but she isn't very skilled at artfully placing them in vases. Perhaps a book might help her learn how to do so."

"I will see you soon."

Wyatt left and Meadow saw more customers nudge one another. A few traipsed after him. Quickly, she moved along the aisle they had stood at the foot of and went deeper into the store. She lost herself, browsing the shelves, until she sensed the presence of someone nearby and looked up.

It was Lord Kibbard.

"Ah, good day, Lady Selfridge." He took her hand and brought it to his lips, causing an unpleasant shudder to run through her.

"Good day, Lord Kibbard," she said stiffly and turned back to the shelf in front of her, hoping he would go away.

"I didn't believe you," he said softly.

Meadow turned toward him, frowning. "I beg your pardon?"

"I went to the country as you knew I might in order to visit the new Lord Selfridge at his estate. I asked about the various item his predecessor had collected. We had a pleasant conversation but it was obvious the new Selfridge hadn't a clue what the old Selfridge secretly amassed.

"But you do, my lady. You most certainly do."

Panic filled her. She glanced to her right and saw it was a dead end. She wanted to get around Lord Kibbard but didn't know how to go about that.

"What do you think of the collection, Lady Selfridge? Do you look at it at night before you retire? Do you think of the pictures as you lie in bed, your hand caressing yourself? Do you imagine the Duke of Amesbury touching you in those very ways? Or do you imagine another female taking liberties with you?"

"Stop!" she hissed, deciding to come clean with him. "I didn't even know of its existence until my husband lay on his deathbed. He mentioned something about a trunk and a Lord Kibbard who would purchase its contents, seeing me set for life. I located it upon Selfridge's death. When I did, I only glanced at a few of the lithographs. They were dreadful. Revolting. I put them away and locked the trunk again."

"But you didn't leave it for the new viscount to find, did you?" He gazed at her for a long moment. "All right, my lady— name your price. If payment for the collection is what Selfridge wanted you to live upon, I can't blame him." He chuckled. "He didn't know what to do with you. You were the most precious thing he ever collected and he was agog when he actually landed you. I, on the other hand, would know exactly what to do with you. Why, we could spend time each night before we retired going through the collection. Letting it guide us down the paths of pleasure and beyond."

"That is disgusting," she spat out.

"If it is, why did you take it and not leave it behind?"

Her face flamed. "I did not want anyone to think that I had

anything to do with it. I haven't looked at it since," she lied. "And I didn't know how to dispose of it."

"I want it," he said, determination filling his face. "I will give you a fair price. I would offer for you but it looks as though Amesbury has won your heart. Who would take a middle-aged, ordinary-looking earl over a young, handsome duke?"

"I cannot sell it to you," she said, equally determined that the lithographs never see the light of day again. "It is disgusting. No one should possess something such as that. It should be burned."

His eyes darkened. "It would be sacrilege to destroy it. You are too inexperienced to know of what you speak."

"I saw it, my lord. At least some of it. The lithographs depicting children. With hideous things being done to them."

His eyes gleamed at the mention of that and she guessed he performed those very acts upon young boys and girls.

"It is too important for you to get rid of it. Especially those special pictures you found. Those are what I am most interested in. Give it to me, Lady Selfridge. The collection is wasted upon someone such as you."

"No," she said firmly. "It is wrong. Children should not be abused in such a way. No one should look upon pictures such as that, much less act out those macabre fantasies."

His fingers latched on to her arm, tightening so that she knew it would leave bruises.

"You *will* give it to me, my lady. If you don't, I will make public the fact you own such a collection. That you possess hidden, dark desires. I will make sure Polite Society knows exactly what they should think of you. It will ruin your reputation. And your chances with Amesbury."

Meadow was torn. This evil stranger held her future in his hands. Yet she knew many of the lithographs were loathsome. That Lord Kibbard would look at them. Most likely, he would share them with others who held such bizarre tastes. That these men would lure unsuspecting children into their clutches in order to perform the very perverse acts pictured.

She couldn't allow that. Even if it cost her her good name.

And a life with Wyatt.

"No," she said firmly, jerking hard in order to free herself from his grasp. "My husband was sick. You are sick. I will not allow you to hurt others."

His face darkened with rage. "What you consider wrong is actually quite accepted by some gentlemen. Men you have danced with. Supped with. There are places in London where you can name any act depicted in those lithographs and, for a price, it can become your reality. Even those acts involving children." He paused. "Not giving me what I want is a mistake, Lady Selfridge. It took your husband a lifetime to collect such precious art. I won't see you have it go to waste."

Lord Kibbard frowned. "I will give you until tomorrow night's ball to make a decision. Either you will turn it over—or you will suffer the consequences and be banned from Polite Society for all time."

The earl turned and strode off.

➤➤➤◄◄◄

WYATT BROWSED THROUGH several children's books and found three that he thought the countess' boys would enjoy. He gave them over to a clerk, who rang up his purchase and wrapped the books in brown paper, tying the package with string.

Setting off to find Meadow, he decided to purchase a gift for her, as well. He asked a clerk and was directed to the poetry section of the store. He did not have the heart of a poet and couldn't begin to remember what iambic pentameter was.

But his soul was beginning to understand the language of love—and desire.

He skimmed the shelves, recognizing none of the names on the spines until he reached William Shakespeare. He had enjoyed the bard's plays, the ones rooted in history, thanks to Miles' tutelage. Wyatt had trouble understanding what the plays were about until Miles, who was devoted to history, gave him the background. Suddenly, Julius Caesar and Prince Hal became as flesh and blood men and Wyatt eagerly read the plays, even beyond what was required by his Turner Academy tutors.

He vaguely remembered studying a few sonnets from Shakespeare and found a slender volume of them on the shelf. Leafing through it, he paused at one and begin to read.

Shall I compare thee to a summer's day?
Though art more lovely and more temperate:

It was as if Shakespeare described Meadow.

He closed the book and took it to the same clerk.

"I'll have this, as well."

"Very good, Your Grace."

Wyatt paid for the book and refused to have it wrapped, slipping it instead into his pocket. He had given Meadow enough time. Today would be the day he asked for her hand in marriage. He would take her back to Marshmore's and they would stroll the gardens. When they came to the gazebo, he would have them sit. He would present her with the book as a token of his affection. Then he would offer for her.

He began roaming the store and cut down an aisle when he saw a viscount he had met at White's yesterday heading in his direction. Wyatt had accompanied Miles to the club in order to see what the fuss was about. He found the place and its inhabitants incredible boring. Men sitting about reading their newspapers, gossiping over coffee or even a whiskey at eleven o'clock in the morning. He could read and drink at a more reasonable time in his own townhouse and told Miles that very thing.

The viscount had been one of several to stop by and chat a bit. He had proven to be dull. Wyatt didn't want to get caught up in another conversation with the man.

As he walked down the long row, he thought he caught sight between the shelves of the gown Meadow wore. He had told her she resembled a daffodil and she had blushed prettily at his compliment. Maybe he was more of a poet than he suspected.

He strode toward the middle where he could catch a bare glimpse of color and thought to move a few books to surprise her.

Then he heard a voice. A man's voice, its tone threatening.

"I will give you until tomorrow night's ball to make a decision. Either you will turn it over—or you will suffer the consequences and be banned from Polite Society for all time."

Wyatt couldn't see the man who threatened Meadow but caught a glimpse of his coat as he whirled. The bright color jarred his memory.

Lord Kibbard.

The earl had paused at their table at Gunter's a few weeks ago, introducing himself as a friend of Lord Selfridge. Apparently, Kibbard thought Meadow had something he wanted, some possession of her late husband.

And he wanted it badly enough to threaten her with ruin.

What could it be?

Quickly, Wyatt raced up the aisle to stop Kibbard and confront him, only to find the irksome viscount hovering, ready to ambush him.

"Ah, there you are, Your Grace. We met at White's yesterday."

Wyatt nodded and brusquely said, "Excuse me."

As he moved quickly to the front of the store, he glanced through the display window and saw Lord Kibbard pass down the pavement, having already left the bookshop. He pondered whether or not he should chase the man down and decided against it. He didn't want to abandon Meadow and he certainly wanted to learn what the earl demanded from her.

Returning to where he had last seen her, Wyatt started down the row. She stood halfway down it, staring at the shelves in front of her as if in a trance.

"Meadow?"

She didn't move. It was as if she hadn't heard him speak.

He touched her arm and she startled.

"Meadow?"

She had tears in her eyes. Quickly, she pulled a handkerchief from her pocket and dabbed at her eyes.

"I am sorry. I have something in my eye. It is causing me to resemble a watering pot."

"Is something wrong?" he asked quietly.

She couldn't hide the panic in her eyes. "No. Not a thing."

She was a terrible liar.

"I was just looking for . . ." Her voice trailed off and she dabbed at her eyes again. "Could we leave? I will look another time." She glanced to his hands. "Oh, I see you've bought something for the boys. They will be so pleased." She gave him a weak smile.

He took her hand and slipped it through his arm. "Are you certain nothing is wrong?" he asked again, giving her a chance to tell him about the encounter with Kibbard.

"Nothing at all."

Perhaps she didn't wish to reveal the conversation in public and might do so in his carriage. Wyatt escorted her from the bookshop and to his waiting carriage.

"Are you still ready for a sweet from Gunter's?"

She mustered a smile. "Of course," she said, the smile false and her voice bright and artificial.

He told Blevins to head to Berkeley Square. This time, his driver found a place to park the carriage near the establishment. A waiter rushed over, handing them a menu. Meadow showed no enthusiasm this time, simply telling him to order something for her. Soon, the ices appeared and they ate in silence.

What was she hiding from him?

Kibbard had asked for her to turn something over to him. Why would she not mention having seen the earl, much less keep the threat to herself?

Wyatt found himself uneasy in her company for the first time. If she would keep secrets from him, was she truly the woman he longed to be his duchess?

CHAPTER TWENTY

M EADOW SENSED THE shift between them. She couldn't put her finger on what had happened, only that Wyatt pressed her to reveal something she couldn't discuss with anyone.

Had he somehow overheard her conversation with Lord Kibbard? If so, he must be curious about what the collection was. And why the earl wanted it. Wyatt didn't ask her outright but had twice wanted to know if she was all right.

She wasn't. She never would be again.

Meadow believed Lord Kibbard was exactly the kind of man who would make good on his threats. She had been warned. Turn over Selfridge's evil lithographs or suffer the consequences. The earl would drag her name through the mud and make certain no man would ever offer for her, much less the Duke of Amesbury.

She glanced to Wyatt, who now sat silently looking out the window as they approached Marshmore's residence. She didn't want to hurt him. She certainly didn't want to hurt her cousin, especially since Tilda had given her a place to stay ever since she'd become a widow.

It would be imperative to leave town as soon as possible. Once Kibbard started the rumors about her—or outright lied about her in public—the news would spread rapidly. Leaving London quickly would be important, so that she might distance Wyatt and Tilda from the gossip. She had in her possession six thousand pounds, or at least of good portion of it. True, some had been spent on gowns for this Season but the majority still remained. It would allow her to find a cottage in the country. If she watched things carefully, she could live off the funds indefinitely, with a single maid and perhaps a cook. The important thing would be to get away. It wouldn't matter where she went. Her life in Polite Society would be over.

She wondered why she was risking everything in order to keep the vile lithographs out of Kibbard's hands. She supposed it had to do with having been collected herself. Selfridge had taken her away from everything she had ever known, keeping her trapped in the country, as if he placed her upon a shelf to be admired but never touched. She related to those children in the lithographs. They, too, were trapped, their images captured in the foul drawings. She hadn't been able to protect herself but she hoped she had the courage to stand up and protect these nameless boys and girls from the men who wanted to leer at them.

Even if it meant giving up Wyatt.

She would leave before tomorrow night's ball, the deadline Lord Kibbard had set. She would plead a headache and skip whatever tonight's affair might be in order to be packed. Selfridge's trunk would go with her and, once alone, she would destroy everything within it.

She admired Wyatt's profile, thinking how she would have loved to bear his children and seen him become a father. She would miss his kiss. She would never know the mysteries of lovemaking, which she had hoped to explore with him once they wed.

Or could she?

Meadow determined in that moment that she would seek what she wanted.

And what she wanted was Wyatt.

They arrived at the townhouse and he helped her from the carriage.

"Would you like to come inside?" she quickly asked, cutting him off before he could leave.

"If you wish."

"I do," she said firmly, her thoughts swirling with places she might take him so they could be alone, knowing it would be almost impossible with servants everywhere and Tilda to hide from.

A footman opened the door and she remembered that it was Wednesday. Tilda gave a majority of the servants a half-day off on Wednesdays, which is why the butler had not answered the door.

"Where are Lord and Lady Marshmore?" she asked, untying her bonnet and removing it from her head.

"They left only minutes ago for a garden party, my lady," the footman informed her.

She had forgotten about the party. It meant Tilda and Marshmore would be gone a good while, however, since they had just departed.

"Thank you," she said dismissively. Turning to Wyatt, she said, "Would you care to stroll in the gardens, Your Grace?"

"Of course," he replied, setting the wrapped books on a near-by table and taking her arm.

She led him to Tilda's sitting room and out those doors. They stepped into the gardens and he said, "I have something for you."

He withdrew a small volume from his coat's inside pocket and handed it to her.

"Why, thank you," she said, moved by such a romantic gesture when she saw it was Shakespeare's sonnets. "I have always loved poetry."

"I know little about it," he shared, "but I hoped you might enjoy this."

Other than flowers, he had given her no gifts. Meadow promised herself to always keep these sonnets by her bed as a reminder of him.

"It will always remain dear to me," she said, moved by his

gift.

Knowing she was wasting time, she gathered her courage and said, "Would you accompany me to the house?"

"We've only arrived in the gardens," he pointed out.

"I know. I have something to show you."

Before her feet could falter, she hurried away from him, lifting her skirts and running back to Tilda's sitting room. With most of the servants gone for the afternoon, she doubted they would see any, the only ones left usually in the kitchens at this time.

She opened the door to the sitting room and quickly sought the staircase, sensing Wyatt had now caught up to her. Sure enough, he captured her elbow as she arrived on the first landing.

"Where the Devil are you going?" he demanded.

"To my bedchamber."

She saw understanding dawn in his eyes. The brown, which usually dominated his hazel eyes, receded, allowing the fire of the green to step forward.

"Meadow?" he asked.

"Come with me."

She led him upstairs and down the corridor to her room, ushering him inside quickly and shutting the door, throwing the lock to ensure privacy.

"Why are we here?" he asked.

"Because I want you," she said honestly.

Before she could explain further, his arms banded about her and his mouth came down on hers, hard and demanding. Immediately, her body quickened in anticipation, knowing a bit of what desiring him meant and how he could fulfill her needs.

This time, though, she wanted to go further. She needed to experience everything.

Before it was too late.

She returned his kiss, hungry for him. For his big, powerful body she was crushed against. For his kiss which drove her wild. Somehow, she was able to free her arms and her hands moved to his nape, playing with the hair there. Then she pushed her fingers into it, running them through his thick locks, hearing the low rumble of satisfaction that came from him.

He broke the kiss and they both panted, breathless from it.

"Are you certain this is what you want?" he asked. "There is no turning back."

She understood what he meant. That when he made love to her, he expected the act would brand her as his. She always would be.

She just wouldn't ever be able to see him again.

The rumors about her and her perverse tastes would spread quickly. Men would give him knowing looks, thinking he had dallied with her as the Season progressed. Wyatt was a duke, though, and dukes were the darling of the *ton*. He would be quickly forgiven for a brief liaison with her, while if she remained, she would be ostracized.

"I need you," she told him, knowing her body did. She hadn't the knowledge to understand why her body throbbed. Meadow only knew that he would be the balm to her body.

And her soul.

"Help me to make a memory," she pleaded. "One which I will always remember."

"With pleasure."

His mouth dipped to hers again, his kiss all-consuming as his hands began to roam up and down her spine. They went lower and cupped her bottom, kneading it, as he held her against him. She reveled in the feelings flowing through her. He would be an expert lover. This afternoon's coupling would be something she took out and played over and over in her mind as the years passed. As she lost her figure. Turned old and gray.

It would be what sustained her throughout the inevitable loneliness.

His lips traveled along her jaw and down the column of her throat, heat left in their aftermath. His fingers pushed her gown off one shoulder and his kisses went along it. She reached up and untied his cravat, pulling it from his neck and tossing it to the floor. Gradually, they undressed one another, sharing kisses and touches until both stood bare.

Meadow had thought she would be self-conscious but instead she was dazzled by what stood in front of her. Wyatt looked carved from stone yet when she touched him, it was warm flesh. Her fingers glided along his ribcage and back up, the muscles flexing beneath her touch. His flat nipples, so different from hers, looked like round discs. The pads of her fingers grazed them and he sucked in a quick breath. She had liked when he played with hers and she now returned the favor, brushing her nails slowly over them.

And then her mouth.

And then her tongue.

Wyatt gripped her elbows. "You've got to stop that or I'll spend right here."

She had no idea what that meant.

But she would soon.

His hands spanned her waist and he lifted her. Her legs wrapped around his torso, placing her intimately against him. She felt the ridge of his manhood as he walked them to the bed and eased her onto it. What had been something small, nestled within his dark hair, now stood at full attention. Her eyes widened as she realized that was what he would put inside her.

It would never fit.

He kissed her everywhere, so thoroughly that she didn't think he missed an inch of her flesh. Every place was touched, kissed, licked, worshipped. They kissed greedily as his fingers parted her folds.

"You are ready for me, love," he told her, stroking the seam of her sex.

Her heart beat like the flapping wings of a frightened bird but she smiled up at him.

"I am ready if you are."

His fingers toyed with her as they had before, causing the pressure to build within before it spilled out in a tidal wave of pleasure as she bucked and sighed. As the waves subsided, he placed the tip of his rod at her core and kissed her deeply as he gave a powerful thrust and entered her.

She cried out in his mouth, tears springing to her eyes. Wyatt stilled, his mouth lifting from hers.

"Meadow?"

She heard the uncertainty in his voice. Thankfully, the hurt already subsided, replaced by a feeling of fullness. Of him being inside her.

"Meadow?" he asked again. Not softly. Sharply.

She refused to reply.

Instead, she rocked her hips into him.

He gasped.

She fisted her hands in his hair and pulled him back to her mouth, taking charge of the kiss. He allowed her to do so as he began to move slowly. Too slowly. She moved against him and they began to match one another, as if he were teaching her the steps of the waltz again. His thrusts became longer. Deeper. More satisfying. Then they came more quickly. She locked her hands behind his neck and clung to him as pleasure exploded within her.

Wyatt cried out and collapsed atop her, their bodies slick with sweat. She delighted in his weight, pressing her into the mattress as she clung to him. Then he rolled slightly and they were on their sides, facing one another.

She saw the questions in his eyes and closed hers, wanting to avoid speaking.

"You were a virgin," he stated quietly.

She had used him for his body. She supposed she owed him an explanation.

"Yes. I was. No longer."

"Could Selfridge not perform? I know he was much older than you."

Thinking that meant that her husband had not been able to enter her because of his age, she nodded. "No. He never could."

It was better him believing that than learning she was merely something he collected and pushed aside.

"You could have told me."

She arched her brows. "Let me see. How might that have come up in conversation? Would you care for a canapé, Lady Selfridge? Oh, thank you, Your Grace. Virgins always enjoy canapés. Or Lady Selfridge, would you care to stroll in the gardens? I would enjoy that, Your Grace. Did I mention that I wish I could have enjoyed my husband's performance but he was incapable of giving one after we wed."

"Meadow," he said, a warning edged in it. "Don't be flippant." He smoothed her hair. "I would have treated you differently had I known. Been more gentle the first time. Did you know it hurts?"

She chuckled. "Yes, I just found out that it does."

He kissed her tenderly. "It never does after that first time. I suppose you had no one to speak about these things with."

"No. My mother died in childbirth when I was twelve. She spent her entire married life trying to give my father an heir. I was the only child that lived and she never gave me any attention, much less love."

He cupped her cheek. "I know you've said your father gambled. I suppose he, too, ignored you."

"Naturally. I was a female. He had no need of a child who could never be an heir."

Wyatt kissed the tip of her nose. "You have spent most of your life with no one to care for you." He kissed her cheek. "That is over now. I am here." He kissed her other cheek. "I am your champion. I will love you."

He kissed her slowly, deepening the kiss as her mind fought what he had just said.

I will love you.

She knew she loved him—but did he truly love her? If he did, what she would do would hurt him beyond measure. Agreeing to be his wife, though, knowing her reputation was about to be ruined would hurt him even more.

Meadow gave herself to his kiss, hoping she would always be able to remember it.

He broke it and she stared at him, trying to commit every detail of his face and body to memory.

"You look at me as if you might never see me again," he teased.

"I am merely impressed by your good looks and muscled frame," she said lightly, not wanting him to touch on the truth.

They lay together for a few more minutes, petting one another and kissing. Then she told him they should dress.

"Tilda and Marshmore will be home soon. I can't have you found in my bedchamber. Marshmore might call you out."

"I doubt it," Wyatt said easily, swinging his legs from the bed and standing. "He knows what I would do to him if he did."

"Was he really a bully in school?"

"The worst," he said. "It doesn't matter. I will accept him simply because I know how close you are with your cousin."

He hinted at marriage with that comment. Meadow didn't want him to offer for her now. She refused to promise him she would wed him, only to flee London. She already lied to him by allowing him into her bed. He would think she had acquiesced and was ready for them to wed.

"No more talk," she scolded. "Dress quickly and then help me. We need to get out to the gardens and come in as if we have been there this entire time."

Wyatt captured her hand and brought it to his lips, placing a searing kiss against her knuckles. "Very well."

He managed to dress by himself and then helped lace her into her corset before slipping her petticoat and gown over her head and fastening the buttons down the back.

"Your hair is a mess," he teased. "It has come totally undone."

Quickly, she removed the few hairpins left and then twisted it into a simple chignon, pinning it into place.

"That style flatters you," he said.

"No time for compliments," she said. "Help me find the rest

of my hairpins."

He did as she commanded and placed them on her dressing table before helping her to bring the bedclothes into place. Meadow ignored the blood on the sheets, the sign of her loss of virginity. She would let her maid think her courses had come, though they weren't due for several more days. Sometimes, she spotted a few days before they began so the girl wouldn't suspect anything out of the ordinary.

They crept down the stairs and returned to Tilda's sitting room. As Wyatt opened the French doors leading to the garden, Meadow heard footsteps.

"Pretend as if we are coming in," she whispered and stepped outside the doors.

Wyatt closed them and then rested his hand on the handle. As the door to the sitting room opened and Tilda appeared, he turned the handle.

"Thank you for showing me the gardens, my lady," he said, ushering her inside and then adding, "Oh, good afternoon, Lady Marshmore."

"Hello, Tilda. How was the garden party? I am sorry I forgot about it."

"Where were you?" her cousin asked, suspicion clouding her eyes.

"I asked Lady Selfridge to accompany me to a bookshop," Wyatt said.

"His Grace bought books for the boys," Meadow added.

Tilda brightened. "You did that for my boys, Your Grace?"

"Yes. I then convinced Lady Selfridge that we should go spoil ourselves with ices from Gunter's."

"Then we walked in the gardens," she added, hoping her face didn't betray what they had been up to.

Wyatt turned to her, mischief in his eyes. Taking her hand, he kissed it. "I have taken up far too much of your time today, my lady. I do look forward to seeing you tonight." He looked to Tilda. "Always a pleasure to see you, Lady Marshmore."

After he left, Tilda asked, "Why would he buy my boys books? How does he even know I have children?"

"His Grace came to call when I was playing with them," Meadow explained. "He is a very thoughtful man."

"I am impressed with His Grace," Tilda said, smiling widely. "I doubt he has done this for any other children. He is most taken with you, Cousin. I expect a betrothal to be announced soon."

Meadow couldn't talk about Wyatt anymore without bursting into tears. She would never see him again. He would go on to wed another woman and buy books for their children. She didn't need Tilda studying her too closely and fanned herself. "The day is so warm. I am in need of a bath. I will see you later."

She left the sitting room and returned to the foyer, where she retrieved her bonnet and reticule as the clock chimed four. She would go now to see her solicitor and make plans to leave London.

For good.

CHAPTER TWENTY-ONE

WYATT DID WHAT he always did when he was conflicted. He walked.

He dismissed Blevins after leaving Meadow and strode along the pavement, not seeing anything in front of him because he was lost in thought.

One thing he did know. He was definitely in love with Meadow.

His growing attraction to her body and mind could no longer be termed a fascination. He loved her. He couldn't imagine a life without her.

And that's where the frustration lay.

Honesty meant a great deal to him. Too many he'd known had been hurt by secrets and lies. Wyatt had no room for such subterfuge in his life and couldn't understand why Meadow hid something of importance from him.

He reflected on what Lord Kibbard had said to her. The earl had demanded she turn something over to him. If she didn't, she would suffer expulsion from the *ton*.

Whatever Kibbard wanted, it had to be something that belonged to the late Lord Selfridge. Something Meadow still possessed. He thought back to her mentioning her husband collected things. Those collections would have become part of the estate, property of the next viscount. Yet Meadow had kept something, something so valuable that Lord Kibbard desperately wanted it for himself. If Meadow didn't give it to the earl, he would ruin her.

But how? What would be so extraordinary that if it were to be found in her possession, it would ostracize her from Polite Society?

If Meadow wouldn't tell him, then Wyatt would make certain Lord Kibbard revealed the truth.

He returned home and sequestered himself in his study. He closed his eyes and leaned back in his chair, thinking on how he had made love to Meadow. Part of him regretted that he didn't directly tell her that he loved her. He had said he would love her.

That wasn't good enough. Tonight, he needed to tell her he did so. Perhaps then she would trust him enough to share with him what Lord Kibbard was up to. He still wondered what object Meadow possessed that Kibbard might want. He knew nothing about the earl, other than he had approached them at Gunter's. Even then, when Meadow had learned Kibbard's name, she had become upset. Lord Selfridge must have told her something terrifying about Kibbard, the viscount's supposed friend, in order for her to react as she had.

He wondered why Kibbard had waited as long as he did before approaching her in the bookstore. Wyatt couldn't remember seeing the earl at any previous *ton* events this Season. Then again, he hadn't been looking for him. He would search tonight to see if Kibbard was in attendance. If not, he would learn everything he could about the man before he confronted him. With the deadline of tomorrow night looming, Wyatt would have to act quickly to discover all he could about the man.

Frame helped him to dress for the ball and Wyatt went downstairs, telling his butler not to call for the carriage because he wished to walk. Fortunately, Winkle took the news in stride and merely wished him a good evening, not questioning such odd behavior in a duke. Wyatt supposed Winkle was getting used to working for a duke who was more eccentric than most.

The ball was only a few blocks from Wyatt's address. Deliberately, he made his way there by heading near Marshmore's townhouse. As he turned the corner, he saw the Marshmore carriage pull away from the curb so he knew that Meadow was on her way to the ball.

By the time he reached his destination, the receiving line was lengthy. He decided to skip it and find Meadow instead. She had played coy with him in recent weeks, not saving a dance for him, instead making him claim one as other gentlemen did.

Wyatt scanned the ballroom and did not see her yet, figuring she remained in the dreadfully long receiving line. He did make his way over to Miles and Emery. Her figure was beginning to change now and a golden glow filled her face.

Taking her hand, he said, "You are looking especially beautiful tonight, Your Grace." He kissed it. "The midnight blue suits you well."

"Miles likes this color," she told him.

"No, I like *you* in this color," her husband corrected, shaking hands with Wyatt.

"Is there any color you don't like Emery in?" Wyatt teased.

They spoke for a few minutes as he constantly looked to the entrance.

"Are you afraid Meadow might turn up with her programme entirely filled?" Emery asked.

"No. I have something important to tell her."

Miles chuckled. "Either he's going to tell her he loves her—or he's about to offer for her."

"Be quiet, Miles," Wyatt said. "You aren't half as clever as you think you are."

"Have you told her you love her yet?" his friend persisted.

"In a way."

"That sounds rather vague, Wyatt."

"I told her I will love her. Not that I do love her," he said. "There's a difference. I need to make sure she understands how I truly feel about her."

"She knows," Emery said. "Just watching the two of you

together, I believe the entire *ton* knows."

He felt his face flush, something that never occurred. "I need to set things straight. If you'll excuse me."

Wyatt had spotted Lady Marshmore but not Meadow, who always accompanied her cousin. He strode toward her as she joined a group of women.

"Good evening, my lady," he said.

"Oh, my, Your Grace!" she exclaimed, turning to face him. "I cannot believe how generous you were to read to and buy *my* boys books. You are so very thoughtful."

The women gathered tittered.

"They are fine boys," he said. "I enjoyed playing with them."

More titters occurred.

"Might I ask where Lady Selfridge is?" he asked.

Lady Marshmore frowned. "The poor dear is ill. She did not feel up to coming tonight."

"What is wrong with her?"

"A terrible headache. She hoped going to bed and getting some sleep would help it to dissipate."

Meadow wasn't sick. She was either avoiding him or Lord Kibbard.

"Good evening, Lady Marshmore," he murmured, retreating to a far corner.

From it, he skimmed the ballroom, looking for Lord Kibbard. He doubted the older man would be present. Dancing was usually a much younger man's sport unless a gentleman sought a bride.

Once the dancing commenced, Wyatt made his way to the card room in case the earl might turn up there. It startled him when he did see Kibbard sitting at a table. Immediately, Wyatt went into spy mode. He had learned that a successful spy traded in the commodity of information. Because of that, he had always studied others at length, looking at their gestures, habits, and reactions.

Now, he made learning everything he could about Lord

Kibbard his mission.

For over an hour, he watched the earl at cards. How he held his hand. The amount he wagered. His reaction when he won or lost. Then Lord Brimmer, who had been a player at the table the entire time Wyatt had observed it, excused himself. He knew Brimmer from being introduced to him at White's and knew the man enjoyed gossip.

This time, Wyatt wanted to avail himself of that gossip.

He met Brimmer and greeted him.

"Ah, Lord Brimmer. It is delightful to see you here."

The viscount gave him a ready smile. "How nice to see you, Your Grace."

"I see you were playing cards. It looked as though Lord Kibbard is on a win streak tonight."

Brimmer frowned. "He seems to be on one far too often if you ask me." He lowered his voice and moved closer to Wyatt. "Frankly, I think he is a cheat but is too clever to have been caught at it."

"Interesting," he murmured. "Do you know anything else about him? I was thinking of joining the table and find it helpful to learn something about my fellow opponents."

Brimmer's floodgates opened. "Lord Kibbard is a bit of a mystery to most. No Lady Kibbard. No bastards. He has invested in a variety of business ventures but claims he knows nothing of business. Rumor has it his finances are in poor shape. Despite that, he is obsessed with collecting unusual items."

"Such as?"

Brimmer glanced around. "Let's just say the items are of a . . . questionable nature."

Wyatt had no idea what that might mean. "How so?" he encouraged.

"Well, Lord Kibbard is a frequent visitor to several brothels. Ones which cater to bizarre tastes."

Brimmer named a few of them and Wyatt immediately knew what abnormal tastes the viscount referred to.

Did that have a connection to what Kibbard demanded from Meadow?

"Thank you, Brimmer. If I win tonight, I will most certainly buy you a drink."

"That would be wonderful, Your Grace."

Armed with some knowledge, Wyatt ventured to the table Kibbard sat at. Though someone had already taken Brimmer's spot, the man to Kibbard's left was rising.

"Are you returning—or might I take your place, my lord?"

Soon, he was seated, waiting for Kibbard to make the first move. No one spoke as a new deck of cards was produced and a hand dealt. The betting went on until only Wyatt and Kibbard remained. When they finally showed their cards, Wyatt proved victorious.

As a new hand was dealt, Kibbard said, "I believe we have met before, Your Grace."

He looked at the earl blankly. "Have we?"

"Yes, you were with Lady Selfridge. It was at Gunter's."

He pretended to think. "Oh, yes. I do recall now. You knew her husband if I am not mistaken."

"Yes, we were quite close."

Knowing now of Kibbard's perverse tastes, Wyatt couldn't help but wonder if Lord Selfridge had shared them, along with his friendship of this man.

After two more rounds, both taken by Kibbard, several players left the table. As they waited for others to take their places, the earl struck up a conversation again.

"It seems you have spent quite a bit of time in Lady Selfridge's company?"

"What is it to you?" he asked sharply.

"Nothing, Your Grace," Kibbard said quickly, looking away.

Wyatt knew offending a duke wasn't done and that Kibbard might even stand and walk away.

"So, you knew Lord Selfridge," he said agreeably, hoping to draw Kibbard back into conversation. "I hear he collected items. I am curious. What kind of things?"

"Anything beautiful," the earl said. "Porcelain snuffboxes. Race horses. Rare gems." He paused. "And his greatest acquisition? His wife."

Anger burned through Wyatt but he said, "How so?"

"Selfridge was obsessed with beauty," Kibbard explained. "Lady Selfridge was the most beautiful girl of her Season. My friend simply had to have her." He chuckled. "It helped that her father was a habitual gambler and deeply in debt. Selfridge purchased her for a very reasonable price."

He fought slamming a fist into the smug face of the earl. "Is that so?"

"You, too, seem taken with her, Your Grace. She still is a stunning woman. It is a shame Selfridge didn't know what to do with her."

"I don't understand."

Kibbard smiled. "Once he had her, he didn't know how to display her as he did his other collectibles. I think her beauty intimidated him. He abandoned her to the country and returned to town for the most part."

"I would think if he claimed her as his bride that he would want to show her off to society."

"No. Selfridge had been a bachelor far too long. He had tastes that ran contrary to a traditional marriage. Unique tastes."

"Such as?"

Kibbard sat back, crossing his arms. "Shall we say that Lady Selfridge was too old for her husband?"

His words sickened Wyatt. "Do you share those tastes, my lord?"

The earl laughed. "I am a man of many tastes, Your Grace. If I had wed Lady Selfridge, I certainly would have known what to do with her. I am sure you will, too, if you see fit to offer for her. I would wait to do so, though."

"Why so?" he asked.

"I hear the lady has a decision to make regarding her future.

Once she has, you may find she could be the perfect duchess—or that she is a pariah."

Rage sizzled through him. "And how do you know Lady Selfridge so well as to have knowledge of this . . . decision?"

"I would ask the lady that question, Your Grace."

Just then, a footman announced that supper was being served.

Lord Kibbard rose. "If you will excuse me, Your Grace. I am to meet a friend. Good evening."

As Wyatt watched the earl leave the card room, along with the others who wished to attend supper, he decided to leave the ball.

Because he needed to speak to Meadow.

Now.

CHAPTER TWENTY-TWO

MEADOW SENT THE maid away and fell into a chair, exhaustion filling her. She glanced to the bed, still covered with items that needed to be packed before she left tomorrow.

And thought of what she and Wyatt had done there that afternoon.

Making love with him already seemed a lifetime instead of merely hours ago. She closed her eyes, remembering the feel of his lips traveling the length of her body. He had introduced her into mysteries she would never explore again with any other man. She couldn't.

Because she loved only him.

Tears streamed down her cheeks. She assumed many more tears would be in her future, especially during the lonely nights when her body longed for the warmth of Wyatt to be next to her.

Suddenly, the very air changed as something descended upon her. Meadow's eyes flew open, only to find Wyatt in front of her. He bent and kissed her cheeks, his tongue licking at the tears.

"Wyatt!" she cried, dissolving into more tears.

He scooped her up and sat where she had, cradling her in his lap. Meadow buried her face against his hard chest, sobbing.

"There, sweetheart. It's all right."

She heard the words but couldn't tell him that he was wrong. Nothing would ever be right again for her. She had made a huge mistake bringing him to her bed today.

Once had not been enough. Once could never be enough. She wanted this man every day. Every hour. Every minute.

And that was impossible.

Meadow raised her head and angrily wiped at the tears. "Why are you here?" she demanded. "Why have you come?"

His eyes searched hers. "Because I love you, Meadow," he said simply.

His words broke her. She began weeping hysterically, pushing against him, trying to escape. He was having none of it, holding her tightly until the fight went out of her and she gave in to him. He stroked her back soothingly. Kissed her hair. Her temple. Linked his fingers with hers.

"I love you," he said again, his voice low and rough.

An ache where her heart sat began spreading through her. She couldn't repeat the words. Not when she was leaving him.

Wyatt lifted her chin until their gazes met. "Do you love me, Meadow?"

Her mouth trembled. Her whole body began to tremble. Still, she refused to speak.

He sighed. "I love you. I hope that is enough for the both of us. That we can build a life together. Have children."

"No!" she protested, scrambling off him, knowing being in his arms caused all rational thought to flee. Swallowing, she said, "I need you to leave. Now."

He glanced to the bed. "It looks as if you are the one leaving, love."

Fisted hands went to her waist. "And what if I am? I don't owe you or anyone else an explanation."

"Where do you plan to go?"

"Away," she said stubbornly, her chin rising a notch.

He stood and started toward her.

"No. Don't come any closer," she ordered. "You shouldn't even be here. If it got out that you were found in my bedchamber, why I—"

"—would be ruined," he finished. "But Lord Kibbard has

already promised to do that to you, hasn't he?"

Dumbfounded, she could only look at him, no words coming out.

Wyatt took a few more steps and then clasped her hands. "Why has he threatened you, Meadow? What did Selfridge collect that Kibbard now wants so desperately from you?"

She knew how determined he could be. After all, he had sat his sights upon her and had been relentless in his pursuit. She might as well tell him so he could gracefully withdraw from her before he was sucked into the mire.

"Lithographs. Selfridge gathered hundreds of them. He told me on his deathbed to sell them to a Lord Kibbard. That the price Kibbard paid would make certain I was taken care of."

He squeezed her fingers. "Did you see them?"

Meadow nodded. "Selfridge told me where to find them. In his study. He went there every night when he was in the country and spent hours behind closed doors. He rarely spoke to me. I had no idea what he did in there. I found the trunk and key." She glanced to where the same trunk sat in the corner. "That is it."

He nodded. "What did you find?"

She shuddered. "Horrible images. Things I couldn't begin to understand. The worst involved . . . children." She choked on the last word.

He enfolded her in his arms. "You shouldn't have had to see that."

She let him hold her. Being in his arms made her feel so safe. So protected. But she had to tell him the rest.

Meadow broke away and went to stand by the bed, holding on to the post for support.

"I took the trunk because I didn't want the new Lord Selfridge to know about it. I tried to never think about it—until Lord Kibbard approached us at Gunter's. He saw through me when I pretended not to know what he spoke about."

"And confronted you in the bookshop today."

She nodded. "Yes. He offered to buy the lithographs. I refused. I told him they were evil and should be burned. He gave me until tomorrow night to hand them over to him. If I refuse, he will make known exactly what I have in my possession. That I shared in my husband's wicked corruption. That I enjoy such foul, depraved activities."

Meadow looked at him, the ache growing within her. "That is why you must disassociate yourself from me, Wyatt. I won't have you tainted by the gossip. I don't want others to believe you, too, enjoy such vile things."

"You were fleeing London?" he asked.

"Yes. And taking the trunk with me. I wanted to burn everything but it would take hours to do so and I couldn't have servants present when I did."

"You could do as he asked. Give the trunk and its contents to him."

"No!" she cried. "Never."

He moved toward her again, placing his hands on her shoulders. "Why? Why would you have your reputation ruined? You could simply hand it over and be done with it."

Her voice shook as she said, "Selfridge was a collector. He collected me. I was treated as a prized possession. Locked into a gilded cage and forgotten. Those children were collected by him, having to engage in acts so heinous I cannot even think of it without weeping. If I give the lithographs to Kibbard, I am just as guilty as he is of passing it on. Allowing others to perversely enjoy it. I know I sound mad but what was done to them is wrong. Just like my father selling me to Selfridge and him removing me from everything I knew and placing me upon a shelf. It was wrong. I won't hand it over to Kibbard so he can sit and enjoy such lewdness. To allow others to see the vileness. I won't let this evil spread any further."

Wyatt's hands slid from her shoulders to her neck, his fingers stroking the tender flesh.

"Yet another reason why I love you, Meadow. You are strong. So strong in your convictions. You do the right thing, which many would not. You would risk everything for nameless faces you don't even know."

He pressed a soft kiss to her mouth.

"We will fight this together. Lord Kibbard may think to bully you. Threaten to expose you in a falsehood he tells Polite Society. I will not let him. You and I will stand strong against him, Meadow. Because we have the unbreakable bond of love between us."

"I do love you, Wyatt," she told him. "I have for some time. I just didn't want you to be trapped in this situation, your good name linked to mine. I couldn't have you dragged through the mud. There's nothing the *ton* likes more than to eviscerate someone through gossip, unfounded or not."

He cupped her cheeks. "I love that you wanted to protect me, sweetheart. But we are stronger together than apart. We will take on Lord Kibbard. And afterward, perhaps we can help the children in those lithographs. Or ones like them, who have been abused by men such as Kibbard."

"You would do that for me?"

Wyatt smiled. "There isn't anything I wouldn't do for you, Meadow."

He kissed her tenderly.

For the first time, Meadow had hope that she could escape this nightmare. Because of the love of this good man.

He led her back to the chair, bringing her onto his lap again.

"You have been honest with me. It is time I am truthful with you."

Immediately, she knew that he was speaking of his past. Once, she had thought she couldn't marry him—much less love him—until she knew the truth. Only now, she understood that whatever had happened to him as a boy had led him to become the man he was today. A good man. One that she loved uncondi-tionally.

"You needn't tell me anything, Wyatt. I love you. I trust you."

"No. I want to tell you. About my past." He paused. "I haven't spoken about these events since I was ten years old. I need to tell you."

Meadow nodded her permission, her throat thick with emotion.

"I loved Amberwood. As a boy, I explored every nook and cranny of the house. I knew every rolling hill of the land. I was often left on my own. My mother showed me no affection. My father demanded perfection from me and was constantly disappointed when I couldn't live up to his impossible standards. Eventually, he simply ignored me. All the attention went to Clive, my older brother. The marquess who would one day become the duke."

"Did you like this brother?" she asked softly.

"I barely knew him," Wyatt told her. "He was almost a decade my senior and wanted nothing to do with me. What I did know of him, I didn't like. You see, we had a parade of maids quit abruptly. One was even let go. Due to her condition."

"I don't understand," she said when he hesitated. "What did that have to do with your brother?"

He brushed the back of his fingers along her cheek. "My sweet, naive Meadow. Clive was forcing himself upon them. I know of at least one that he got with child."

"Oh!" she said, startled. The idea of something like that happening had never occurred to her.

"The staff ignored me as did my family," he continued. "All except one maid. Joan. She always had a kind word and ready smile for a lonely boy. Thinking back, I probably had a bit of a crush on her since I was so starved for affection."

Meadow began to realize where his story might go. She took his hand, lacing her fingers through his.

"One night, I had been sent to my bedchamber, punished again for simply doing the things a little boy did. As I watched from my window, I saw Clive appear, dragging Joan along with him. They headed toward the stables. I knew something terrible was going to happen to her and that I had to stop it."

He hesitated a moment, closing his eyes, and Meadow knew he must be going back to that long-ago night.

His eyes still shut, Wyatt said, "I found them in an empty stall, Clive assaulting her. She begged me to leave, wanting to protect me. I refused—so Clive told me he would make me leave. He was going to be the future duke and he didn't want anyone crossing him."

Opening his eyes, she saw the pain that still lingered there after all these years.

"He attacked me—even breaking my ribs—but he was careless as he did so and knocked over a lantern. Joan's skirts caught fire. Clive fled like the coward he was as the fire spread quickly to the hay and wood of the stables. Joan helped me up and we stumbled from the burning structure. I wanted to go back. To try and save at least some of the horses. But she wouldn't let me. The fire spread too quickly. She had the sense to know if I went back inside, especially in my injured condition, that I would never return."

Tears brimmed in his eyes as he said, "I can still hear their screams sometimes. I dream of them and wake up, terrified. Ashamed that I couldn't save them. Or Joan."

"Oh, Wyatt."

Meadow's heart ached for the brave little boy who had wanted to rescue a servant and had been beaten by his own flesh and blood.

"I tried to tell my father what had happened but he wasn't having any of it. My gut tells me now that he knew he truth and chose to turn a blind eye as Clive accused me of starting the fire. Of being the monster who was responsible for the death of over two dozen horses."

Wyatt sighed. "Clive got me alone and told me to accept his lie as truth. That if I continued my protests, he would slit Joan's throat."

She gasped. "No!"

"I believed him, Meadow. He was drunk on power. Of being a marquess who would one day be a duke. I accepted my fate. My father washed his hands of me. I was sent to Turner Academy, a school known for taking on troubled boys." His jaw tightened. "It was the best thing that could have happened to me. I received a superb education at the hands of the Turner brothers and their tutors. The two Turner wives were warm and affectionate.

"And I came to know the four boys who would become my true brothers. Brothers of choice. Brothers of my heart. Being sent to the academy made me the man I am today. I wouldn't change any of it. It brought me to my fellow Terrors. And to you."

"I can never imagine all you went through, Wyatt. I only know you are the best man I have ever known."

"I have tried my utmost, Meadow. Once I became the Duke of Amesbury, one of the first things I did was search for Joan. She had left Amberwood and had wed a local dairy farmer. They had a son together. Joan recently became a widow. I offered her the position as my housekeeper and she and her boy have returned to Amberwood. Philip is working in my stables. It is a small way for me to try and right the wrongs of the past."

Meadow melted at his words. That action alone proved to her what a decent man Wyatt truly was. She kissed him, willing him to understand that.

"I must tell you two things now, Meadow."

She couldn't fathom what else he had to say after hearing about his tragic past.

"I offered for you far too soon. And then I smugly knew you would accept me in time. First, I must say again that I love you. I should have told you as soon as I realized it. I promise I will do it often. Every day."

He cleared his throat. "That leads to the second thing. I have assumed you would wed me but I want to ask you again. Officially."

Her heart began beating quickly.

"I have come to the realization that I cannot even comprehend living a day without you. Will you marry me, Meadow? Will you be my duchess? My partner in all that comes our way? Bear my children and love them with me all the day long?"

Love bloomed within her. "I cannot imagine a day without you, Wyatt. You are everything I could have ever dreamed of when I wished for a husband. This time, it is my choice. *You* are my choice. Now and always."

She framed his face with her hands and kissed him softly.

"I don't want to wait," he told her. "I want you to have the protection of my name."

"You mean before tomorrow night's ball—when Lord Kibbard wants my response to his blackmail."

"Yes. I can purchase a special license first thing tomorrow morning. I will send my carriage for Finch."

"Finch?" she asked. "Oh, you have mentioned him. He is the Terror who is now a vicar."

"Yes. I can have him in London by early afternoon. I hope you don't mind that I want him to perform the ceremony."

"Not at all. I have already met one Terror and like him quite a bit. I would be happy to have another officiate at our wedding."

He frowned. "It wouldn't be the usual ceremony and wedding breakfast. Perhaps a late afternoon wedding and a wedding supper before tomorrow night's ball?"

"That would be lovely."

"Emery expects to have it at their townhouse. Would you be agreeable to that?"

Meadow laughed. "I would wed you in the middle of Berkeley Square if that's what you wished."

"Then shall we say five o'clock?" Wyatt asked. "While the *ton* parades their carriages through Hyde Park, we can pledge ourselves to one another."

"All right. As long as you allow Marshmore to escort Tilda to the wedding. I can't do this without her."

He kissed her soundly. "Invite them and anyone else you

choose."

"Just the two of them," she said. "And Miles and Emery."

He took her hand and pressed a kiss to her palm. "Thank you for agreeing to marry me, Meadow."

She warmed at his words. At his touch. "Thank you for asking me properly, Wyatt."

CHAPTER TWENTY-THREE

WYATT PACED THE room, constantly looking out the window in order to see when Finch arrived. When his carriage pulled up, its ducal seal gleaming in the sunlight, he left Miles' study and hurried to the foyer where the butler admitted his friend.

"Finch!" he cried, greeting his old friend with a bear hug and then stepping back to look at him. "It's been far too long. Since before I left for war."

"You're right about that."

A footman took Finch's valise and hurried up the stairs with it.

"So, I have been called to town to perform your marriage ceremony," Finch added. "The last letter I received from you told me you were the new Amesbury. Then I get a second letter—if you could call it that. One of two sentences in length." He paused and looked up, reciting from memory. "Come to London today. I need you to marry me to my soulmate."

Finch laughed. "You didn't even bother to sign it, Wyatt. Since it was a ducal carriage that stood outside the vicarage—and since I know only two dukes and had already married off one of them—I assumed it was you."

Wyatt couldn't help but laugh, too. "I am sorry, old friend. I have my reasons for wanting a speedy wedding."

"I already think your bride is too good for you. I thought the same about Emery."

"I heard that."

Wyatt looked up and saw Miles descending the stairs. He greeted Finch and then said, "You're absolutely right. Wyatt and I chose women far above us."

"What do I need to know about the future Duchess of Amesbury, Miles?" Finch asked. "Wyatt will be much too prejudiced in his description of her."

"Suffice it to say that Emery and Meadow are already as thick as thieves."

Finch burst out laughing. "Since Emery is an excellent judge of character, that is testimony enough to the bride's good character."

"Come to the drawing room," Miles invited. "Emery is waiting for us there."

The three men went upstairs and Finch greeted Emery enthusiastically.

"You are aglow, Emery," he told her. "Being with child suits you."

She placed her hands on her growing belly. "We cannot wait to see the babe. Come and sit, Finch. I have already rung for tea. It should be here soon."

The teacart arrived and Emery poured out as the men fixed themselves a plate.

Finch then asked, "What is Meadow like? That is, if I am allowed to address her thus."

"She won't mind at all," Wyatt assured him. "She is rather like me in that she had parents who ignored her. Her mother died in childbirth, trying to provide an heir. Her father had no interested in her since she was a female. He devoted his time to gambling and amassed huge debts."

He paused, wondering how much he should reveal and then decided these people were his family and they should know all.

"Meadow's father sold her to Lord Selfridge, a man much older than she was, during her come-out Season. The viscount agreed to pay off all his friend's markers if he could claim Meadow as his bride."

Finch sucked in a breath but said nothing.

"It seems Lord Selfridge accumulated the very finest of things, from walking sticks to horses to paintings. That including acquiring the most beautiful debutante of the Season. He added her to a collection of one and then left her in the country. She learned to run a huge household on her own and she tended to Selfridge's tenants, learning quite a bit about his estate, while he remained most of the year in London."

"Why would he do such a thing?" Miles asked. "It seems as if he would have wanted to flaunt his new viscountess to Polite Society."

"Meadow only learned upon his death that her husband had very perverse tastes," Wyatt explained. "She found a collection of prized lithographs. I am sure you can guess at their content—and why he left her untouched."

He saw Emery's eyes brim with tears as she said, "Poor Meadow. I had no idea."

"As to your original question, Finch, Meadow is the strongest woman I know. She is clever and compassionate. She makes me happy. And she has me wanting to be the best man I can be for her."

"Then you have chosen well, Wyatt," Finch said. "I look forward to meeting her." He hesitated. "But why the rush? Is it because you simply cannot wait another day to consummate your relationship?"

"Meadow is being blackmailed," he said. "By Lord Kibbard."

"Wasn't he the man who stopped by our table at Gunter's?" Miles asked, frowning.

"That's Kibbard. He was close friends with Selfridge and enjoys the same depraved tastes. He knows Meadow is in possession of her late husband's lithographs and wants them. If she doesn't surrender the collection, he will make known to the *ton* that she shares the same sexual tastes as Selfridge—in effect, ruining her."

"You want to protect her. As her husband," Finch said, nodding. "It would be very hard for this lord to cross swords with a duke. Has Meadow thought of giving the viscount what he wants?"

"She refuses. She relates to the children in the lithographs. She feels she was used by her father and Selfridge, being forced to wed a stranger to settle her father's gambling debts. Meadow knows the children depicted also were forced to do unnatural things. She doesn't want them exploited more than they have been, having Kibbard and his other corrupt friends pass the collection among themselves. She would rather her own reputation be ruined than see them further abused."

"She certainly has great moral character," Finch pointed out. "I doubt any other woman in the *ton* would sacrifice herself on such principle. You know I would have performed the marriage regardless of what you told me. Now, though, I know just how special your Meadow is."

"Kibbard's deadline is tonight. If Meadow doesn't give him the trunk containing the lithographs, he says he will spread his lies."

"But she will now go to the ball as the Duchess of Amesbury," Emery said with a smile. "Lord Kibbard would not dare try to make a move against her with you as her husband."

"That is my greatest hope," Wyatt revealed. "I assume he will drop the matter. I will help Meadow to destroy the lithographs, which is what she wants."

Miles held up his teacup. "It's not the usual means of a toast but to Meadow. For her fortitude in standing up to a dissolute Lord Kibbard and for taking on a Turner Terror."

The other three raised their cups. "To Meadow!" they said in unison.

MEADOW DRESSED WITH a maid's help as Tilda looked on.

"I don't understand why you didn't tell me Amesbury had offered for you," her cousin complained. "You didn't even bother going to last night's ball. We could have celebrated there."

"I wanted to pack," she said.

Tilda snorted. "A maid could have done the packing for you."

"I wanted to supervise her. You know I can be very particular." She looked to the maid. "Thank you. That will be all."

The servant left as Meadow seated herself at the dressing table. Tilda came over and picked up a brush and began brushing Meadow's hair.

"Shall I arrange it for you? I am not the best at that. Perhaps I should call the maid back."

"No, I will do it myself. Wyatt likes it when it is simply styled."

"You call him Wyatt?" Tilda asked, looking perplexed.

"Yes, it is his name."

"But . . . you *use* it? Why, I never call Marshmore by anything other than his title. It simply isn't done, Meadow."

"I won't use it when in public. He shall be Amesbury, of course. But in private and with family or friends, I certainly plan to address him as Wyatt."

Her gaze met that of her cousin's in the mirror and she added, "I love him, Tilda. Perhaps that is the difference between me and most wives. I never called my husband anything other than Selfridge or my lord. In fact, I don't think I even remember what his Christian name was. I must have used it at our wedding ceremony but that day was a blur to me."

Tilda's hands came and squeezed Meadow's shoulders. "You looked very unhappy that day, I remember. You never smiled once."

"Why would I? Father bartered me to Selfridge in order to keep his own head above water. He had lost a great deal of money at the gaming tables. I was his way out."

Tilda's mouth quivered. "I never knew that, Meadow. I only

knew he had told you he had chosen a husband for you. Many fathers do so. My own did for me."

She reached a hand up and covered Tilda's with it. "What matters is that, this time, it is my choice. I have had the opportunity to once again meet men in society and I found the only one meant for me."

"I had thought Lord Pomeroy might be your choice until His Grace continued to come around. What woman could resist that title? You will be a duchess, Meadow."

"That matters not to me, Tilda. I am marrying Wyatt for him. He could be a common bricklayer for all I care. He is smart and handsome and a wonderful kisser. And he wants to be a father more than anything. We plan on having a very large family."

Tilda squeezed Meadow's shoulders and lowered her hands. "I wondered if you had kissed him or not."

She thought her cousin would be scandalized if she learned Meadow had made love with Wyatt in this very room.

"I have. Several times. Each kiss is better than the one before, I assure you."

"Looks fade. At least you will be wealthy and a duchess."

She shook her head. It was obvious Tilda hadn't a clue what love was. How strong and lasting it would be. Meadow felt sorry her cousin would never experience the joy she had with Wyatt as she wound her hair around and inserted pins into it. When she finished, she admired her image in the mirror.

"This hairstyle quite suits you," Tilda said. "As does that shade of gown. I can't quite decide if it is more blue or gray. Either way, it makes your eyes sparkle."

Meadow stood. "You look lovely, as well, Tilda."

"I would hope so. I am going to one duke's home and witnessing my cousin marry another duke," Tilda said, only half in jest.

They went downstairs, where Marshmore awaited them.

"You look quite nice," he said, the only time he had ever given Meadow a compliment. She hoped things might thaw between him and Wyatt.

"Thank you, my lord."

They went to the carriage and were driven the few blocks to the Duke and Duchess of Winslow's townhouse. The butler granted them entrance, where a tall, blond man with an athletic frame and sparking blue eyes stood in the foyer.

He came toward them and took her hand. "I am Reverend William Finchley, my lady," he said in a deep tone.

She introduced herself and the Marshmores and then the vicar asked the butler to take the couple out to the gardens, saying they would join them momentarily.

"I wanted a private word with you, my lady," he said. "Wyatt may not be my blood relative but we are brothers, all the same."

"He speaks of you and the other Terrors with great fondness, Reverend," she replied.

"That is the first thing I must clear up. If you do not call me Finch and allow me to address you as Meadow, then I am not certain I can perform this ceremony."

She laughed. "I would be happy to add you to my impromptu family. I have already made our host and hostess members of it. I find being able to choose one's own family is infinitely more enjoyable than being stuck with the one you were born into."

"I will give a loud amen to that," Finch said, smiling broadly. Then he sobered. "Wyatt has told us of the blackmail threat to you. Know that Miles and I will stand with him and prevent any harm coming to you, physically or otherwise."

She blinked at the sudden tears. "Thank you," she said softly. "I am grateful for your support. It is odd, to have gone from having no one to depend upon, and now having a good man who loves me and his chosen brothers who stand by him. Not to mention Emery, who is probably the strongest of all of us."

"That, I would agree with," Finch said. "I was happy to come to know her and thrilled for Miles that he had found the perfect woman for him. It seems Wyatt has done the same."

"Wyatt is my everything," she admitted. "The past is but a

distant memory. My present and future are with him."

"Then let us go and see you wed to him."

Finch took her arm and guided Meadow through the house, saying, "Since the day is so calm and pleasant, Emery thought you might like to speak your vows in the garden."

"What a delightful idea!" she exclaimed.

He led her outside and waiting there was Miles, a bouquet in his hands.

"I hope you don't mind if I escort you to your fiancé," he said.

"I can't think of a better Terror to do so," she said cheekily.

Finch handed her over and strode off as Miles handed Meadow the flowers he held.

"Emery thought you might enjoy carrying these."

He slipped her hand through the crook of his arm and led her to the entrance of the gardens and down the path. After a few minutes, they reached a gazebo surrounded by flowers.

In it, Wyatt waited for her.

Her breath caught at how handsome he appeared. This man would be hers.

All hers.

Miles led her to the stairs, where Emery, Tilda, and Marshmore had gathered. He placed her hand in Wyatt's and her groom guided her up the stairs to where Finch awaited them in the center.

As they spoke their vows, Meadow marveled at how different her life would now be, with a husband who loved her completely. She hoped even now that they had already made a babe and it grew in her belly. She wanted to give Wyatt at least half a dozen children.

They promised to be faithful and love one another always. Then Finch pronounced them husband and wife and Wyatt took her in his arms for a slow, delicious, lush kiss that went on and on.

Someone cleared his throat loudly—but Wyatt did not break the kiss.

"We're going in now," Miles announced. "There's cake and you know how I enjoy my cake. If you care to join us, that would be lovely, seeing as to how my beautiful wife arranged a wonderful wedding supper for you at the last minute."

Wyatt finally lifted his lips from hers. "Shall we go in and have cake?" he murmured.

"I do like a slice of cake at a wedding," she admitted. "Especially if it is my own."

He laughed and looked to their guests. "Then cake it shall be."

With a quick move, he swept Meadow into his arms and carried her all the way from the gardens to the house.

"Miles thinks he has the market on romantic gestures," her new husband told her. Grinning, he added, "I think I shall challenge him."

She fluttered her eyelashes at him. "As long as I am the beneficiary of your romantic gestures, I say have at it, Your Grace."

Wyatt brought her to her feet and enveloped her in his arms. "You will always be the one, Meadow."

He kissed her passionately until she felt the kiss down to her toes.

"I find I quite like being married," she told him.

He laughed all the way into supper.

Chapter Twenty-Four

MEADOW WENT THROUGH the receiving line with Wyatt, Emery, and Miles. No mention was made of today's marriage. Wyatt had told her in the carriage that he preferred it being announced as they entered the ballroom. She doubted Lord Kibbard would be there to witness this since she had only glimpsed him twice at *ton* events and had never seen him inside any London ballroom. Wyatt told her he had found the earl in the card room last night and she supposed he would remain there until he approached her.

It wouldn't matter. She had her husband by her side and had total faith in him. He promised her that he would handle the situation and they would be rid of Lord Kibbard's blackmail after tonight.

As they reached the ballroom, he entwined his fingers with hers.

"Wyatt, no one in the *ton* holds hands," she whispered to him.

He grinned. "We do. We are newlyweds. We will be forgiven anything."

He looked so boyish as he said this. Her heart did flip-flops just thinking this man was all hers now.

Wyatt stepped to the butler and said something to him. He raised an eyebrow and merely nodded before announcing, "The Duke and Duchess of Winslow . . . and the Duke and Duchess of

Amesbury."

As they stepped into the room, she heard the gasps before enthusiastic applause broke out. Of course, she saw disappointment on the faces of a few mamas, seeing another duke had been felled in marriage and was no longer available to their hopeful daughters.

The four made it only a few paces into the ballroom before they were surrounded by well-wishers. He had warned her they would be fawned over. After all, they were a duke and duchess.

Miles and Emery slipped away, leaving them to face the gathered crowd. She spoke to more people in those minutes than she had the entire Season. Several of her previous suitors, including Lord Gimble and Lord Airedale, made a point of wishing her well and telling Wyatt how fortunate he was to have found his duchess.

"I knew you would wed His Grace," Lord Pomeroy said. "Amesbury oozes charisma. He is intelligent, as well. I hope he takes good care of you." The earl smiled wistfully. "And I hope you have many children."

"I wish you well, my lord," Meadow said. "You are a good man and will make for a good husband."

"Just not to you," he said ruefully. "Good evening, Your Grace. And the best of luck."

Their hosts for the evening made their way over, asking for Wyatt and Meadow to open the ball with them. Wyatt agreed and led her to the center of the dance floor. Meadow scanned the room but didn't locate Lord Kibbard.

The musicians commenced and she found herself being twirled about by her new husband, knowing every eye in the ballroom must be upon them. She was glad to be wearing the gown she had donned for her wedding, knowing it emphasized her best assets.

The dance concluded and others now joined them on the floor. Wyatt had told her she would accept no dance card this evening. He would dance the first few dances with her and then they would seek out Lord Kibbard. After meeting with the earl, they would go home. Since almost everything she owned had already been packed, Tilda's maid had finished the job early this afternoon and her trunks had been taken to Wyatt's townhouse during the wedding.

Including the battered one containing the lithographs.

He agreed with her that disposing of them in town might draw too much unwanted attention from his servants. Once they reached Amberwood, he said it would be the first thing they did, burning the entire trunk and its contents within. Meadow didn't think she would breathe easily until that had been accomplished.

They danced thrice more, the room tittering each time because even newlyweds never did so. She realized she had married a man who didn't care for conventions.

And was glad she had.

"Shall we get some ratafia?" he asked.

"I would like that. I am feeling parched," she replied.

They received more congratulations as they made their way to the punch bowl.

As Wyatt handed her a cup, Meadow said, "I wonder if he is here."

"He is. I spied him during our last dance."

Immediately, a chill rushed through her.

"Come, let us stroll leisurely on the terrace. I have the feeling that Lord Kibbard will join us."

Her husband led her through a set of French doors. A slight breeze cooled the evening air. They moved along the terrace, passing two couples, and then paused at its end, waiting.

As Wyatt had predicted, Meadow saw Lord Kibbard step from the ballroom and begin to move toward them. Her heart sped up as he approached. It still surprised her. He seemed so ordinary. Why would such a bland man have such perverse inclinations?

"Ah, I hear that congratulations are in order," Kibbard began. "You thought to protect Lady Selfridge."

"It is Her Grace, the Duchess of Amesbury," Wyatt corrected. "And yes, naturally, my wife is under my protection. You are to never speak her name—nor mine."

The earl chuckled. "Salacious gossip has a way of getting out, Your Grace. You cannot control everything."

Wyatt took a step forward. "Your finances are shaky, my lord. You have made some very poor investments as of late. You owe quite a few merchants around town and beyond."

The earl's brows arched. "Oh? Are you telling me that you will pay me to keep silent?"

"You misunderstood."

Meadow heard the cold, deadly words and almost flinched, seeing a side of Wyatt he had never revealed before now.

"If you even think of speaking ill of my wife, Kibbard, I will destroy you. You won't receive a farthing from me. Do I make myself clear?"

"Of course, Your Grace. But wouldn't it be wise to allow me to take the lithographs off your hands? That way, you would no longer have to worry about them."

"My wife wishes them destroyed," Wyatt said. "No one is to see them—or sell them to others."

"How disappointing," Lord Kibbard remarked, as if they were talking about rain disrupting a planned garden party instead of the vile pictures. He looked to her. "There is a beauty in them, Your Grace. Perhaps you will change your mind."

"Never," she vowed.

The earl took a threatening step toward her. Wyatt stepped between them.

"This is the last time you will ever approach either one of us, Kibbard," her new husband growled. "I mentioned your debts. I can assure you that they would only be the beginning of your very public downfall. I am giving you an opportunity to stand down. I reiterate—there is to be no contact between us. No gossip which you spread. Else I will crush you. Your reputation will be shattered. I will pulverize you financially so that you

haven't even a farthing to feed or clothe yourself.

"And that would only be the beginning, Kibbard. My annihilation of you will break you physically and emotionally. By the time I am finished, you will be obliterated and wish you were dead."

Meadow saw fear spring to Lord Kibbard's eyes, the first sign of any weakness the earl had displayed.

"I am a duke," Wyatt continued. "One of the most powerful men in England. I have the ear of many influential men. You know I am capable of destroying you. Walk away before I do so and never threaten my duchess or me ever again—else you will live to regret it."

The earl now quaked in fear.

"If you will excuse us," Wyatt said politely, his menacing tone replaced by one of civility.

He led her back inside the ballroom. Meadow found herself trembling from their encounter.

"Might we leave?" she asked him.

Before he could reply, Miles and Emery joined them.

"Emery is exhausted after planning the wedding supper and all of today's excitement," Miles told them. "We were thinking of leaving and wondered if you might join us. If not, we would like to borrow your carriage, Wyatt, and then send it back."

"We were ready to depart ourselves," he said easily. "After all, we are newlyweds and eager to celebrate our marriage."

Meadow found herself blushing.

They found their hosts and thanked them for the invitation to the evening's event and said they were leaving early.

"I quite understand, Your Grace," said the earl. "You have a wedding night to enjoy. Thank you for gracing us with your presence this evening."

They returned to the carriage and Blevins dropped Miles and Emery at their townhouse before proceeding to take her and Wyatt home.

Home . . .

Meadow had never really thought of any place as home. She had lived in houses. First, with her parents and then with Lord Selfridge. After his death, Tilda and Marshmore had taken her in. They had all been places. Not a home. She realized that home wasn't a place. It was a person.

It was Wyatt.

They arrived and her new husband escorted her upstairs to her bedchamber, where he removed the pins from her hair and ran his fingers through her locks. He helped her undress until she stood naked before him. Lacing his fingers through hers, he led her through her dressing room and into his and beyond to the ducal bedchamber.

"Your turn," he said, an impish smile on his face.

Meadow took her time undressing him, admiring his broad shoulders and flat stomach. The perfectly shaped calves. The light dusting of hair on his chest. His manhood jutted out and she clasped it, causing him to suck in a quick breath.

"Join me in our bed, Your Grace," he said huskily, leading her to it.

They made love, discovering things about each other's bodies, giving and receiving pleasure. A whole new world was opening to her, thanks to this wonderful man.

"I love you," he said as she lay nestled in his arms afterward. "I hope you will stay with me each night. I know it isn't usual for a married couple to sleep together but if you don't remain here, I fear I will only follow you to your bed each night."

She kissed his chest. "You are my home, Wyatt. Where I always want to be. By your side."

"Good," he said, his satisfied tone pleasing her. "Go to sleep, my love. I will always be here when you awake."

Meadow closed her eyes, feeling secure.

And most of all, loved.

SHE AWOKE WITH Wyatt's arms encircling her, her back pressed against his front. From his even breathing, Meadow knew he was still asleep. She luxuriated in his arms, thinking back on last night. He had made love to her twice. Once when they had arrived home and once when he had awakened her in the middle of the night. It seemed that he shared the hunger she had for him. She didn't know if it would ever be satisfied but knew they had a lifetime to explore it.

Together.

Funny, she had never felt a part of anything. Not her own family. Her mother rarely saw her, only having Meadow's nanny or governess trot her out occasionally. Once Meadow arrived, her mother never seemed interested in talking to her or sharing anything. She saw her father even less. He had made known his disappointment in only having a female child. She could count on one hand the times they had been alone in one another's company. She hadn't even known about his death until weeks later. Selfridge mentioned it casually in passing, that he had received word and hadn't wanted to bother her with the news. Hearing of her father's death had meant nothing.

Her marriage had been an empty one, with no closeness between her and Lord Selfridge. He had acquired her and then forgotten about her, spending a majority of his time in London and only returning home for brief periods of time.

Now, though, she had Wyatt. A man who loved her completely. One who seemed interested in everything she had to say. She knew they would build a new life together and couldn't wait for children to appear. She also had Emery as her friend. Her very first one. It pleased her greatly that Amberwood and Wildwood were only twenty or so miles apart, with Amberwood about ten miles southeast of Maidstone and Wildwood ten miles north of the city. Meadow envisioned spending many good times with Emery and Miles, watching their children play with one another. Perhaps there might even be a marriage or two between their children.

Wyatt stirred and his arms tightened about her. His lips brushed her nape and traveled along the curve of her shoulder before he made his way back up, licking and nipping.

"You taste divine, Duchess," he murmured, his palm splayed against her belly, slowly traveling downward.

Her breath hitched as he touched the thatch of curls and slid a finger inside her.

"You like that?"

"I like everything you do to me," she admitted.

He continued stroking her until ecstasy made her call out his name. Quickly, he replaced his finger with his rod, thrusting slowly at first until she begged him to move faster. Her husband followed instructions well, bringing her to the heights of pleasure again as he cried out his own.

"Happy?" he asked as he hovered over her.

"Deliriously," she replied.

"Shall we rise—or stay in bed all day?" he asked, his finger skimming lightly down her arm.

"We can do that once we reach Amberwood. Besides, we have a houseguest. We better go meet him for breakfast."

Wyatt helped her dress and then returned to his own room, calling for Frame. Meadow went downstairs and found Finch already in the breakfast room.

"Good morning," she said. "I hope you slept well."

"I did. The duke's guest bed is far more comfortable than the one at my vicarage."

A footman brought her tea and she added cream and sugar as another placed a plate before her.

"Do you enjoy being a vicar?" Meadow asked.

"I suppose so. At least I get to marry off my friends to beautiful women," he teased.

"Why did you choose that path? Especially since the other four Terrors all went to war."

He sighed. "I suppose because I thought I might be able to save my own soul. Along with a handful of others."

"Why do you need saving?" she asked, curious about this new Terror, remembering that Wyatt had told her each of the Terrors shared with the others their tales—except for Finch.

"Don't we all?" he asked, obviously wanting to avoid the topic. Then he said, "I have quite a bit of anger inside me, Meadow. If I had gone to war and allowed it free rein, I might have lost myself completely."

His honesty startled her but she said, "Wyatt and Miles are here for you whenever you need them. Emery and I are also here, as well. If you ever need an escape, you are more than welcome at Amberwood."

Finch gazed at her a long minute and then said, "Thank you. I shall keep that in mind."

Wyatt joined them and the mood lightened considerably, the two men comfortable with one another and teasing each other unmercifully.

"So, this is what it is like to have brothers," she said, laughing. "Maybe it is a good thing I didn't have any."

"You have them now," Finch said, smiling. "You'll never get rid of Miles and me. And hopefully, one day Bonaparte will be defeated and Donovan and Hart can finally come home."

"Yes, but they will always be in the king's army," Wyatt pointed out. "Who knows what conflicts lie in England's future?"

"You and Miles never thought you would sell out," Meadow said. "And yet here you are, both dukes. Anything could be in your friends' futures."

Wyatt took her hand and kissed it. "What is in your future today, Your Grace?"

She loved the tingles shooting through her at his touch.

"I plan to spend the morning looking over your house."

"Our house," he corrected.

"Our house," she agreed. "I want to become familiar with it and the staff before we leave tomorrow. Will Frame be packing for you?"

Her husband nodded. "I have told him we are leaving in the

morning. It's up to him to be ready to go. What of a lady's maid for you? Now that you are not at your cousin's, surely you need one. Unless you wish to allow me to take on that position," he said suggestively.

"You are worse than Miles and Emery," Finch proclaimed. "And I didn't think that possible."

Meadow ignored him, knowing it was all in good fun. "This afternoon, I will be at Emery's. She and Miles are also leaving for Wildwood tomorrow morning and we are spending the afternoon together."

"You seem like fast friends," Finch noted.

"We became close quickly," she said. "We have much in common. I am happy our country estates are located as close together as they are." She glanced to Wyatt. "I have told Finch that he may come and visit us anytime he likes."

"Gad, we'll never be rid of him," Wyatt complained. "He'll come so often, he'll expect to have his own rooms."

"One room will do," Finch said. "Or perhaps a sitting room and a bedchamber." He smiled. "I do appreciate the invitation, Meadow."

"I hope you will take us up on it," she told him.

They finished breakfast and then she walked the townhouse from top to bottom with the housekeeper, making note of little things she might want to change for when they were next in town. Once she finished, she took the carriage to Emery's townhouse, where a flurry of activity occurred.

The butler took her up to the drawing room and Emery asked for tea while they chatted.

"Your household seems quite busy today," Meadow re-marked.

"Yes, we are getting ready to depart for Wildwood. I don't have much to do with it. The butler and housekeeper know what needs to be accomplished. Besides, Miles told me to rest today. He thinks I overtaxed myself yesterday. He worries about the baby."

"Are you feeling well?"

"I am. I was only nauseous for a few weeks in the beginning. Right now, I have an amazing amount of energy. My mother told me that will eventually fade, the closer I get to the birth."

"Have you missed her while you've been in London?"

Emery nodded. "I have. I have never been apart from her until Miles and I came to town. Mama and I are very close."

"I envy you."

Her friend reached to take Meadow's hand. "I will share her with you. I am so grateful to have met you, Meadow."

She smiled. "I feel the same."

"I know. Why don't we go to Gunter's once more before we leave town? We can celebrate our friendship."

"I would like that very much. Their ices are marvelous. It is not something we can get once we return to the country. My carriage is still out front. Shall we use it?"

"Yes. Let me fetch my reticule. I will meet you outside."

Meadow returned downstairs and went out the door. The carriage was just past the townhouse's entrance.

She called up to the driver. "Blevins, Her Grace and I would like to go to Gunter's."

His back remained to her, which she thought odd. Usually, the coachman was very friendly.

"Blevins?" she asked.

Still, he remained focused straight ahead, frustrating her.

Meadow started to march toward him, afraid he might not have heard her, when fingers tightened about her arm. She glanced up.

Lord Kibbard had hold of her. Panic seared her.

"I've got her," he said.

The driver finally turned around. It was not Blevins. Meadow opened her mouth to scream.

"I wouldn't, Your Grace," he warned, his free hand pressing something into her side. "If you make a noise, I will gut you here and now on the pavement."

He moved her toward the carriage. The driver leaped down from his seat and opened the door. The earl forced her up the stairs that had already been set out, entering behind her, shoving her into the seat as the door slammed. Quickly, the carriage set off.

Meadow had never been more terrified.

CHAPTER TWENTY-FIVE

"WHERE ARE YOU taking me?" Meadow demanded, sounding far braver than she felt as she scrambled to the far side of the bench, bracing her back against it.

She glanced down and saw the blade in Lord Kibbard's hand, the steel gleaming.

"Away," he said cryptically.

"My husband will kill you."

She knew Wyatt would. He would tear this man limb from limb for taking her.

The earl chuckled. "You might think so but I doubt it. Amesbury will be reasonable. He will give me what I want."

"The lithographs. Why do you want them so badly?"

"Why do you want to keep them from me?" he countered. "Unless you have developed a taste for them."

"Never!" she spat out. "They are depraved. I want nothing to do with them."

He cocked his head. "Then why not turn them over? I would have paid you for them."

"It's wrong to look at something like that."

A gleam shone in his eyes. "Oh, not all of them depict children. I know. I have seen many of them. Selfridge shared them with me. I think you would enjoy trying out some of the positions with your new husband."

Her cheeks burned—because she and Wyatt had actually

done a few of the things.

"Oh, it seems you already have," he commented. "Just think, Your Grace—if you enjoyed those things, surely you might wish to experiment more. Branch out and try other enticing things. Dark pleasure is the best kind of pleasure."

He reached over and brushed a finger along her cheek. She pushed his hand away and crossed her arms protectively, only to have him laugh.

"It is too bad you married Amesbury. I told you I would have done the same. There is much I could teach you." He paused. "Actually, I may do just that before I return you to him."

"Don't think to touch a hair on my head, my lord. It is already bad enough that you kidnapped me in broad daylight. My husband will come after you with a fury you have never known. It would be best if you stopped the carriage now and got out."

Suddenly, a thought occurred to her. "Where is my driver? What did you do with him?"

"He is back at Winslow's house, probably nursing a monstrous headache."

At least Blevins was alive.

Suddenly, Kibbard reached over and yanked hard, tearing away the locket she wore. Meadow hadn't a clue why he would want it. It was the only piece of jewelry she wore, a gift from Tilda, and it contained images of Tilda's boys inside it.

The vehicle slowed and the door opened. She saw a boy standing there, his face terrified as he looked up at Kibbard.

"Here," the earl said, tossing Meadow's locket at him. "You know what to do."

The boy nodded grimly and slammed the door. Immediately, the carriage started up again.

She chastised herself. She should have tried to leap out when the door had been opened briefly. Or at least tried to scream. That chance had been lost, though. Perhaps she could reason with Kibbard. He had acted rashly. He hadn't thought through the consequences of what taking her might mean.

"Please, my lord," she begged. "Return me to my husband. Or stop the carriage. Let me out. You may take it. Just—"

"I will do no such thing!" he roared, anger rising in him. "I want that collection. I will have it."

A thought occurred to her. "You don't want it for yourself, do you? Oh, you might keep one or two lithographs—but you are going to sell it, aren't you? In fact, I suspect you already have a buyer and that is why you are so eager to put your hands upon it. Wyatt said you were in debt."

He shook his head. "Beautiful and clever. Too clever, if you ask me. Yes, I have a buyer. One who enjoys unique items. I promised it to him upon Selfridge's death. Your husband told me the collection would come to me when he passed. Since it didn't, I will take it for myself. That—and a hundred thousand pounds."

"What? I don't understand?"

"Oh, I will ask Amesbury for the lithographs. And I will also require a ransom for your return to be included."

"One hundred thousand pounds? Are you mad?"

"Not at all. Amesbury is incredibly wealthy. He will think you worth it. Selfridge paid seventy-five thousand for you."

Meadow shuddered. She had been sold for a fortune. Her father must have been terribly in debt. Selfridge must have wanted her desperately by agreeing to pay such an outrageous sum.

Would Wyatt pay for her return?

"It is too bad you aren't a virgin any longer and you've had your wedding night with your husband," the earl said. "I would have enjoyed claiming your virginity."

Her eyes went wide at the remark.

"Oh, you think just because I might enjoy sex with children, both boys and girls, that I would not want it with a grown woman?" He shook his head. "I have had men. Women. Young. Old. Children not yet five years of age."

Her belly tightened in fear and loathing.

"You are disgusting," she told him.

"I enjoy all kinds of amusements, Your Grace. I delight in all pleasures of the flesh and take satisfaction wherever I can find it." He gazed at her hungrily. "I still may find it with you. Married or not."

Fear filled her.

"You cannot do that," she said.

"I can do anything I want," he said, his gaze piercing her. "I hold all the cards now."

Would Wyatt even want her back if this man had abused her? She didn't know.

"Where are we going?" Meadow finally asked after some minutes had passed.

"Just south of Hertford. My country seat is in Hertfordshire. We should be there in less than two hours' time."

"How will Wyatt know where I am? Or what you want from him?"

"Oh, that has been arranged. He will receive a note, delivered by an old friend of mine. It will contain the instructions he needs. Hopefully, it will cause him to go mad with worry. He will be desperate to have you returned to him. I plan to claim every advantage I can."

Wyatt would tear London apart looking for her. Would he suspect that Lord Kibbard had kidnapped her and left town? Would Blevins be able to tell Wyatt anything to help him find her?

With confidence in her husband, she stared at the earl and said, "You have made the worst mistake of your life, my lord. My husband will annihilate you. On that, you have my word."

⁂

WYATT TOSSED HIS reins to a groom, as did Miles and Finch. The three had gone for a ride along Rotten Row and now adjourned to his study. He rang for refreshments since he was ravenous.

At least for food now. For Meadow later.

When tea and cakes arrived, he asked, "Has Her Grace returned home yet?"

"No, Your Grace," the maid serving them replied. "She said she would be spending the entire afternoon with the Duchess of Winslow."

"Let them have their fun," Miles said. "We are having ours." He sat back in his chair. "It's just so good to have you with us, Finch. We need to find you a parish near Maidstone so we can see you more often."

Finch shook his head. "Lord Markham has been quite good to me. I wouldn't think of abandoning the living he has provided me. It would have to take an act of God for me to leave."

Suddenly, the door flew open and Emery rushed in.

"He's taken her!" she exclaimed.

Wyatt didn't have to ask who *he* was. Instinct gave him the answer.

"Lord Kibbard," he said, his voice filled with venom.

"Come sit, my love," Miles urged, leading Emery to a seat and kneeling beside her. "Are you all right?"

"I am fine, Miles. But we must find Meadow."

Wyatt joined Miles, kneeling on the other side of Emery. "Tell us everything you can remember. Don't rush. Every little detail is important."

She nodded. "Meadow came to visit me. We decided to go to Gunter's one last time. To rejoice in our friendship and the bond that has grown so quickly between us. I went to retrieve my reticule and bonnet. Meadow offered her carriage since it already sat ready in front of our townhouse. I was to meet her downstairs."

Emery paused and drew a breath. "She wasn't in the foyer. Our butler said she had stepped outside. I did the same and saw Lord Kibbard—that man from Gunter's—shoving her into the carriage. He climbed in after her." She bit her lip.

"What?" he urged.

"I saw a knife in his hand, Wyatt."

He went cold inside. Then the part of him that had been a spy and faced the ultimate dangers took over.

"He won't harm her. He needs her. The blade was but a threat to make her fear him. Go on."

"The driver slammed the door behind them and leaped into his seat. They took off. So fast that even the stairs were left behind."

"Which way did they head?" he asked.

"North. And I saw a man lying in the street. It was your driver, Wyatt. Blevins. He was unconscious. I had him brought inside and a footman went to fetch the doctor. I don't know how he is. I came here as fast as I could."

"You did well, sweetheart," Miles said, pressing kisses upon her hand.

"He took her because of those drawings, didn't he?" Emery asked.

"Yes," Wyatt confirmed. "He is desperate for them. It goes beyond wanting them for personal pleasure. Perhaps he has promised them to another. He is in heavy debt. He might have agreed to sell the lithographs and that is why he is fighting so hard to obtain them, having sold something he doesn't even possess."

"He won't get them," she declared. "You three will see to that—and getting Meadow back."

He had admired Miles' choice in a wife and now saw how steel lay under her surface. Just as Meadow's core was firm with steel.

"Should we call in the Bow Street Runners?" Miles asked. "They have had success with these types of situations."

"No," Wyatt said firmly. "A Bow Street Runner may be good—but we are three Terrors. No one stands a chance against us."

"He's right," Finch agreed. "We should go to Kibbard's townhouse first. Do either of you know where it is?"

"No," Miles answered. "But we can find out easily."

Wyatt rang for Winkle and asked him to learn the location of the earl's townhouse.

"Servants talk," he explained when Finch looked puzzled. "Kibbard isn't very social. It would take time to learn who his friends are. The network of servants rivals anything I put into place during my spying days."

"Let me take Emery home and –"

"You will do no such thing," she declared. "I am not some delicate, hothouse flower, Miles. I want to be here. I want to help."

Within half an hour, after his servants had checked with others in neighboring houses, they had an address for Lord Kibbard.

"Something odd is going on in the household, Your Grace," Winkle said once he had informed Wyatt of the address. "A majority of the servants have been let go in recent months. There is only a handful left in the household. Apparently, Lord Kibbard has sold off most everything of value within his London townhome. Rumor has it he will sell it by next Season."

"Thank you, Winkle," Wyatt said. Once the butler left the study, he added, "Debts. Kibbard was trying to cut costs by letting servants go."

"Do you think he is holding Meadow there?" Finch asked. "It would be easier with fewer servants to ask questions."

"We will go there first," he said. "If Meadow isn't there, we'll quiz the staff and ascertain where Kibbard's country estate is located."

"You need to stay here, my love," Miles told Emery. Before she could protest, he added, "I will not have you risk your health—or that of our child's."

Wearily, she agreed. "If you go to the country, though, I want to come."

"We'll see," Wyatt answered in order to keep the peace between the spouses. "It could be hundreds of miles from here, Emery. You do not need to undergo a journey such as that."

"I would," she said stubbornly. "Meadow would do the same for me." She paused. "If she isn't in town, you will come back and tell me, won't you? You three won't leave without letting me know where you head?"

"I promise," Finch said. "My word should be taken more seriously than these two since I am a man of the cloth." He smiled wryly.

"Let's go," Wyatt said.

They took the carriage Emery had come in since Wyatt now had none of his own. His other vehicles, such as the phaeton or curricle, were too small to seat the three of them. He recalled driving Meadow to the park, just the two of them, the feel of her lush body pressed against his in the tight quarters. He pushed the notion aside.

He would get her back. They would get her back.

They spilled from the carriage and marched up to the door. Wyatt pounded upon it fiercely, as if his raps could knock the door from its hinges.

A servant answered. "Yes?" he asked timidly, confronted by three large, angry men.

It was obvious he wasn't a butler from his dress and bearing. No London butler would be so cowed.

"Lord Kibbard. We must see him at once," he said.

"His lordship isn't here, my lord. My lords," he corrected.

"Where the bloody hell is he?" Wyatt demanded and the footman flinched.

"He said he would be out of town, my lord. He didn't say for how long. We never ask. Lord Kibbard comes and goes as he pleases. I'm not certain if he went back to Hertfordshire or to a house party but he isn't here."

"Hertfordshire is damned close," Miles said. "Where in Hertfordshire?"

"Just a few miles south of Hertford." The servant provided them with the name of Kibbard's estate and the closest village.

Wyatt stormed back to the carriage, the others following.

Miles ordered the driver to return to the Duke of Amesbury's residence and the three men climbed inside.

"We'll need to be armed," he said. "We don't know what we will be stepping into."

They remained silent until they arrived, going straight to Wyatt's study. Quickly, they told Emery what the servant had said.

"Then you'll go to Hertfordshire?" she asked.

"Yes," he confirmed. "The footman had no reason to lie."

Suddenly, something crashed through the window, sending glass flying. Wyatt glanced out and saw a boy standing there, his mouth agape.

"Get him!" he shouted and Miles and Finch immediately fled the room.

He looked to the floor and saw it was a brick which had been tossed through the window. Tied to it with brown string was a folded page.

His gut told him this was a ransom note from Lord Kibbard.

Chapter Twenty-Six

W ITH TREMBLING FINGERS, Wyatt reached for the brick. He lifted it and untied the string, freeing the note. Placing the brick on his desk, he opened the page. Inside was a small, gold locket. One which he had fastened about Meadow's neck only this morning.

At the time, he had thought about never having seen her wear any other jewelry. He had determined to lavish some upon her. She would never ask for anything extravagant but he wanted to give her the world.

Now, he held something of hers. He only prayed he would get her back, safe and whole.

Wyatt glanced to the sparse writing on the parchment.

Bring the collection to my estate—but only after you have obtained banknotes which issue me one hundred thousand pounds. Once you produce the notes with my name as the payee and a cashier's signature, I will exchange what I have for what you want.

He refolded the note. Kibbard had been clever. He hadn't signed the ransom demand and had worded it vaguely so anyone reading it would have no clue as to what was offered in trade. Anger seared through him. He would use the very knife Emery had seen in Kibbard's hand and slice the earl into a thousand pieces.

Miles and Finch appeared, a boy held fast between them. He was gaunt but decently dressed, no obvious holes or tatters in his clothing.

"Let me go!" he shrieked, struggling to free himself as a bevy of curse words flew from his lips.

"Enough!" Wyatt shouted and the boy fell silent. Their gazes meeting, he said, "You cannot flee. My friends will only bring you back each time you try. It will get old very fast. What I need from you is information and then you will be allowed to leave. Agreed?"

The boy contemplated Wyatt's words and then spat out a sullen, "Yes."

He looked to Finch and Miles and nodded. Reluctantly, they released the boy. Wyatt held up the note. He wanted to shake the boy and shout at him but something held him back.

Instead, he asked, "What is your name?"

The question surprised the child. "Scrunch."

"Scrunch. I see. Well, Scrunch, how old are you?"

The boy shrugged. "Dunno. Eleven. Maybe twelve?"

So, he was from the streets. Yet he was dressed much better than any urchin Wyatt had seen.

"How long has Kibbard used you?"

The boy's mouth trembled. "I can't remember," he admitted. "But he's done with me. He always is when you get too old."

He kept from flinching.

Scrunch added, "He told me if I delivered the note, that would be it. I would finally be free. I didn't have to come back. If I didn't bring it here, he'd hunt me down and do terrible things to me." Fire lit in the boy's eyes. "I know when to believe him, my lord. That's why I did it. I had to do whatever I could to win my freedom."

Scrunch had said he might be eleven or twelve, close in age to Philip, Joan's boy. Yet Scrunch looked years younger, underfed, his eyes haunted. All because he had been trapped by Lord Kibbard. Pity filled Wyatt.

"I have a stable boy named Philip. He's only a bit older than you. Would you like to come to Kent, Scrunch? You could work in my stables with Philip."

The boy frowned, his eyes wary. "No. I'll take my chances here. In London. I ain't never been anywhere else."

"Kent is very pretty. The country air is clean and fresh. It would give you a new start, Scrunch," he said. "A paying job. A roof over your head and good meals. If you remain here, what will you do?"

He saw the boy wavering. "Why should I trust you?" he asked warily.

"Because I am nothing like Lord Kibbard," Wyatt revealed. "He is evil incarnate. I want to help you—and any boy like you. Free you and them from the earl."

"The girls, too?" Scrunch asked.

He went cold inside. "Yes. The girls, too," he promised.

"Would they also get a job?" the boy asked, hope in his eyes.

"Yes. Every last one of them."

"All right. What do you want in return?"

"Tell me everything about this locket," he said, holding it up. "And the note you were to deliver. Where Lord Kibbard might be now."

"He told me to wait at a street corner. I already had the note he wrote. I don't know what it says. I don't read. The carriage stopped and I went to the door. He threw the locket at me."

Scrunch paused. Swallowed. "There was a lady inside with him. She was pretty. She looked scared." His eyes welled with tears. "I shut the door. They drove away. I was to come to Mayfair. To your address, my lord. Lord Kibbard showed me which house before. I put the necklace in the note and tied it up so it would stay. Then I was to throw it and run."

"Besides looking frightened, did the lady seem hurt?"

"No, my lord. Just scared," Scrunch said. "He was taking her to Hertford. I heard him tell Bovry this morning. Bovry was the one driving the carriage."

"Are there other children in the country?" Wyatt asked.

Scrunch shrugged. "Dunno. I ain't never been before."

Once Wyatt got Meadow back, he would claim all the children Kibbard had stolen from the streets. After all, what good was it to be a duke if he didn't use the power that came with it for good?

He placed a hand on Scrunch's bony shoulder. "You did very well, Scrunch."

"I did?"

The boy looked as if he had never heard a word of praise in his life.

"Very well," Wyatt echoed. "Ring for Frame," he told Finch.

"I'll fetch him instead," his friend said, opening the door.

Wyatt saw a group of servants gathered outside it, including his valet. "Frame, come in here."

The valet hurried inside. "Yes, Your Grace?" he asked eagerly.

"You're a duke?" Scrunch said, his eyes round with wonder upon learning that.

"I am," he confirmed. "This is Frame, my valet. Frame, this is Scrunch. He will be going to the country with us and serving in my stables. He needs a good meal in him. And a bath. An extra set of clothes would also be nice."

"Of course, Your Grace. I will see to it now. Come along . . . Scrunch."

"Wait," Wyatt said. "Scrunch is more like a nickname. Do you recall your true name?"

The boy sadly shook his head. "No, Your Grace. I've been Scrunch as long as I've been at Lord Kibbard's. I don't remember much before that."

"Then you and Frame will work on coming up with a name for you. A proper name."

The boy's eyes lit up. "I get to pick my name?" he asked.

"You do. Take your time. Don't rush it. But make sure it is a good one. One that you will enjoy hearing being called for the rest of your days."

Suddenly, Scrunch rushed to Wyatt. He threw his arms about Wyatt's waist.

"Thank you, Your Grace. Thank you."

He patted the child's back. "You are very welcome, Scrunch. Go along with Frame now."

"Yes, Your Grace."

The pair left and Frame closed the door.

"I wonder how many children are at the London home," Finch said. "Much less in the country."

"We will take care of them between us," Miles said. "We have enough estates to do so."

"Let's prepare ourselves," he said, happy his friend would share in the burden of finding the abused children homes. "Although Amberwood is better stocked with weapons, I have enough here to aid us on our mission."

Once they had gathered several pistols and ammunition, Wyatt asked Emery to remain behind.

"I hope we will return by this evening," he told her. "Until then, look after Scrunch. Perhaps you can help him choose his name. If you can, see if you can find out how many children are at Kibbard's townhouse. Their names. Approximate ages. It would be helpful to have as much information as we can."

"I would be happy to, Wyatt." Emery kissed his cheek. "Give Meadow my love. I will remain here until you return."

He left with Finch, allowing Miles to have a private goodbye with his wife. Glancing up, he saw a footman carrying the battered trunk upon his shoulder, the lewd lithographs inside it. Wyatt wanted to bring it with them.

Because he wanted to watch Kibbard's face as the trunk burned.

Soon, they were on their way, heading north toward Hertfordshire.

Finch said, "I saw the trunk placed atop Miles' carriage. Are you going to force Kibbard to see its contents destroyed?"

"Yes," he ground out, thinking of all the ways he would punish the man who had taken his wife.

"Wyatt, once we have Meadow in hand, you must stay with her," Miles said. "Leave Kibbard to us."

"No," he said, shaking his head angrily. "He is mine."

"Vengeance is mine, sayeth the Lord," Finch said. "I am an instrument of His will. You will need to tend to Meadow. No matter how strong she is, she will have gone through a horrific experience. She will need you. No one else."

"Leave Kibbard to us," Miles affirmed.

"What will you do to him?" Wyatt asked.

Finch gave him a grim smile. "You don't want to know."

MEADOW'S STOMACH GURGLED noisily. She hadn't eaten anything since breakfast this morning.

Once more, she tugged at her wrists, bound together behind her back. Already, her shoulders and back screamed in agony, as if they were lit on fire. No matter how hard she pulled, the cords binding her held fast. Her ankles had also been secured with heavy cords to ensure she wouldn't run off.

The most humiliating thing had been when, after she had been restrained, Lord Kibbard had yanked her fichu free from her neckline. He'd taken the triangular scarf and used it to gag her. Then the earl had run his fingers along the low neckline, now revealed with the fichu missing. Meadow had shouted at him to stop but the gag muffled her response.

Kibbard had laughed, his fingers plunging inside her gown to squeeze her breast painfully. Then he'd pinched her nipple hard. Tears had come to her eyes but she had glared at him all the same.

Wyatt wouldn't have to kill the earl when he came for her. Meadow decided she would be the one to do it herself.

Kibbard and his man, the one who had handled her roughly

as he restrained her, had left after that. Kibbard angered her.

Bovry frightened her.

She had seen the gleam in his eyes and worried he might come back after he did whatever his employer had tasked him to do.

And she would be helpless to defend herself from him.

Once again, she pulled at the ropes in frustration.

They had left her on her side but Meadow had pushed herself up soon after they left, resting her back against the stable's wall. Her belly growled again.

Food was the least of her concerns now. Freeing herself was what was important.

She scooted toward the empty trough, surrounded by old hay. She hadn't seen any horses when she'd been brought inside. Knowing Kibbard was in debt, she assumed they had been sold off. Bovry had brought in the team that had driven Wyatt's ducal coach and she had heard the sounds of the horses being rubbed down and fed after he placed them in various stalls.

Would Wyatt ride his horse to her? Would Finch or Miles accompany him?

Meadow fought the tears that wanted to flow, knowing they would serve no purpose. She needed to save whatever strength she had in order to try and escape.

Finally, she reached the trough and pushed her back against its edge. It wasn't sharp by any means but she began rubbing the cords binding her wrists against it, moving her arms slightly up and down. Though it sent jolting pains through her, she continued the action, desperate to escape the madman who had kidnapped her.

She wondered if Wyatt had received a ransom note by now. It must have included her locket, the one Kibbard gave the sad-looking boy. She wondered what link the child had with the earl and feared it was an unholy one.

She heard a noise and stopped what she was doing, on alert now. Footsteps sounded, light enough to let her know it wasn't

Kibbard or Bovry returning.

A young girl of about twelve or thirteen appeared at the stall's door, peering in at her. She saw a tray in the girl's hands.

"I brung you something to eat."

She balanced the tray on her hip and opened the stall's door, stepping inside and setting the tray on the ground.

"He said I was to untie the gag only. I'll feed you."

Meadow nodded, her jaw weary of being restrained for so long.

The girl reached behind Meadow's head and unknotted the scarf, pulling it away. Immediately, the corners of her mouth ached as the rest of her mouth and jaw throbbed.

"What's your name?" she asked, wanting to establish some kind of rapport with the child. She didn't think she would be able to persuade the girl to remove the bindings but she might be able to learn valuable information.

"Sally," she mumbled.

"Sally. That is a lovely name."

The girl lifted a slice of apple to Meadow's lips. She bit into it, the juice flooding her mouth, making her realize how dry it had grown. She chewed carefully, not rushing, not wanting this time to be over too quickly.

Sally placed another slice up to Meadow and she eagerly took it. The girl watched as she chewed.

"You're old," she observed.

Meadow swallowed. "I am five and twenty. How old are you?"

Sally frowned. "I don't know."

"How long have you been here?"

"A long time. I hardly remember London at all."

"You lived in town?"

The girl nodded. "Mum died. I didn't have nowhere to go. I ate out of bins. I stole. Until *he* found me."

She didn't need to be told it was Lord Kibbard Sally referred to.

"He promised me things. Food. Nice clothes. I just had to come with him."

"I don't blame you. I would have gone, too."

"You would have?" Sally frowned. "I wish I didn't. He hurts me."

Meadow thought of the lithographs and shuddered.

"Has he hurt you, too?" Sally asked.

"He took me from my husband. He has me tied up." She paused. "You could free me."

Sally's eyes grew wide. "He would kill me. No. No, I can't."

"My husband is a duke, Sally. That is a very powerful lord. If we escape Lord Kibbard, then my husband will take you in. I need a maid. A lady's maid. Perhaps you would like to be one."

Longing filled the girl's face. "Do you live in London?"

"Sometimes. I just wed my husband and we were leaving for the country. For Kent. You would like it there. The estate is called Amberwood."

The girl fed Meadow a piece of cheese. She chewed it, letting Sally think. Meadow accepted several more bites and then tried again.

"I know he hurts you, Sally. No one wants to be hurt. I can help you. But first, you must help me."

The girl shot to her feet. "I can't. He's a lord. He would find us."

She reached for the fichu. Before she could place the gag, Meadow said, "My husband is much more powerful than Lord Kibbard. Help me, Sally. He will take you with me. And any other child who is being hurt."

The scarf was forced around her mouth again. Sally tied it—but not nearly as tightly as Bovry had.

The girl studied Meadow a long minute and then quickly fled the stall. Meadow only hoped she had planted a seed in the girl's mind, one which might grow, convincing Sally to help them both escape.

CHAPTER TWENTY-SEVEN

MEADOW CONTINUED RUBBING the cords against the edge of the trough, feeling she was getting nowhere. Her neck, shoulders, and back radiated pain. She stopped for a minute, unable to wipe away the perspiration which trickled from her temple down to her jawline.

At least she had freed herself from the pesky gag. Sally hadn't fastened it well, probably feeling sorry for Meadow. It had only taken a few turns of her head and bobbing her head up and down for it to come loose. It now rested against her throat.

She wondered what time it was. She had gone to Emery's just before one o'clock and had only been there a short while before they decided to leave for Gunter's. Lord Kibbard had said the journey to his estate was about two hours. Sally had visited her most likely an hour after her arrival. Her best guess was that it was close to six in the evening now. Sunset wouldn't be for another three hours this time of year.

Would Wyatt have received the ransom note by now?

Even if he had, her abductor had asked for an astronomical amount of money. Wyatt would have to wait until the banks opened tomorrow morning before he could arrange to have the money to hand over to Kibbard.

Once, Lord Selfridge had thought her worth seventy-five thousand pounds, a veritable fortune. Meadow considered it wasted money since the viscount had spent it for her and gotten nothing for his purchase, save a wife in name only. Knowing her father, he probably had gone right back to his old ways and begun gambling again, once he had used the money he had received for his daughter to pay his debts. She pitied the man who had inherited the title, sorry for him because she doubted anything would have been left beyond the title itself.

Meadow stilled. Listened. Yes, she heard footsteps, so faint they were almost imperceptible. She prayed it was Sally again, coming to help her escape. With hope, she looked to the stall door, waiting to see who might appear. The faint glow of a lantern moved closer. She held her breath.

After a moment, she saw the blond of Sally's head visible above the stall door before it opened.

"Hello, Sally," she greeted. Not wanting to press too hard to start, Meadow added, "Have you brought me something else to eat?"

The girl set down the lantern and moved hesitantly across the stall. Then from behind her back, she revealed a knife.

"No." Her gaze bored into Meadow. "Did you mean what you said before?"

"That you could be my maid? Of course. Do you know how to sew?"

Sally nodded. "My mum taught me. I haven't done so in a long time, though."

"Well, a lady's maid does need to know how to sew," she said, wanting to draw the girl into conversation. "Did you learn to sew on a button? Or hem a gown?"

Sally nodded. "Both. I would have to practice again. What else?"

"You would take care of my clothes. Make sure they were washed and pressed. Clean my shoes. Help me to bathe and dress each morning and arrange my hair. You'd also assist me every time I needed to change clothes throughout the day."

The girl frowned. "Why would you change your clothes after you got dressed?"

Meadow chuckled, knowing the girl would have no idea how Polite Society worked. "Sometimes, I think that very thing. In London—especially during the Season—ladies must change gowns several times a day."

"What's the Season?"

"It is when many social events are held. I would dress when I rose in a morning gown. I would change in the afternoon if I went to a garden or tea party or if I entertained guests at home. I would change again if I went riding or driving in the park. Again when I went out that night, to a ball or rout or musicale. And then I would certainly need help undressing for bed."

The girl's eyes were round. "You must own a lot of clothes."

"I do. I realize I am very fortunate. Most of my year will be spent in the country, though, instead of town. Would you like that? You would have your own room and—"

"My own room?"

"Yes. It would be small but all yours. Unless you decided you wished to share quarters with another maid."

"Another lady's maid?"

"No, a house maid. You would be my only lady's maid."

"Oh." Sally thought a moment. "I've never had a room to myself. I remember we lived in one room before my mum died. And now . . ." Her voice trailed off.

"Are there other girls here that the earl hurts?"

"Yes." Sally whispered the word. "There are three of us. One went back to London with him a few months ago but he brought another one—a younger one—to take her place."

Meadow's heart ached for these abused girls. "Do you share a room with them?"

Sally nodded. "It's small. We used to always stay inside it until lately. His lordship now has us cleaning the house and doing the cooking. There ain't no one else left to do it."

"Why haven't you run away?" she asked gently.

"Bovry stays in the country with us. He's charged with keeping us in line." She shuddered. "He's worse than the earl."

"He also hurts you?" she prodded.

The girl nodded, misery written across her face.

"If you help me now, Sally, I promise you that not only will you have a place at Amberwood, but the other girls would, as well. If you find that you don't like being a lady's maid, you could do something else on the estate. Work as a parlor maid or even a scullery maid if you want to learn how to cook. It would be honest work."

Sally squeezed her eyes closed. Meadow held her breath.

"I'll do it," the girl finally said. "But we'll have to come back for the others. We can't chance going inside and having Bovry or his lordship finding us. He would kill us."

Meadow believed the girl.

"His Grace and I will make certain we return and free your friends."

"His Grace?"

"That is what a duke is called. I am his wife and a duchess so others address me as Her Grace."

"Not my lady?"

"No. A duke is elevated above other titled gentlemen. The only men above a duke are a prince or the king."

"Blimey," Sally whispered. "No wonder you say I can have my own room. You must be filthy rich."

"My husband is very wealthy but he is also very kind."

Sally began wringing her hands. "He won't like me. Not when he knows what his lordship does to me. He won't want me around you." She began to back up.

"No, Sally, you're wrong. He hates men such as Lord Kibbard. And he loves me. Very much. If I say I want you as my maid, he won't question it."

"He loves you?" the girl asked.

Meadow's throat tightened. "Very much. And I love him. I miss him. I want to be with him again. I want you to come with me."

She prayed her words had persuaded Sally to stay and free

her.

Once more, the girl headed toward Meadow. "All right." She knelt. "Lean up, my lady. Oh, Your Grace."

Meadow did as asked and Sally put the blade to the cords, sawing back and forth. After working some minutes, she felt it loosening. Suddenly, she tugged and her arms came free.

"Yes!" she cried, enveloping Sally in a hug and then crying out as a fierce, painful stinging rippled through her upper body.

"Here, let me help," Sally said, rubbing Meadow's wrists as the feeling came back in them.

Her shoulders and back smarted, now feeling as if they had been set afire. She whimpered and then bit her lip. She was not going to acknowledge the hurt. She needed to move quickly.

"Give me the knife," she said, taking it and bending toward her bound ankles, despite her back protesting the move.

With determination, Meadow gripped the hilt of the blade, moving it back and forth as quickly as she could.

As she did, she asked, "Do you know how to saddle a horse?"

"No. Why?"

"Lord Kibbard abducted me in my own carriage and that man, Bovry, brought the horses into the stalls. If there was a saddle somewhere, we might try to use it to saddle a horse and ride away."

Sally shook her head sadly. "There are no saddles. All the horses were sold off months ago and almost everything with them. The house is bare except for a few pieces of furniture."

Meadow had never ridden without a saddle and wondered if it would even be possible. If they could mount one of the carriage horses and stay on it, it would give them a better chance to elude her kidnappers. Maybe she could lead the other horses from the stables and set them free so that Kibbard or his minion would have to follow them on foot.

The knife finally did its work, slicing through the last bit of cord and she pulled her feet wide.

"Help me up," she said, leaning on Sally for support and then hobbling around the stall while the feeling came back into her legs and feet. Once again, it was as if they had been set on fire. She continued moving about the perimeter of the stall until she could remove her arm from Sally's shoulders and walk on her own.

"I've a plan," she told the girl, the knife still in her hand. She would keep it for protection in case they came across Lord Kibbard or Bovry.

"What?" Sally asked, excitement filling her face.

Suddenly, the stall door opened. Bovry stood there.

"I've a plan, too," he said, moving menacingly toward them.

He grabbed hold of Sally since she was closer and slammed her against the stall's wall. The girl cried out. Bovry pulled her away, striking her in the face before he shoved her back into the wall again. Her head hit it hard and bounced off.

Sally crumpled to the ground and didn't move.

Bovry looked to Meadow, his eyes gleaming with desire. "Want to hear my plan, Duchess? It involves me spreading your legs and having my fun. Just as I do with all those street urchins I bring home for Kibbard and me."

Disgust filled her, knowing this man did the same to Sally and the other young girls Lord Kibbard had taken from the streets of London.

"Do you know who my husband is?"

He shrugged. "Some fancy duke. What of it?"

"Not just some duke. He was in the military. He served as an officer and a spy for Wellington. He is not a man you wish to tangle with. He has killed, both with weapons and his bare hands. If you touch me, he will hurt you beyond anything you could ever imagine. Yours will be a slow death, Mr. Bovry. A horrific one."

Meadow saw his confidence wilt slightly and pressed on.

"See me returned to Amesbury and he will reward you. He is very wealthy. He will make it worth your while to restore me safely to him."

The man hesitated a moment and then shook off her warning. "Kibbard is my half-brother. He is the one I trust. He has promised me enough money so that I need never work again. From the ransom he will get for you. I have been with him many years. I can take him at his word. You make glib promises—but your duke would not have to honor them. He might turn me over to the authorities for my role in your abduction. He might kill me."

Bovry shook his head. "I'll take my chances with Kibbard if it's all the same." He paused. "And I'll have my taste of you now."

Meadow tightened her grip on the hilt in her hand. She had kept it by her side, hidden by the folds of her gown. She would only have one chance. She would have to make the most of it.

Bovry advanced. She stood waiting.

He closed the gap until he stood directly in front of her. "You're a brave one, aren't you? No blubbering. No begging." He grinned. "You will be fun to break."

He reached and clasped her nape, drawing her to him.

Meadow brought the knife up swiftly and jammed it into his gut. As he shrieked, she pulled hard, moving it up inside his chest. Bovry looked at her, stunned, as she shoved him hard and he stumbled backward.

Into the lantern.

It turned on its side, oil spilling out, lighting the hay on fire. Meadow turned and ran to Sally, who still lay motionless.

Shaking her, she cried, "Sally, wake up! Wake up!"

She raised the girl to a sitting position and saw a bit of blood on the ground. It must have been from where her head hit the wooden planks. She tried to lift Sally but the girl was dead weight. Meadow glanced about, panicking, as the fire began spreading.

She had to save Sally.

Bending, she grabbed the girl's ankles and dragged her to the stall's opening, trying to avoid the spreading flames and Bovry's motionless body. She managed to pull Sally down the length of the stables to the entrance, trying to ignore the alarmed whinnying of the horses that had been brought in.

Meadow thought of Wyatt and how he had wanted to save his family's horses from the fire his brother had started.

And as she dragged Sally through the opening, Wyatt was suddenly there.

CHAPTER TWENTY-EIGHT

WYATT HAD RAPPED on the ceiling as they reached the turnoff to Lord Kibbard's estate. The carriage slowed and came to a halt.

"I think we should approach on foot," he told Miles and Finch. "I always preferred getting the lay of the land during my spy days. We can use the trees to hide our approach."

"I agree," Miles said.

"I bow to your military knowledge," Finch told them.

Finch might not have the military experience he and Miles did but Wyatt knew Finch was probably the best shot of the three of them.

They exited the carriage and Miles said, "How long should my driver wait before he approaches?"

"An hour," he replied. "If we need him sooner, one of us can come fetch him. By then, we should have located Meadow."

"And any children Kibbard has here," Finch added, grim determination on his face.

It sickened Wyatt to think of the children such as Scrunch who had been violated at the earl's hands. He had heard of other deviants who had their tastes catered to in various London brothels. But for the earl to have children kept in his homes for his own sinful pleasure was almost more than Wyatt could comprehend.

Death would be too good for Lord Kibbard.

Miles instructed his driver to remain for one hour before coming up the lane and the three men set out, weapons in hand, moving from tree to tree.

"I doubt he has men other than this Bovry," Finch said quietly. "If he's let so many servants go and sold off items of value, he won't have the coin to pay for men to guard his country estate."

"He has to know we're coming," Wyatt insisted.

"I think he's foolish enough to believe you'll actually wait until tomorrow when the banks would be open before you arrive here with the ransom he demanded," Miles noted. "If he was thinking clearly to begin with, he would know not to tangle with you, Wyatt. Desperation has clouded Kibbard's judgment. He needs the money you are supposed to bring, as much as he needs the contents of Selfridge's trunk. Because of that dire need, he believes you will do as asked."

"Then I suppose it's a good thing he has no idea who I really am. What I have done for my country in the name of the king," Wyatt said, knowing he would never tell his friends—nor Meadow—of the acts he had committed during his time at war.

They reached the house, which had a forlorn look about it. Just as the trees lining the drive had lacked being pruned, the landscaping surrounding the house also seemed neglected.

He glanced to his right and saw his ducal coach standing in front of a structure which he assumed to be the stables and pointed it out to his companions.

"The horses must be inside the stables," Miles said. "It will help to have another carriage in case Kibbard has additional children here."

Suddenly, Wyatt saw a billow of smoke coming from one end of the stables.

Fire!

Without waiting for his companions, he took off running toward it. As he ran, he could hear the cries of those horses from long ago. Smell the acrid smoke as the barn burned to the ground. Feel the eyes of so many upon him, pronouncing him guilty.

He reached the entrance and Meadow appeared. Wyatt gave a strangled cry. Dropping his weapons, he threw his arms about her. She was here. Safe. He had her.

He kissed her, grateful that he had found her.

She broke the kiss. "Wyatt. The horses."

He glanced down and spied an unconscious girl on the ground as Finch and Miles rushed up. Finch scooped the girl up and hurried away with her.

"Take Meadow," he said, pushing her toward Miles.

And raced inside the barn.

Everything from years ago rushed back at him—except this time, these were no memories. He cringed at the sound of the fire crackling, eating at the wood and hay. The whinnies of frightened horses, bumping against stall doors in panic, trying to free themselves. The pungent, sharp smell of smoke already filling his lungs.

It didn't matter. He hadn't saved the horses before. He would this time.

He ran to the sound of stomping and bumping and found the first horse, its eyes wild with panic. Ripping the cravat from his throat, Wyatt entered the stall and quickly wrapped the material around the horse's eyes, effectively blinding him. He grabbed the mane in his left hand to guide the horse and stroked it with his right.

"Good boy. That's it. Come along, my friend. We'll get you out of here."

He passed Miles and Finch, who raced by him, knowing they would get the next two horses free. Both men tugged upon their cravats, seeing how Wyatt had used his to calm the horse he led from the stables.

He reached outside, where Meadow sat on the ground, the girl's head in her lap. He realized she had blood all over the front of her.

Racing to her, he fell to his knees.

"You're bleeding."

"No, it's not my blood," she assured him. "Get the last horse."

He looked and saw the horse he had brought out had run away.

"Here, take this." Meadow loosened something about her neck and threw it at him.

Wyatt ran back inside, once again passing Finch and then Miles as they, too, brought a horse from the burning barn.

Something crashed to the ground and he knew the structure was beginning to break apart. Still, he couldn't abandon the final animal to death. Holding the scarf to his nose, he hurried along, blinking rapidly as his eyes burned from the swirling smoke.

Reaching the final horse, he moved quickly, tying the scarf around the horse's eyes. Knowing the barn could come crashing down at any moment, Wyatt gripped the horse's mane and swung atop it, kicking his heels as he gulped air and then held his breath. The horse bolted from the stall and he yanked its head to the right. As they rode through the opening, the building behind him collapsed.

He slowed the horse and leaped off it, heading to join Miles, who tried to move the carriage away.

"We can't do it," he said after joining his friend and pulling with all his might. "Back away. Let it burn."

They abandoned the carriage and returned to Meadow. The girl she tended sat up.

"You're him," she said, her eyes round with awe. "You're the duke. She said you were nice."

"And brave," Meadow added, squeezing the girl's shoulder. "So very, very brave." She looked up at him, her eyes shining with love. "I would like to introduce you to Sally, Your Grace. She is to be my new lady's maid."

His gut told him Sally had somehow helped Meadow and that she wished to reward the girl.

"I am pleased to meet you, Sally. I know you will do a fine

job caring for my wife."

"But first, I must care for Sally," Meadow said. "She will need to see a doctor. She has a nasty bump on the back of her head and it has bled some."

"Is that the blood you wear?" he asked.

Her eyes clouded. "No. I will tell you about that later."

Miles' carriage roared into the open space, the driving yanking back hard on the reins.

"I saw the smoke and then fire, Your Grace," Miles' driver told him. "I hope it's all right that I came."

"A good move on your part," Miles praised. "Let's get Her Grace and young Sally into the carriage."

Wyatt held out a hand and Meadow took it. He brought her to her feet and then bent to retrieve Sally.

A shot rang out, whizzing above his head. Right where he had stood a moment ago.

Lord Kibbard . . .

He whirled and pushed Meadow toward Finch, knowing his friend would protect her, then ran pell-mell toward the earl before he might reload. Reaching him, Wyatt hurled himself at the man, knocking him to the ground. The pistol went flying.

"You dare take what is mine?" roared Wyatt, slamming his fists repeatedly into Kibbard's face. "You abuse children? You are worse than pond scum."

Something caught his fist and he was pulled off the bruised, bleeding earl.

"Wyatt!" Miles shouted at him. "Wyatt!"

The red that had clouded his vision receded. He took a deep breath, trying to gain control of himself, still needing to punish this evil man.

Wheeling, he hurried to the carriage and climbed up it, unfastening the straps that held the ancient trunk. He pushed it until it toppled to the ground, breaking open, lithographs spilling out.

Lord Kibbard pushed himself to his feet and stumbled toward it, falling to his knees as he gathered lithographs, clutching them to his chest.

"No!" he cried, his voice breaking.

Wyatt began collecting the spilled contents until he had all but the ones in the earl's hands back inside what was left of the trunk. He dragged it to the burning building and shoved it into the flames. They immediately licked at the trunk, igniting it.

The earl's keening filled the yard. He came to his feet, lithographs still held to his chest, and ran toward the stables. Wyatt watched in horror as Kibbard leaped into the blaze. A long, piercing scream filled the air.

Then silence.

Wyatt hurried to Meadow, pulling her into his arms, forcing her head to his chest so she wouldn't see the fire eat away at Kibbard's prone body. He saw Finch lift young Sally and take her to the waiting carriage.

Meadow pulled away and gazed into his eyes. "Thank you for coming for me."

He gazed at her with all the love he held in his heart. "I had to. You are the woman I want to share all my important moments with. The only one I want by my side."

He kissed her tenderly, knowing he would walk through the fires of Hell and beyond for this woman.

"There are others," she told him. "More like Sally. We need to go inside and find them."

He would tell her about Scrunch on their journey home. They would go to Kibbard's London townhouse and rescue any children locked within it.

"I killed a man today," Meadow told him, her eyes filling with tears.

"What?"

"He was like Lord Kibbard. He took children off the streets and brought them here."

Wyatt kissed her brow gently. "Then you have rid the world of an evil man, my dearest. Think of the children that you have saved." He stroked her cheek. "Let's go save some more."

EPILOGUE

Amberwood—March 1812

MEADOW WOKE, ENVELOPED in her husband's warmth, his hand cradling her belly.

"Good morning, love," Wyatt said huskily in her ear, his hand now stroking her.

He made love to her tenderly, each kiss, each touch sweet and gentle. She didn't know it was possible to love him more each day than she had the one before.

But she did.

He kissed her. "I'll be back."

She watched him shrug into his banyan and leave their bedchamber. Meadow loved that they slept together every night. They had grown close in these months of marriage, especially now that she was carrying their child.

Time seemed to fly by these days. She had begun to keep a journal, wanting to capture all the feelings she felt and keep a record of all they did at Amberwood. Like her husband, Meadow had fallen in love with Amberwood. They would remain here this spring and summer instead of going to town for the Season since she would give birth in July.

Meadow hoped for a boy so that there would be an heir to Amberwood. Wyatt said he preferred a girl, one who would be just like her mother. Whatever gender, she knew her husband would be the best of fathers and hoped she would give him many children. She had seen him with Ben, Miles and Emery's newborn son, and love burst from her as Wyatt held the babe, cradling Ben in his large hands and singing to him.

So much had happened since they had returned to the country. They had brought with them several of the children Lord Kibbard had ordered abducted off the streets, some from the earl's country estate and a few found in his London townhome. Miles and Emery had taken on the other children. Between the two dukes, all of these children from the streets now held positions and not only had a roof over their heads and adequate clothing, but people surrounding them who truly cared for them.

Sally had been a delight. While terribly young to be a lady's maid, the girl was quick-witted and learned fast. She proved skilled with a needle and was ferociously loyal to Meadow. While Sally enjoyed caring for Meadow, Sally had recently approached her and asked about the possibility of her becoming the babe's nursemaid. Knowing how protective Sally was of her, Meadow knew she would transfer her loyalty to the newborn. After talking it over with Wyatt, they had agreed Sally could serve as the nursery governess to all their children. It would mean training someone else to be her lady's maid, but Meadow didn't mind that at all.

Wyatt appeared again, carrying a cup and saucer along with a plate, and she pushed up to a sitting position. He set the saucer and plate down and found her dressing gown, bringing it to her and wrapping her in it before climbing into bed beside her.

"You don't have to bring me tea every morning," she told him.

He had begun doing so when the nausea was so great that she couldn't climb out of bed in the morning. Only tea and dry toast would do—and Wyatt had fetched it every morning, bringing it to her and sitting with her, holding her hand as she tried to eat or holding her hair back as she vomited over the chamber pot. The nausea had finally subsided but her husband still brought her tea and toast each morning.

Wyatt slipped an arm about her. "Of course I want to bring you tea each morning," he said. He smiled and cupped her cheek. "I do so because I want to win your heart each day."

"My heart has been yours from the moment we met," she murmured and then took a sip of the sweet brew.

He smoothed her hair. "Ah, but you made me work for it, didn't you?"

Meadow grinned. "Perhaps a bit."

Wyatt took her hand and kissed her fingers. "Have I told you I love you today?"

"No, but I expect you will. Several times, in fact."

It was true. Her husband was generous with his affection and also gave her the words she longed to hear each day.

"I love you, Wyatt," she said. "More than words can ever say."

He nuzzled her neck, his hand coming to rest atop her belly. "You show me your love in a thousand ways, Meadow." Then he stilled. "Wait. Was that . . ." He voice trailed off as he focused on her belly.

Meadow felt the flutter of a kick. She had begun to sense the baby's movement recently but this was the first time that Wyatt had been able to feel a kick.

"Your son—or daughter—wants to tell you good morning."

He beamed and moved his lips to her belly, kissing it, and then placing his ear against it. Waiting, he nodded. "Yes, there it went again."

A knock sounded and before they could say anything, the door crashed open. Michael—formerly known as Scrunch—rushed in.

"You better come quick, Your Grace," the boy said.

"Do you remember that you are supposed to wait for an answer before you come barreling into a room?" Wyatt asked, raising his head but keeping his hand possessively on his wife's belly.

"I forget sometimes," Michael said. "Sorry, Your Graces."

Miles bent and pressed a kiss to Meadow's belly and then climbed from the bed. He slung an arm about Michael and winked at Meadow.

"Show me what needs my attention," he said, leading the boy from the room.

She smiled as they left the room. Michael had already grown a few inches since they had brought him home with them to Amberwood. The boy had also put on weight and looked happy and healthy. He'd become fast friends with Phillip and it seemed he had put the darkness in his past behind him.

Meadow sat contentedly, sipping her tea, her hand on her belly, until Wyatt returned.

"Dare I ask what Michael needed?" she asked as he closed the door and climbed back into bed with her.

"No." Wyatt slipped a hand around her nape and brought her to him for a sweet, lingering kiss.

When he broke it, her husband said, "I think we should stay in bed today. What do you think, Duchess?"

Meadow smiled. "I think you have the most wonderful ideas, Duke."

They kissed again—and Meadow thought how lucky she truly was.

About the Author

Award-winning and internationally bestselling author Alexa Aston's historical romances use history as a backdrop to place her characters in extraordinary circumstances, where their intense desire for one another grows into the treasured gift of love.

She is the author of Regency and Medieval romance, including: Dukes of Distinction; Soldiers & Soulmates; The St. Clairs; The King's Cousins; and The Knights of Honor.

A native Texan, Alexa lives with her husband in a Dallas suburb, where she eats her fair share of dark chocolate and plots out stories while she walks every morning. She enjoys a good Netflix binge; travel; seafood; and can't get enough of *Survivor* or *The Crown*.

CPSIA information can be obtained
at www.ICGtesting.com
Printed in the USA
LVHW082137080921
697407LV00024B/700